Dvarsh

An Introduction

by Robert Stikmanz

STIKMANTICA

AUSTIN, TEXAS

Dvarsh, An Introduction © 2017 & 2018 by Robert D. Lewis
Cover art, book design & entire contents by Robert Stikmanz
0814021

ISBN 978-0-9838137-6-7

Cataloging Data -
Dvarsh, An Introduction / Robert Stikmanz
      p. 162   cm.
      ISBN 978-0-9838137-6-7
      I. Stikmanz, Robert
            1. Languages—Glossaries, etc.
            2. Imaginary languages in literature
            3. Fictive art
      II. Title

Stikmantica
Austin, Texas
stikmantica.com

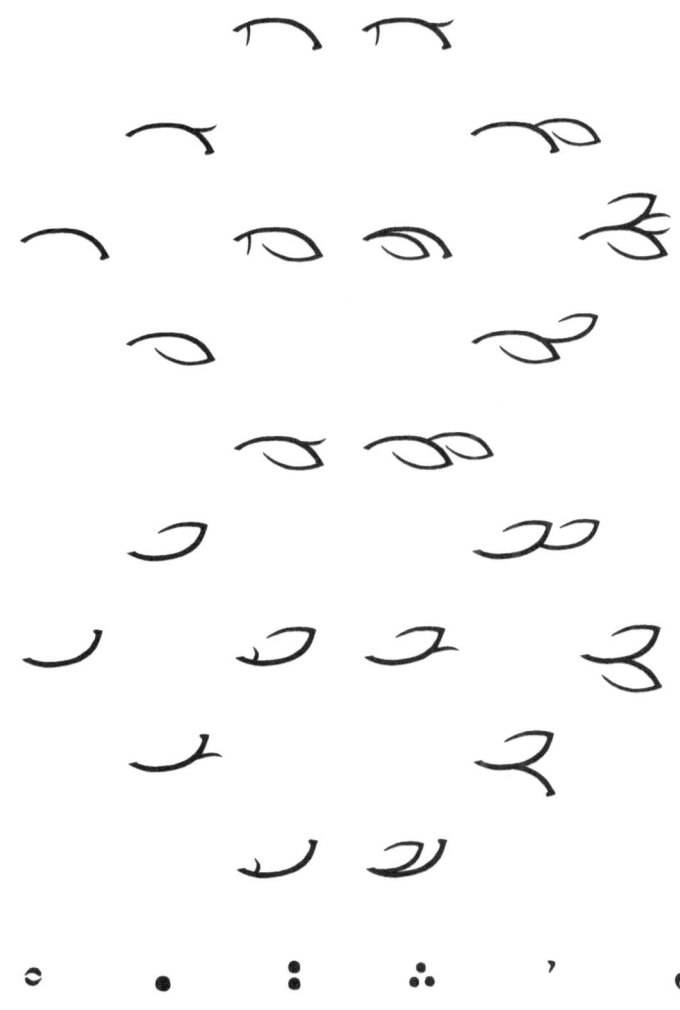

The Jayelu, *jayĕlufvē* [ɔ.⌒:.ɔ.⌒:], the character set of the Dvarsh writing system, shown in handwritten script.

A note about the font

Dvarsh Book, the font used to render the Dvarsh language in this volume, was created by Robert Stikmanz as part of this project. The font is © Stikmantica, all rights reserved. It is available with a limited, noncommercial license and disclaimer information on *stikmantica.com.*

Table of Contents

The first public sentence in Dvarsh known from a human source.
A minor decorative element in a 2006 cover design, the attention it
attracted was unexpected.

Preface

Now it passes from these hands. Since the first use of Dvarsh script on the cover of a novel more than a decade ago, I have been asked repeatedly when a dictionary and grammar of the language would be available. That question finally has an answer.

A point to stress is that this is not a comprehensive reference. In ambition and scope, it is a primer. The information it presents on Dvarsh grammar amounts to a sketch of essentials. Its dictionaries feature significant vocabulary, but they do not include anything like the complete lexicon of a still evolving tongue. As with any introductory work, a wealth of information that could have been included has been left out. Some of these decisions may seem arbitrary. Some of them no doubt were.

Dvarsh, An Introduction is the second attempt to publish the language's fundamentals. Its predecessor, *The Way it Grows (TWiG)*, was handicapped by imperfect understanding of the subject and an inconsequential word list. Hastily prepared from raw field notes, *TWiG* overlooked much of the rich nuance of Dvarsh, and, on several details, was simply wrong. Subsequently distilling material from a stack of notebooks showed both that I had collected more substance than I had realized, and that details had slipped from mind. Built on systematic organization of all available information, *Dvarsh, An Introduction* supersedes *TWiG* utterly.

In the face of that statement, one may ask, "supersedes how?" Inevitably, this slender volume serves a double purpose. Clearly, it is an instrument for language learning, but it also contains the first significant account of a culture long suspected and an idiom little known. Two hats have meant that in every particular the struggle has been to maintain clarity and access for non-specialists without sacrificing entirely the rigor observed by academics. Aiming for accessibility, I have avoided the jargon of professional linguists; at the same time, I have tried for a presentation those professionals may respect.

One feature of the language that has affected presentation is lack of a written practice comparable to capitalization. On the page, common and proper nouns are distinguished largely by familiarity and context. When writing about these things in English, the very word, *dvarsh*, becomes a headache, as it labels the people, their language, their civilization, their species, its individuals, and their core commonalty. Present purposes demanded a work-around.

The plan I have followed anglicizes proper nouns—first letter capitalized, non-italic, no diacriticals or accents—to produce, for example, names of languages, like Dvarsh, Hazl and Zek. Common nouns and other parts of speech—such as *zĕktha, wotúk charlsa,* or *dvarsh*—have been rendered in italic, all lower case, with necessary accents and diacriticals, thus emphasizing transliteration from a foreign tongue. My hope is a distinction that leads to less confusion instead of more.

This project has been a very long time in the making. Learning curves have been steep, resources few, and stubbornness often a stand-in for the competent team of relevant experts that never was. Mostly alone, I have made this book. Regardless of how the world greets it, I am proud of having carried the work to completion, and of its odd beauty.

Mostly alone, I have made this book, and that also means I am sole author of whatever flaws haunt an introvert's passion. There is no finger to point. Errors belong only to me.

Fortunately, when it comes to virtues, I have not been left with only my own small store. Many, many people have shared comment over the years, and I have been quick to seize benefit when I have had the snap to recognize it. A constant few deserve more than mere words of thanks: Paul E. Cooley, Carol Daeley, Thomas Fang, Gary Warner Kent, M. S. Lewis, Carla Maywald, Martin McCreadie, Bram Meehan, Monica Banko Meehan, Stephen Radney-Macfarland, James Rossignol, Nancy Salay, Mary Saunders and Genevieve Sprinkle. In a spirit of love and regard, I offer this artifact to them, and to the worlds unseen that travel alongside us.

–Robert Stikmanz

Production of this edition was assisted by generous sponsors Carol Daeley, Mark S. Lewis, Thomas Mahler, James Rossignol and Siu Ping Rossignol, with additional support from Alycia Christine, David Gray, James Jarnagin, Rose Vitola, Tom Wheeler, and others who asked to remain anonymous.

Dvarsh

An Introduction

Who are the Dvarsh?

Some generations after the *dzazan'm* [ɔ͜ɔ.ᷮᷮ͜] branched from our common ancestry, the succeeding lineage split into three. First to diverge was a wandering population that evolved into small, gracile foragers, the *thrm* [ᷮᷮ͜]. After separating from the *thrm*, the lineage split again, one group becoming the people who are the subject of this essay, the *dvarsh* [ɔᷮ͜]. We know the third group, the *hoomanth'm* [ᷮᷮᷮ͜.ᷮᷮᷮ͜], as modern humans.

First, the *thrm*

The path of *thrm* development took a turn markedly different than that of its sister taxa. Most visibly, both men and women sport lush manes, and their index fingers have shifted on each hand to become a second opposable thumb.

Although some of their adaptations are astonishing, much about them remains primitive. Their vocal signaling, for instance, never differentiated into language and song. Vocalizations became melodiously complex and improvisatory, but did not transition from meaningful call to speech.

One proposal for why the *thrm* never stopped singing long enough to learn to talk points to a permanent mental state of hypertrophic empathy. This effect on mindedness appears driven by a neurological quirk that makes the thrmmic brain sensitive to neural activity in the near environment, especially that of their own kind. The result, a biologically sustained group awareness, seems to have made much of the exchange of language irrelevant.

Long after removal of these near kin from landscapes once shared, humans retain fragmentary memories of wee folk and little people pieced into stories surviving from a time when the world and its explanations were more magical. Once common among us, the *thrm* now live protected by the second lineage, the *dvarsh*, removed to exile along with the last *dzazan'm* and a few others.

After the divide

It is the *dvarsh* that sit at the heart of this book. Also known to humans primarily through stories, they are sometimes accounted another race that walked this earth in an earlier age. Rarely does anyone consider that they survive beside us.

Though they average a head taller than the *thrm*, the giants among them barely top four feet. Robust, often described as broad and lean, agents of their civilization manage to pass through margins of human society where variation is great and scrutiny lax.

11

They are extremely long-lived.

For millennia, they shared a landscape with humans as an elder, wiser, less populous civilization. Stories remember them by different names at different times in different places. One name by which they have been known in English, "dwarves," is corrupted directly from the name by which they call themselves.

The *dvarsh* argue various hypotheses about when and where they split with modern humans. Some of the ambiguity stems from a dearth of fossil and artifactual evidence. This is the archaeological downside of a typically *dvarsh* behavior, that of picking up after themselves. Lack of bodies and abandoned things also explains why human excavators have never recognized traces of ancient *dvarsh* inhabitance for what they are. From any place these people leave, they remove every sign of their passage. They still observe the practice scrupulously. It seems they cannot help it.

Whatever their specific origin, their spread around the planet, although at low density, appears to have been rapid. Cultural ties and technology exchanges survived dispersal, which helped maintain attachment to a sense of common origin despite extensive linguistic and ethnic diversification.

The rare human observer of the *dvarsh* may comment on three races, *atwĕzlo* [ ] (brown), *ahĕzlo* [ ] (red), and *awomuzl* [ ] (white). The *dvarsh* themselves scoff at this description. Race, their ethnographers insist, is a nonsensical construct. In terms of their sociobiology, *atwĕzlo*, *ahĕzlo* and *awomuzl* are understood as historical "attractors" around which different combinations of traits tend to cluster.

By whatever method the types are defined, *dvarsh atwĕzlo* are most numerous, diverse and widespread. They have occupied most landmasses since time immemorial. The *dvarsh ahĕzlo* and *awomuzl* developed in isolation for thousands of years, but descend from *atwĕzlo* progenitors.

In point of fact, though, after millennia of global community, there is no longer any such thing as pure *atwĕzlo*, *ahĕzlo* or *awomuzl*. Significant numbers even have human DNA sprinkled through their genomes. Despite mixing, however, the variety of traits of the source populations survive. Residents of many historic centers not only hold fast to ancient clan and family traditions, but collectively resemble local ancestors as far back as memory can trace.

During the long age before emergence of the global polity, or *"wotúk charlsa"* [ ] (lit. "world dream"), virtually all *dvarsh* across all subpolar landmasses were *atwĕzlo* until climate change segregated the extreme west of Eurasia. As an ethnographic term, *atwĕzlo* covers tremendous variety, with some clans tending very dark, some very light, and most somewhere in between. Though of robust build, the *atwĕzlo* type tends to be lean and, for *dvarsh*, of medium height. Observers mention the strangely liquid colors of the irises of their eyes.

Roots of the *wotúk charlsa* reach into an ethic of pan-dvarshism that took shape within a number of *atwĕzlo* clans concurrently with the earliest phase of paleoliteracy.

The *dvarsh ahĕzlo*, the Red Dvarsh, arose in an area beyond what is now the Western Isles, back when their homelands spanned the dense forests at the tip of what was, in that distant age, the Great Western Peninsula. An old poeticism, *"hogmĕchokth'm ahĕzl'm oa taltagop'mfvē"* [ꙮ], "Red Clans of the Glades," acknowledges those sylvan roots.

Rather than *ahĕzlo*, the red clans call themselves *dvarsh hazl* [ꙮ], after their ancestral complex of languages, itself called Hazl after the most widely spoken variant of the group. Referring to people, *haza* [ꙮ] is an individual; *haz'm* [ꙮ] is plural.

If a little taller on average than the *atwĕzlo*, *haz'm* tend to slightly less breadth. What really sets them apart as outliers on the family tree, however, is the fact that they are red. This is not a hyperbolic "averaging up" from ruddy or rubescent. When the *dvarsh* say that someone is "red," they mean the person so-called is red, the way a tomato is red. Scarlet to crimson, their skin color is unequivocal. In the Americas, they are stalked by hummingbirds. Virtually all *haz'm* have green hair and and green eyes in striking shades. Green eyes, green hair, and red skin make it difficult for *haz'm* to pass among humans, even for those with only slight point to their ears. As a result, contact is infrequent.

Dvarsh awomuzl, the White Dvarsh, also evolved in isolation. Their clan territories lay in the circumpolar region of the far north, even during glacial maximums. Among humans, once in a while still, a story crusted with age will raise its venerable head to tell of mysterious little people of the ice and their strange arithmetics.

Just as the *hazl* are red, the *dvarsh awomuzl* are white—like snow, like new paper. Their skin is white, as are their hair and lips. The absence of color results not from pigment, but from defractive structures embedded in proteins of skin and hair. Their eyes are completely black, both iris and sclera. On average shorter than *atwĕzlo'm* or *haz'm*, the *awomuz'm* are also most solitary in general. Their ancestral languages have made the least impact on modern Dvarsh. Even fewer in number than the *hazl*, they, too, are covered by a single ethnonym. *Zĕk* [ꙮ] yields the plural, *zĕkth'm* [ꙮ], and *zĕktha* [ꙮ] as a term for an individual.

Agreement is unanimous that *atwĕzlo* splinter populations were ancestral to both *hazl* and *zĕk*. Whether distinct clan identities preceded or followed the mutations that produced the marked physical differences of the *haz'm* and *zĕkth'm* is an open question. What may be stated with certainty is that over thousands of years of isolation, mutated traits within their respective suites came to predominate. The complexions of these two subtypes are unique among primates.

Social organization

Clans were the basis of social organization through the first few thousand years after emergence of a kind of mindedness that the *dvarsh* call *shabvch'dĕ athlobvan'* [ॽ,ॸॷ୰,,୰, .ॷ୰ॸ,୰,], or modern consciousness. What began as extended family groups are now more properly called *extensive*, sometimes intricate, family groups. These have come to function within the *dvarsh* polity in a way similar to provinces.

The clans were independent and competitive for generations after *shabvch'dĕ athlobvan'* emerged. Groups affiliated loosely within tribal confederations, but it was not as though anyone took orders from or owed much to these larger bodies. Tribal identity tended to associate more-or-less with complexes of related languages. Only the *atwĕzlo* clans were numerous and varied enough to comprise more than one tribe. Identification with clan was far stronger, and in the epoch before *wotúk charlsa*, the competition and parochialism occasionally tipped over into hostility.

Intradvarsh warfare was rarely fatal. Even in disagreement at its most furious, a sense of common origin and values persisted. Engagements were less battles than matters of ambush, startlement and intimidating display, like outsized sibling rivalry. Rarely—the stuff of saga and legend—conflict would escalate into pitched manipulations of weather, terrain shifts, and orchestral soundtracks deployed with elaborate brass machinery of uncertain purpose.

Once *ahoomantha* populations started burgeoning, internecine quarrels were abandoned. Felt worldwide, the territorial pressures from human encroachment lent urgency to the earliest expressions of pan-dvarshism.

Nod's visit

A pivotal figure in *dvarsh* history appeared on the scene at this time of transition. From where has never been determined. Stories in the thousands—some of them, perhaps many of them, factual— evoke a mysterious, clownlike entity who arrived among the *dvarsh* "to set things in motion and shake things up." There is no specifically personal information consistent enough across the tales to be considered well-attested. One school of thought even argues that the entity was not a person at all, but an elemental force interpreted variously by those who encountered it.

Whatever the visitor's nature, the visit lasted several centuries, and left enduring marks. Remarkably, this character, known to the *dvarsh* as *nodz* [ᢣ୦୨], is celebrated under a similar name, Nod, by a once secret human tradition. Immersion in *Nod* arcana is what first brought the present author to notice by *dvarsh* agents.

Overstating the importance of Nod's residence is impossible. Tradition has it that the eight signs and thirty-six auspices at the heart of *dvarsh* ethical teaching were revealed by the visitor. Terse comments attributed to the entity illustrate each auspice, providing a framework for the wisdom book, *sosnodz* [⏃⏃⏃⏃], or *Nod's Way*, into which later texts were integrated. This influence, by itself, has been profound.

A revered work, *Nod's Way* is deceptively small. Brief enough that schoolchildren learn it by copying out the text, the book is an ethical guide, an oracle, a game, a surrogate for intuition and an engagement with chance. Its thirty-six chapters, or "auspices," illuminate the path of a responsible life. Re-arranged, they also serve as the basis for the *dvarsh* calendar, *bvatachatazlnodzfvē* [⏃⏃⏃⏃⏃⏃], which is sectioned into neither weeks, nor months but into periods of ten days each, with names drawn from the oracle. Even casual examination suggests a numerological system coded into the book, but about this the *dvarsh* say nothing.

A larger legacy opens out from *Nod's Way* and its ethic. Also credited to the visitor are twin concepts that permeate every aspect of *dvarsh* culture. The idea that dynamic phenomena exhibit a pair of qualities, *akthĕshl'* [⏃⏃⏃], Rising, and *ayushl'a* [⏃⏃⏃], Falling, may actually trace back to the stirring of *shabvch'dĕ athlobvan'* in the *dvarsh* paleolithic age; even so, themes of succession and alternation are inextricable from Noddist worldviews.

An innovation that can be traced with certainty to Nod posits rising and falling as the engine of a cycle that embraces movement and change. Each instant rises, then falls, in a manner likened to respiration, ever changing with circumstance. The same is held to be true of a day, a year, an event, or a life. The consonants of the *dvarsh* writing system sort into falling characters and rising. Motifs of rising-and-falling recur throughout the history of *dvarsh* music, design and art.

Nod's visit and its effects were watersheds in the formation of *wotúk charlsa*. Certainly, the spread of pan-dvarshism went hand-in-hand with embrace of *Nod's Way*, and the roles of the book in subsequent *dvarsh* culture are manifold. A treasured tie to the deep past, the poetic statement of a living ethic, and a serious instrument for oracular play, the book is a tangible emblem of commonalty.

Nod's eventual departure was without fanfare. One evening the sun set on a world in which the visitor still walked. The next morning dawned on a new-minted absence. No one heard anything unusual in the night. Occasional rumors of unconfirmed sightings continue to this day.

15

Hypnarchy and The Sleeping Court

With the stage thus set for change, a little more than seventeen thousand years ago the clans began to unite under Queen Mabv I. Four centuries after succeeding her mother as *nochutha* [ꞏꞏꞏ], or Sleeper, of the *maĕkthĕnas* [ꞏꞏꞏ] clan, Mabv was acclaimed first *wotchuthanotcha* [ꞏꞏꞏ], or Hypnarch, of all *dvarsh*. Evidence suggests a process of assimilation that was peaceful, voluntary, and complete within two hundred years of the first enlargement of her Dream.

The institution of unity traces through the person of Mabv to her parents, whose pairing was negotiated between chiefly houses of the two largest *atwĕzlo* clans. Her mother was *maĕkthĕnas*, while her paternal grandmother was *(h)r'dj'dst'k* [ꞏꞏꞏ], a larger sept of the *ĕshĕn'lokdĕ* [ꞏꞏꞏ]. Once these two lines came together, Mabv channeled her Dream through *thom'mókfvē anotchl'* [ꞏꞏꞏ], the Sleeping Court. This created a pull on other clans that became irresistible.

The Hypnarch of all *dvarsh* reigns through the Sleeping Court, but does not rule. The position is no longer dynastic. Heirs are selected from among candidates named to the royal house.

The signal charge of the hypnarch is to dream the well-being and prosperity of Habdvarsha, serving awake and in slumber as the personification of a common vision. She sways practical affairs by nominating lists of candidates from which officers of the court— i.e. Dozing Plenipotentiaries, *wus(h)ruth'm alĕknotchl'm* [ꞏꞏꞏ], and Companions in the Dream, *modz'm 'a wotúkfvē* [ꞏꞏꞏ]—are chosen, but her only real power springs from the moral authority of intentional sleep.

An oft-quoted quip captures the reverence and constitution of an anarchist nation:

> *"mabvmo nĕth wotchuthaga ēta kth'th'nguthafvē ēst"*
> [ꞏꞏꞏ]
> "Mabv is queen, but not the boss."

Every hypnarch except two has taken Mabv as a regnal name. Okthomolaga, who succeeded Mabv XXVIII, hoped one day to be known as Okthomolaga I. She is not yet. Following Mabv LXII, the other exception announced at her investiture, *"g'gromfvĕsh mofvē luúsēl,"* [ꞏꞏꞏ], "Call me Lucille."

Dvarsh governance

Actual government among the *dvarsh* esteems the hypnarchy, but operates through other channels altogether. An unchartered, shifting, permanently sitting committee of the whole—the "whole" meaning everyone who chooses to show up at any given moment—

functions as the living institution of the realm. Despite its age-old place at the helm of the nation, it has never gotten around to assigning itself a name. Informally, it is often called *omomuthloafvē* [⌐ˑ], "the Assembly." Its only published or broadcast self-reference is *dvarsh fvē* [⌐ˑ], the *dvarsh*. The body sits at what passes for a capital city in *habdvarsha* [ ], the exile realm.

Instead of a house of parliament or a capitol, *omomuthloafvē* teems in permanent session across the grounds of a vast open park known as *hazuchafvē oa fva'rhĕ* [ ], the Field of Fva'rhe. Legislating, lobbying, making speeches, bargaining, conferring, pondering, hearing and being heard, those who assemble on *fva'rhĕ* represent the nuts and bolts of the Dream.

At one end of *fva'rhĕ* sits an enormous compound maintained jointly by all the clans. Designated conveners work from its facilities, moderating convergent and divergent threads of hundreds of simultaneous discussions. It is here that ambassadors are received.

An ancient road runs over a modest hill, across a dale, and into a grove, linking the compound's outfacing gate to the sheltered heart of *dvarsh* identity, *taltagopsfvē akthocho'* [ ] the Still Glade. In this woodland sanctuary, *yatafvē oa thom'mókfvē anotchl'* [ ], the Inn of the Sleeping Court, reposes protected from but nevertheless convenient to the din of government. Traffic on the road is muffled but steady. Availability for consultation with her government is the obligation even of a Dreaming queen. Perhaps especially of one who Dreams.

Settlement patterns

The *dvarsh* have only lived in aggregations large enough to qualify as towns since retreating from the consensus shared with humans. No trace of large, concentrated settlements can be found outside the exile realm. The word generally translated as "town," *m'thl'mata* [ ], applies to a less dense, less built-up, less insistently transformed landscape than anything found among the unrestrained cousins.

Smaller than *m'thl'mat'm*, a more common type of community is called a *m'thlom* [ ], usually translated as "village." The basic plan is older than even *dvarsh* memory. Consisting of a developed center and surrounding lands, *m'thlom'm* range in size from a few dozen to a few hundred residents.

The seat of a *m'thlom* is a place of congregation and activity. Always, there will be school facilities and a place of assembly. Typical industries may include a machine shop & smithy, specialty workshops, a mill, a coffee house & pub (or vice versa), an inn, and an apothecary. A few households also locate centrally, but most *m'thlomot'm* [ ], or villagers, live in single households or small clusters spread among lands under their *m'thlom*'s steward-ship. Away from the center is quieter.

Since removal to exile, several historic clan seats have become substantial *m'thl'mat'm*, or towns. Major factors driving this growth relate to infrastructural needs of modern industry; however, one cannot discount an appetite for cultural activities of a sophistication that only hatches when populations reach a threshold density.

Contributing to the arts and spectacle that spring into being when a *m'thlom* enlarges into a *m'thl'mata* are nomads of no fixed address, the *smosat'm* [ꕭꕡ]. People of the road, they circulate throughout *habdvarsha*, pitching in where they can, jamming with the locals, listening and learning. An "estate" of *dvarsh* society from its inception, the wanderers of this free form, free floating cultural exchange serve to carry insight and inventive thinking from any one place to every other. Before exile, the vast majority of notable *dvarsh/hoomantha* encounters involved these itinerants. As the tales record, meetings were sometimes friendly and sometimes not.

In all of *habdvarsha* there exists but one organized population large enough and complex enough to justify the label, *m'thl'matĕdza* [ꕡ], or "city." This is the seat of government, mentioned above. Like the government itself and the polity it governs, the city has never been given an official name. It is sometimes called metonymically, *"fva'rhĕ,"* after the field in its midst; more often, one hears simply, *"m'thl'matĕdza fvĕ,"* the city.

In terms of municipal structure, the "city" actually consists of discrete, village-like enclaves maintained by each clan and some of the larger septs of clans. These nest within public infrastructure arranged around *fva'rhĕ*. Ringing the enclaves in turn are districts of the kind that grow up where purposeful enterprise concentrates busy people who need stuff. Gardens, parks and wild places are many, as are areas of public quiet and natural light.

At the other extreme from the very social citizens of *m'thl'matĕdza fvĕ*, a small but non-trivial number of *dvarsh* find company of any kind difficult. Hermits by temperament and choice, *mosm'm anĕw'm* [ꕭꕡ .ꕡ], or hidden people, move to the most remote, forbidding locations they can find, bake gingerbread, meditate, and become native to the places they inhabit. Historically, these individuals suffered more than others from accidental encounters with humans. Having no friends, family or neighbors within call, a solitary individual was often rewarded brutally for welcoming strangers into her home. Abuse, robbery, even murder, at the hands of questing knights, doughty woods-men, and—especially—young children lost in the forest was the outcome of virtually every such meeting of which an account survives. Exile, at last, provided the safe seclusion they crave.

Households

Marriage as we conceive it is not completely unknown in *habdvarsha,* but it is rare. Domestic arrangements come in all sizes and variations. A lifelong, monogamous commitment between two adults is actually considered semi-monastic by most *dvarsh,* and more than a little nuts within the bastions of tradition.

It is important to stress that establishment of a household, or *jamno(h)rota* [ଠୄୠୢୄୣ.], has no direct or necessary connection to marriage. An entirely unrelated set of priorities underpin *dvarsh* notions of family and home.

Jamno(h)rot'm are founded as partnerships, most often by four partners, all of whom are usually women. The number and makeup are customary, rather than set in stone. Groups of four hold special significance in the culture, but one finds partnerships of two, three, five or more. Functionally, *jamno(h)rot'm* are equal parts family and small corporation. This is to say that love and economics temper each other in decision-making.

Partnership structure varies considerably. Very conservative segments of *dvarsh* society adhere to a version of *jamno(h)rota* in which a man negotiates entry as an independent associate under contract, rather than as a partner. Terms of hire may or may not address questions of intimacy between an associate and one, some, all or none of the partners. The positions are viewed as primarily social and economic, and many associates fulfill contracts with distinction while conducting private lives exclusively outside the households to which they belong. Although an integral part of the fabric of his *jamno(h)rota,* an associate may not receive an equity stake until completion of a significant period of employment.

That is the way of the old guard. Recent centuries have seen progressive elements define partnerships rooted in other dynamics and other gender roles. Defying change, however, the "four plus one" arrangement and its variants remain prevalent. Familiarity, habit and cultural bias contribute to its persistence, but so does an oddity of *dvarsh* reproduction.

For reasons unknown, *dvarsh* mothers resorb approximately three fourths of all male fetuses during the first days of pregnancy. Human investigators, such as there are, unanimously state that the mechanism at work is unclear. As with most things that set them apart from humans, *dvarsh* researchers share little of what they know. However it comes to pass, female live births outnumber males by a factor greater than four to one. Males that survive the winnowing are, like females, for the most part extraordinarily healthy and long-lived. That fact doesn't change the relative numbers between adult women and men, which stand at 4.67 to 1. Instead of competing for scarce males, the *dvarsh* solution since prehistory has been to share them.

19

Another survival from "four plus one" that has a place in even the most progressively evolved *jamno(h)rota*, divorces the role of paternal parent from biological fatherhood. In fact, asking a mother about a child's biological father is considered vulgar, unless there is very good reason. Whether a partner in the new style or associate in the old, a man stands as guardian and guide to every child entering the household by birth, adoption or fosterage. While he may be the biological father of some or all children under his care, his status as parent under contract exceeds that of any sperm supplier, himself included. This relationship surpasses those with maternal uncles as the closest, most profound, and most enduring beween children and men.

Technologies of mind

Unique to *dvarsh* culture is a group of mental disciplines that act transformatively upon the material world. Developed from the applied sciences of recontextualization and reimagination, they loosely associate under the term, *sĕthyoshuky'm aprĕshananukkth'm* [ꙮꙮ ꙮꙮ], which can be understood to mean, "ontotronic technologies." These technologies fall into three areas:

- *najath'lopĕm* [ꙮ], or 'pataphysics.

- *jokm'hochoanthē* [ꙮ], or metamathemagics.

- *j'kth'kth'* [ꙮ], or intuition.

The first of these, *najath'lopĕm*, deals exclusively with the particular, including ramifications of particularity. It is, thus, the science of all things exceptional. Known in human languages by a word associated with playwright Alfred Jarry, *dvarsh* practitioners specified this term as a translation for their field because "several of Jarry's definitions correspond exceptionally and particularly with our own."

Within 'pataphysics are fields of research and application. Its practitioners achieve status as *mojabvth'm* [ꙮ] (adepts) by demonstrating proficiency in both. Only *mojabvth'm* are admitted to *j'thachĕfvē oa najath'lopĕmuth'm* [ꙮ], The College of 'Pataphysicians.

The second technology, *jokm'hochoanthē* (metamathemagics), involves manipulation of unquantifiable aspects of quantifiable things. Working at conceptual/physical boundaries, practice deals with application of four basic operations: extending, condensing, narratizing and guesswork. If 'pataphysics engages phenomena with precise locality, metamathemagics advances by perspective, association and derivation. The one is a scalpel; the other, a trowel.

As with 'pataphysicians, only *mojabvth'm* who have shown mastery of the field may enroll in *khonfvabvuulfvē ajokm'hochoanuthē* [ꦪꦱꦤꦶꦴ꧇ ꦢꦩꦪꦱꦴꦴꦤ꧆]. The name of this body usually translates as, "The Metamathemagical Confabule."

J'kth'kth' [ꦢꦪꦩ], or intuition, completes the ontotronic triad. The Dvarsh term signifies, at once, the sense of "intuition" familiar in English, and a refinable skill of anticipatory perception. As with any trait, sensitivity varies from individual to individual. For a notable minority, persistently heightened access to things they do not yet know provides an uncanny ability to pluck future fact from present ignorance.

Neither common nor rare, the enabling predisposition occurs at the exact frequency that sustains its social value. Correlation has been noted between expression of the ability and some degree of mixed *thrm* or *hoomantha* ancestry.

Sēthlomfvē achěz(h)ro ota atědzorchěmthl'a oa j'kth'kth'mot'm [ꦱꦴꦢꦩꦤꦶ꧇ ꦱꦴꦢꦴ ꦴꦢ꧆ ꦢꦴꦢꦴꦢꦪꦴ꧆ ꦴ꧆ ꦢꦩꦩꦩꦴꦤꦴ], The Ancient & Venerable Guild of Intuits, long ago established an inflexible threshold of minimum perceptivity for membership in their company. The successful candidate knows intuitively that she or he surpasses the threshold.

While in other ways *dvarsh* and humans explore similar fields of science, these three disciplines have been isolated and elaborated as technologies by the *dvarsh* alone. Each provides a toolset for taking the measure of reality and altering it. Underpinning the evolved techniques are fundamentals of Dvarsh cosmology, which they sorted out not long after the last glacial maximum and have maintained with remarkable consistency ever since.

Proponents of one or another closely related "many worlds" hypotheses, the *mojabvth'm* of *habdvarsha* push far beyond concepts of a multiverse. That ours is but one universe among an infinity they take for granted. Also taken for granted is that the world at hand is but one *jamo'dě* [ꦢꦴꦤꦴꦢ꧆], or consensus, within infinite possibility.

The notion is a bit slippery, but *jamo'dě,* or consensus, as conceived by the *dvarsh* refers to something like a massed average of knowledge, belief and opinion. It is also that rarest of formations, an article of *dvarsh* orthodoxy. All schools accept that the world of the averages is the real world of physicality.

While facts underpinning knowledge may change only slowly, belief and opinion are subject to dynamic shift. With each shift the world remakes. Consequent possibilities of changing the world by changing mind propogate across the rich pastures of intuition, metamathemagics and 'pataphysics. It was through manipulation of *jamo'dě'm* that the *mojabvth'm* engineered the realm of their exile.

Where have they gone?

The *dvarsh* are unquestionably of this world, having emerged from common ancestry alongside humans. Their long ages of co-existence with our kind left an imprint on human culture that shaped the stories by which we define our past. A telling body of evidence—not least, the volume in hand—suggests they remain our contemporaries. Where are they?

A short, if unsatisfying, answer is, "Standing right beside us." Wags may prefer, "Standing firm against us." However one chooses to spin their exile, it is clear they choose to stand out of our path.

A way of suggesting where to find *habdvarsha* is to realize that the *dvarsh* left, not our material world, but rather a shared under-standing of the world. Without putting too much literal stress on the terminology, a poet might say that, in a way, they have made themselves *largely but not completely* beings of the imagination. Four hundred twelve 'pataphysical laws of conservation of particularity require that this work both ways. You may be the hobgoblin with which they scare small children.

Time frames of their migration are hard to define. Departure did not happen all at once, and has never been total. For one thing, constructing a second, fully elaborated reality took time. Even after extensive searches through possibility narrowed to one hospitable *jamo'dě*, the unprecedented process of imagining a world into being proved more than an overnight affair. The necessary level of detail, in and of itself, presented a challenge. False starts, wrong turns and unforeseen obstacles earned mention in the eventual sagas.

With these caveats in mind, one may suggest that the period of establishment and growth of *habdvarsha* correlates loosely with the ebbing of magic from the human sphere—meaning the magic of a way of knowing, not symbolical muttering of conjures and spells. For the *dvarsh*, conjures and spells are matters of technology.

As for why they chose to relocate from our shared consensus, most will insist there was no alternative. Even when relations were good, humans were—are—possessive of resources and territory. It is one thing to share an understanding of the world, and another altogether to share real estate. The friction this created in ancient days only increased as it became clear the tall cousins had neither vision nor will for a population cap.

If this had been the sole provocation, the *dvarsh* likely would have drawn conflict to a head and declared war while they still possessed technological advantages. They did not because through the Dream of the Sleeping Court they knew that this would delay the problem without solving it.

The *dvarsh* are convinced there is a truth *hoomanth'm* urgently need to understand if we are to survive. It is an understanding they cannot reach for us. This does not stop them from trying to shape outcomes. At this point in history, a vast, clandestine, multidimensional struggle to push unfolding *hoomantha* society toward shared benefit defines the policy of their civilization.

In the meantime, while they like some humans very much, by and large we make lousy neighbors. Trashy, loud, we also stink. *Habdvarsha*, their home in exile, is a safety valve, an escape from the constant human press. Ultimately, it is also a preserve in which a different relation to being flourishes in the *wotúk charlsa.*

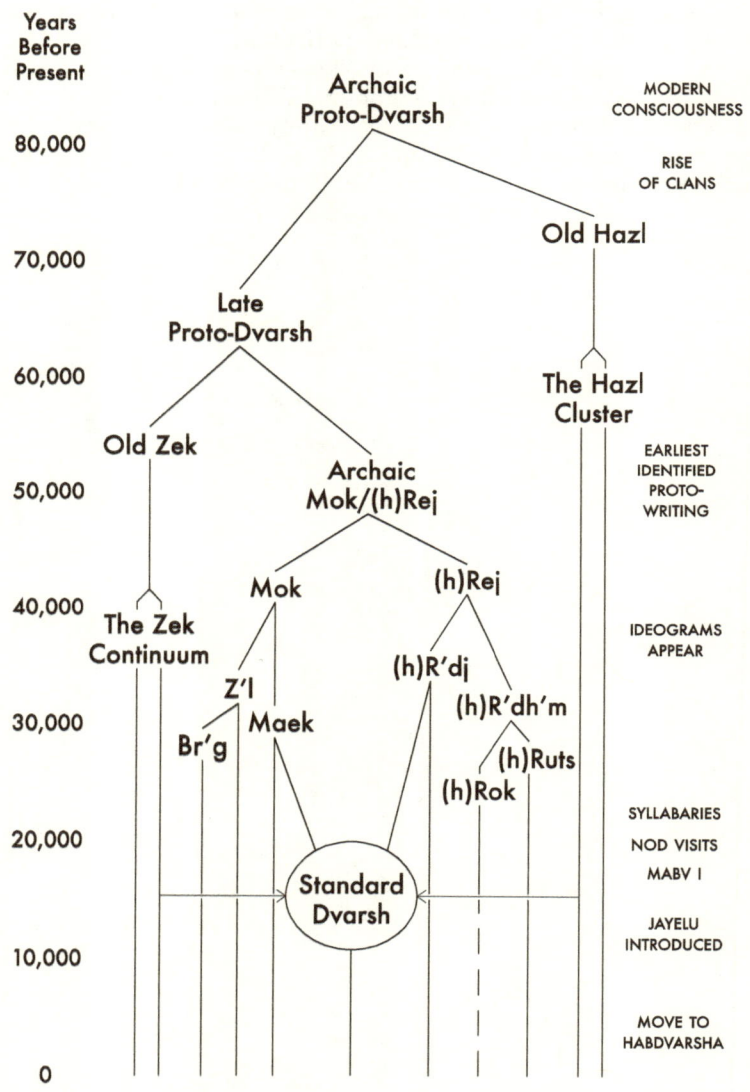

A timeline reconstruction of Dvarsh language descent.
Only major groups are shown.

A Short History of the Language called Dvarsh

Unlike the *thrm*, the *dvarsh* talk. Sometimes they talk and talk and talk. In the past they have done so in many exotic tongues, which they still do within contexts of local tradition; however, the modern instrument of their world spanning conversation, the lingo of the whole people, is one partly constructed and partly evolved. Like their government, like their species, like their society and like their persons, in anything like an official context the language is called only and always, "*dvarsh.*" The present text will continue to refer to it in the English style, Dvarsh, to distinguish between their speech and the people who speak it.

Formation of the language is bound up with establishment of their collective identity. While the *dvarsh* have allowed very few of their ancient clan languages to go extinct, even the most unyielding traditionalists embrace the *abvathraldza* [ˌ◌.◌.◌.], or "standard," idiom as a badge of the whole community. A common proverb has it that,

"*gĕjmo aa o' yolmĕt'm bva nĕth bvambvaps ajēnl'*"

[◌ ◌ .. ◌ ◌ ◌. ◌ ◌.◌.◌ .◌:◌ ◌]

"A head with two tongues is twice wise."

Evidence assembled in the Repository of the Dvarsh suggests the kind of mindedness they call *shabvch'dĕ athlobvan'* (modern consciousness), arose circa 80,000 years ago. This is the period of the earliest verifiable metalworking and fabric production. By 20,000 years ago, a few syllabaries had taken shape from earlier proto-writing, and variations of these were used to write many of the old languages and dialects. One in particular, a 121 character set called the *jaz'zl* [◌.◌] came to predominate after one of the larger clans of *dvarsh atwĕzlo*, the *ēshĕn'lokdĕ*, adapted it for their dialect cluster and many of their allies followed suit. The twenty-two consonants of modern Dvarsh survive from this syllabary in *ēshĕn'lokdĕ* usage.

The formation of standard Dvarsh came about because of the union of all *dvarsh* into a single hypnarchy under Queen Mabv I more than seventeen thousand years ago. Before her reign as first hypnarch of the *dvarsh*, clan languages—varying widely from place to place—tended to abstract the growing passion for a single, integrated community. Eventually, the Sleeping Court embraced all. Eight language families encompassing more than two hundred distinct languages and dialects were documented extensively in the generation after the clans, one by one, called upon good Queen Mabv to accept them into her *wotŭk charlsa*.

Waking the morning of the day after the final clan entered the Dream, her first act was to request creation of a repository charged with compiling knowledge of each clan, its history, culture and characteristics. Later, she asked that this repository also document the Dream as a whole going forward. Unfortunately, while this institution, *ts'hat'jakfvē oa dvarsh fvē* [꒪ᴕ.ᴊᴕ.ᴕᴕꞀ: ꜱ. ꒱.ᴕ Ꞁ:], the Repository of the Dvarsh, is a matchless trove on old clan tongues, its archive from the earliest phase of standard Dvarsh consists of several "to do" lists, a few internal memoranda by its own mid-level clerks, and a remarkably good recipe for almond cookies.

Over millennia, the function of the repository has morphed, as has the role of seventeen Dozing Plenipotentiaries who collectively lead it. Despite the changes, it continues to preserve a wealth of information about *dvarsh* life before the hypnarchy's establishment. Records made in some symbol systems predating the *wotúk charlsa* require specialists to interpret. By contrast, even the first, broken passages in proto-Dvarsh are comprehensible (if stilted and quaint) to contemporary readers.

The *abvathraldza*, or standard idiom, evolved from a lingua franca assembled on the fly as clans unified in the Dream. Scholars hold that primary contributing languages were Maek and (h)R'dj, tongues of the *maĕkthĕnas* and *ēshĕn'lokdĕ* clans, respectively.

Despite a somewhat distant linguistic relationship, Maek and (h)R'dj were closely related through the person of Mabv I. Child of a negotiated pairing of chiefly houses, her mother was *maĕkthĕnas*, while her paternal grandmother was *(h)r'dj'dst'k*, a major sept of the *ēshĕn'lokdĕ*. Evidence suggests the earliest form of the language was improvised within Mabv's household, and was then copied by her kin as these two largest *atwĕzlo* clans shaped the first mud bricks of a Dream.

A third source, mostly of names of many plants and animals, and of objects and activities associated with woodland existence, is the complex of languages spoken by the *hazl*. The mother tongue, also called Hazl, diverged from the archaic roots very early, and evolved for thousands of years in isolation on the fringes of what became, after the ice, the Western Isles. By the time these populations integrated into the hypnarchy, the daughter dialects of Hazl had grown as weird as it gets in *dvarsh* language. They remain living speech, as the *hazl* clans have aggressively maintained each dialect within its enclave.

Significant jargon connected to the *dvarsh* mental technologies, *jokm'hochoanthē* (metamathemagics) and *najath'lopĕm* ('pataphysics), derives from languages of the *zĕk*, residents of the far north. The majority of these terms have roots in *zĕk* mysticism. They have been adopted as technical terms by *mojabvth'm* because ancient esoterica, as metaphor, still informs even rigorously constructed ontotronic expressions. Enthusiasts should note that continuity between old lore and namesake precepts is poetic rather than scientific.

One language of the *zĕk*, recorded as Zkhul, may be extinct. No one among the *atwĕzlo* or *hazl* knows for sure. None among the *zĕk* cares to comment. On rare occasions when hackberry brandy has flowed, one tipsy *zĕktha* or another has stood and broken silence to declaim furiously from what seems to be an epic about a Zkhul speaking "Clan of the Ice." From what listeners have gleaned, the *zkhul'm* of the poem never removed to exile, surviving invisibly in frozen retreats of the human realm, unknown in *habdvarsha*. To date, every recitation has ended with the reciter abruptly sitting and passing out. Sober, no *zĕktha* admits knowledge of any such poem, much less of a hidden clan.

Interestingly, there is also, or was, a language of an *atwĕzlo* clan, the *okka* [₆ᴈᴈᴈ.], that may or may not have died out. A few generations ago, *okk'm* stopped revealing to outsiders whether or not they still use it in private. They are never known to consult files related to the language in the banks of the Repository. Other *dvarsh* consider this the business of the *okka* alone, and assume they will say something on the subject if it is ever relevant.

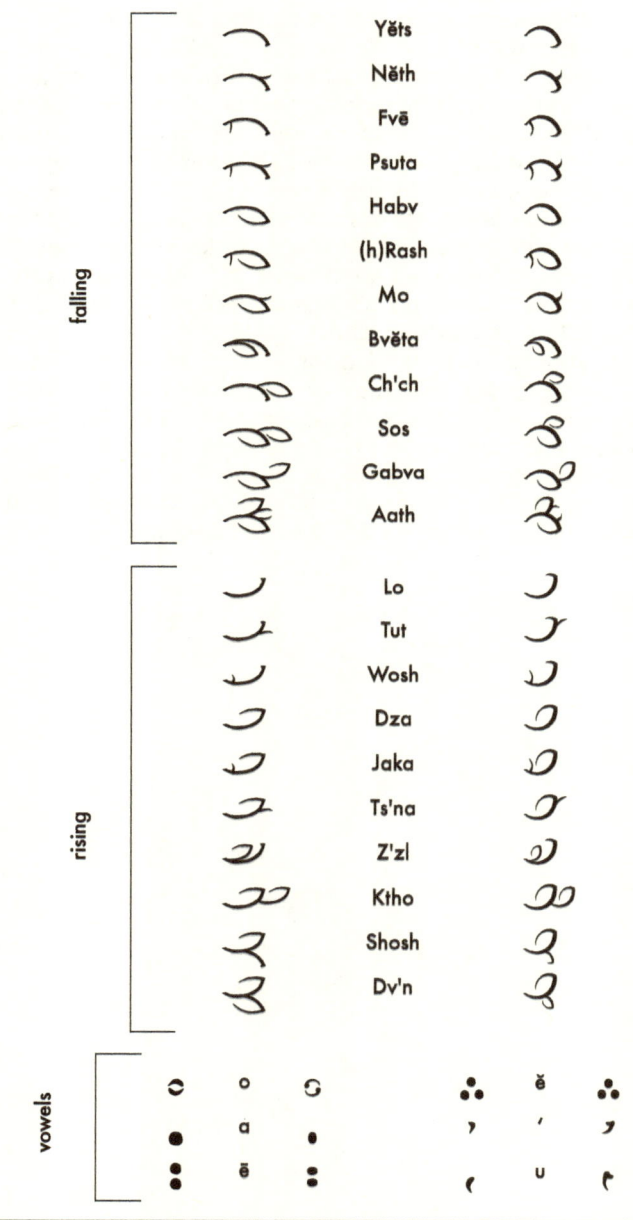

falling

- Yĕts
- Nĕth
- Fvē
- Psuta
- Habv
- (h)Rash
- Mo
- Bvĕta
- Ch'ch
- Sos
- Gabva
- Aath

rising

- Lo
- Tut
- Wosh
- Dza
- Jaka
- Ts'na
- Z'zl
- Ktho
- Shosh
- Dv'n

vowels

- o
- a
- ē
- ĕ
- u

Comparison of calligraphic and typographic characters.

Guide to the writing system and pronunciation

The Dvarsh language is written with with a set of twenty-two characters, the *jayĕlu* [ɔ͵ᴧ∴ᴧͺ], that function both as consonants of an alphabet and as a syllabary, depending on context. Each is also, in its own right, a word. Additionally, there are six vowel symbols used with the main characters in their function as consonants. Only the twenty-two consonant characters are viewed as part of the *jayĕlu* proper. Even after thousands of years, vowels are seen as an innovation, occupying a status beneath letters but above diacritical marks. This despite their obvious utility.

Transition from the old practices has never been absolute. Although Dvarsh is mostly a regular, rule-based idiom, there are plenty of weird holdovers from the remote past, and odd cases where time has eroded a once conforming use into an irregularity. Most obvious are the consonant characters themselves, each of which is both a letter and a discrete word identical to its name. Thus the character *wosh* [ᴜ] is read like English "w" in a word such as the noun, *wopta* [ᴜ₆ᴧᴊͺ], meaning "rice," but standing alone it is read, "wosh," which is the verb, "to see."

Because the source of the characters, the *jaz'zl*, is a syllabary and not an alphabet, otherwise straightforward rules of Dvarsh pronunciation are complicated by interesting exceptions. A number of these involve words spelled without vowels. It is usually—but not always—the case, that when a word is written without vowels its pronunciation is based on the ancient syllabaric reading. Most such words are quite old. Things get tricky when one of these is inflected with latter-day affixes that include vowels. Sometimes spelling of the root is regularized. Sometimes it is not.

The syllabary remains a living tradition. Some clans still use the *jaz'zl* for writing their historical clan languages, reserving the *jayĕlu* for standard Dvarsh. A very few clans, mostly *hazl* and *zĕk*, use archaic writing systems unrelated to the *jaz'zl* for their ancestral tongues. The only parts of any of these systems to enter general use are the numerals, which were originally *hazl*.

Attributes of the characters. The forms of the *jayĕlu*, like the *jaz'zl* from which it derives, were inspired by plant shapes: leaves, buds, thorns, and berries. Written lines may go left to right, right to left, top to bottom, bottom to top, in spirals, winding switchbacks, or whatever. Words and texts are imagined and often discussed as a living vine. One always reads in the direction "the vine grows." This metaphor has been worked to death in *dvarsh* poetry.

The characters sort into two categories: twelve falling and ten rising. Several feature both rising and falling elements, which can lead to confusion about which category includes which. The stem's curve is the definitive indicator. Compare two characters:

aath   *dv'n:*

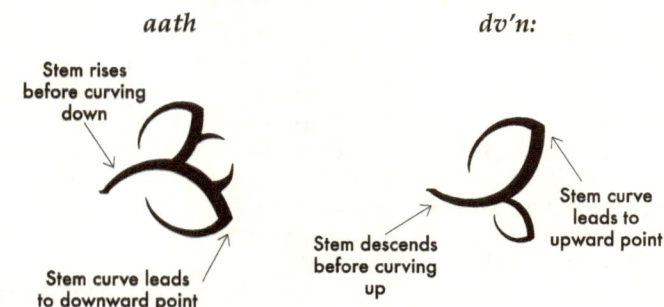

The curve of *aath*'s stem starts upward, but finishes pointing down. Consequently, it belongs to the falling group. By contrast, the stem of *dv'n* drops slightly at first, but swings up to its point. *Dv'n* is a rising character. *Aath,* by the way, is the most complex character retained from the *jaz'zl*.

Phonetic values of the consonants

- *yĕts* is like "y" in yellow.
- *nĕth* is like "n" except at the ends of words and in conjugated forms of verbs, where it takes the verb form "-nth."
- *fvē* is always a blend of English "f" and "v."
- *psuta* is usually pronounced "p" at the beginnings of syllables and in combination with other consonants, but "-ps" at the ends of words and some syllables. There are exceptions to both rules. As a verb auxiliary it is always pronounced, "psuta."
- *habv* is always like "h" in house.
- *(h)rash* mostly corresponds to an English "r." When it begins a syllable, however, the "r" sound is preceded by a suggestion of an "h." Another of the verb roots, it is pronounced with the verb form "-rsh" at the end of words and in their conjugations.
- *mo* is like "m"
- *bvĕta* is a blend of English "b" and "v." This is the character used by Dvarsh to replace both these letters when transcribing from English. In some combinations the "v" sound is subsumed into the consonant that follows, especially if *fvē* [⌐] or *dv'n* [ⱬ].
- *ch'ch* is always "ch," as in church. Its verb form is the same.
- *sos* is like "s" in sun.

૨ৢ *gabva* is a hard "g," as in game.

ᘧ *aath* is always "th," as in thought. Its verb form is the same.

ᒍ *lo* is like "l."

ᒍ *tut* is like "t."

ᒎ *wosh* is like "w" at the beginnings of syllables or in combination with another consonant. It is a verb root, pronounced "-wsh" at the ends of words and in their conjugated forms. Pronunciation of its verb form has the effect of drawing out an immediately preceding vowel.

ᒍ *dza* is pronounced "dz" in all cases except when it is followed by the consonant *habv* [ᔔ] or vowel "ĕ" [ᤫ], in which case it is "d." In some combinations with other consonants, the "z" sound is also subsumed or lost.

ᒍ *jaka* is pronounced like "j" in jar.

ᒎ *ts'na* is pronounced "ts."

ᒎ *z'zl* is "z" as in zeal when it begins a syllable and in many consonant combinations, but it is "-zl" at the ends of words and some syllables.

ᒎᒎ *ktho* is a tongue-twisting "kth" when followed by a vowel. It is "k" when followed by a consonant or at the end of a word.

ᘧ *shosh* is always "sh" as in shush. Its verb form is the same.

ᘧ *dv'n* is a blend of "d" and "v," except in some combinations where the "v" sound is lost."

Vowels. Dvarsh vowels are quite clipped, sounding almost like abbreviations of the English counterparts used here. Other than a very slight drawl in combination with *wosh* [ᒎ], vowel pronunciations do not vary. Without exception, every written vowel is sounded. There is a so-called "unwritten mute vowel," but it is considered separately below.

The six written vowels are:

ₒ "o" as in go.

· "a" as in father.

: "ē" as in be.

∴ "ĕ" as in get.

, as much a hitch in the voice as speech. Form the mouth for a short "i" (as in wit), but skip saying most of it.

ᵣ "u" as in push.

31

Syllabification. Every vowel is pronounced, so a word has at least as many syllables as it has vowels. A consonant always syllabifies with an immediately following vowel. If two vowels are separated by two consonants, the split is between the consonants. If two vowels are separated by more than two consonants, the split is between the first two consonants, unless another exception applies.

Stress. With the vast majority of words of more than one syllable, primary stress falls on the next to last syllable. A small number are stressed on the last syllable, which is indicated in writing by a doubled final consonant.

The unwritten mute vowel. This term refers to a sparse handful of exceptions—such as *thrm* [ɜ̣ꞵꞷ]— that have no vowel indicators, but do not follow the rules of either alphabetic or syllabaric pronunciation. These words feature a so-called "unwritten mute vowel" incredibly difficult for most humans to master. All words associated with the exception originate in the Hazl dialects, and all are characterized by combinations of either *aath/(h)rash* [ɜ̣ꞵ] or *(h)rash/mo* [ꞵꞷ] clustered with another consonant before and/or after. Fortunately, examples are few.

Plurals. The *-'m* [ˌꞷ] ending generally indicates the plural. It often replaces a terminal *"a"* [ˌ], but simply attaches to words with any other ending. Occasionally, *-'m* or its Maek form, *-om* [ₒꞷ], grafts into a singular concept that embodies multiples or repetition. Many beats make a rhythm; many birds make a flock.

Adjectives modifying a plural noun must agree in number, also taking the plural ending when needed.

A note on word formation. Roots in Dvarsh typically consist of combinations of two or three consonants combined with vowels or not. Most often the etymological bases are obvious in combinations of ideas associated with the roots, although sometimes connections can be obscure. There are also words that were apparently coined because they looked or sounded really cool.

When deriving new forms from existing words, the following tips are useful. A review of the dictionary will show that most often the relationship is straightforward between such a coinage and its source.

- The vowel, *"a"* [ˌ], suffixed to a verb makes it a noun.
- *"a"* prefixed to a noun makes it an adjective.
- *"a"* prefixed AND suffixed to a verb makes it an adjective.

A Few Words about Dvarsh Grammar

Word order and noun case. The most common word order in both Maek and (h)R'dj is subject/verb/object. That is typical for most other Dvarsh speakers as well. However, the most common word orders in Hazl and its derivatives lead with the verb. Hazl itself has a verb/subject/object bias, but two of its derived tongues, Hz'l and Hm, tend to lead with the verb and end with the subject. The solution in Standard Dvarsh is to attach the suffix *-mo* [ᴤᴄ] to the subject of a verb, flagging it regardless of position in a sentence.

In ceremonial speech, the suffix *-ĕt* [ˌ.ᴊ] is attached to objects of prepositions. This practice does not survive in ordinary usage. It shows up often in proclamations and sentimental poetry.

Modifiers. Modifiers of nouns and adjectives always follow the word being modified. If the relationship between modifier and modified is seen as essential, then the modifier may be suffixed to the modified to form a compound; otherwise, the modifier follows the modified as a separate word. Subtle differences in meaning lurk in the choice to form a compound or not.

Adverbs follow the verbs or adjectives modified. The verb auxiliary *apch* [ˌᴧᴄ] and its inflected forms, used when conjugating compound tenses, always precede the verb modified.

The definite article, *fvē* [ᴧ: or ᴧ], attaches as a suffix when it is part of a proper noun. It follows common nouns as a separate word except in cases of emphasis. There are exceptions to both practices.

Possession. Possession is shown most often by suffixing possessor to possessed. There is a suffix, *-fvĕ* [ᴧ.], that indicates possession of an object by a subject, but its use is now a little old-fashioned.

The interrogative. Questions are formed by making a declarative statement followed by a question word or phrase. For example, no Dvarsh would ask, "What is your name?" Rather, she would phrase it, "Your name, what?" Omission of the verb in such formations is not unusual. Note: when written, the question marks bracket only the question word or phrase, not the entire sentence:

> *g(h)romfvĕ mēfvĕ ?ĕbvu?*
>
> [ᴤᴐᴐᴤᴨ. ᴐ:ᴨ. ˢ .ᴐᴦ ˀ]

Pronouns and pronominal adjectives

I, me		mofvē
we, us		momofvē
you (sing.)		mēfva
you (plural)		mēfva'm
it, she, her, he, him		mo
they, them		moomo
who, whom (sing.)		mobvu
who, whom (pl.)		mobvu'm
which (sing.)		dvabvu
which (pl.)		dvabvu'm
this		bvum
these		bvum'm
that		yĕbv
those		yĕbv'm
what		ĕbvu
such		fv'u
my, mine		mĕfvĕ
our, ours		momĕfvĕ
your, yours (sing.)		mēfvĕ
your, yours (pl.)		m'mēfvĕ
its, his, her, hers		mĕĕ
their, theirs		m'omĕ
whose		mobvufvĕ

Gender adjectives

female		ag
male		u'g
neuter		ēgo

Conjugated verb forms indicate subject person and number. Subject pronouns are typically only used when clarity requires. Using them otherwise is not wrong, but it is wordy.

Pronouns are gender neutral. When a gender distinction is necessary or convenient, the pronoun is followed by *ag* ("female"), *u'g* ("male"), or *ēgo* ("neuter").

Verb Conjugations

There are six single-character verbs in Dvarsh, given below. In the infinitive, every other verb ends with one of these.

All verbs fall into one of two conjugations, *akthĕshl'* [ˌ๏฿ˌ๖ɔ], rising, or *ayushl'a* [ˌ๛ˌ๖ɔˌ], falling, determined by the rising or falling nature of the terminal character. The single exception is the auxiliary, *apch* [ˌ๛๛].

Verbs ending with one of the following characters in the infinitive belong to the falling conjugation:

๛	*nĕth*	to be
๏	*(h)rash*	to have
๛	*ch'ch*	to seek; to want
๛	*aath*	to build; to make

Verbs ending with one of the following characters in the infinitive belong to the rising conjugation:

๛	*wosh*	to see
๛	*shosh*	to go

The auxiliary, *apch* [ˌ๛๛], ends in *ch'ch*, but is neither rising nor falling. Some of its inflected forms differ depending on the conjugation of any verb with which it is combined.

Partial Conjugation of the Falling Verb, *Neth*, (to be)

	Singular		Plural	
Present Indicative				
1st Person	⟶	*nĕth*	⟶	*nĕthtu*
2nd		*nĕthktho*		*nĕthkthotu*
3rd		*nĕth*		*nĕthy'tu*
Imperfect Indicative				
1st		*nĕthkl'*		*nĕthkl'tu*
2nd		*nĕthkthol'*		*nĕthkthol'tu*
3rd		*nĕthy'kl'*		*nĕthy'kl'tu*
Preterit				
1st		*nĕthklo*		*nĕthklotu*
2nd		*nĕthktholo*		*nĕthktholotu*
3rd		*nĕthy'klo*		*nĕthy'klotu*
Future				
1st		*nĕth psuta*		*nĕthtu psuta*
2nd		*nĕth psutaktho*		*nĕthtu psutaktho*
3rd		*nĕth psutakth'*		*nĕthtu psutakth'*
Conditional				
1st		*nĕth ēpsuta*		*nĕthtu ēpsuta*
2nd		*nĕth ēpsutaktho*		*nĕthtu ēpsutaktho*
3rd		*nĕth ēpsutakth'*		*nĕthtu ēpsutakth'*

Present Participle	*nĕthtĕ*	Imperative	*kth'nĕth*
Past Participle	*nĕthlo*	Gerund	*nĕthl'*

The falling conjugation includes all verbs ending with *neth* [⟶], *(h)rash* [ ], *ch'ch* [ ] and *aath* [ ].

Verb auxiliary inflected forms, Falling conjugation

	Singular		Plural	
[has, have]				
1st Person		*apch*		*apchtu*
2nd		*apchktho*		*apchkthotu*
3rd		*apch*		*apchtu*
[having]				
1st		*apchl'*		*apchl'tu*
2nd		*apchl'ktho*		*apchl'ktu*
3rd		*apchl'*		*apchl'tu*
[had]				
1st		*apchlo*		*apchlotu*
2nd		*apchloktho*		*apchloktu*
3rd		*apchl'o*		*apchl'otu*
[having had]				
1st		*apachl'*		*apachl'tu*
2nd		*apachl'ktho*		*apachl'ktu*
3rd		*apachl'*		*apachl'tu*
[had had]				
1st		*apachlo*		*apachlotu*
2nd		*apachloktho*		*apachloktu*
3rd		*apachl'o*		*apachl'otu*
[shall have, will have]				
1st		*apchp'*		*apchp'tu*
2nd		*apchp'ktho*		*apchp'ktu*
3rd		*apchp'ĕ*		*apchp'ĕtu*
[would have]				
1st		*ēapchp'*		*ēapchp'tu*
2nd		*ēapchp'ktho*		*ēapchp'ktu*
3rd		*ēapchp'ĕ*		*ēapchp'ĕtu*

Partial Conjugation of the Rising Verb, *Wosh*, (to see)

	Singular		Plural	
Present Indicative				
1st Person		*wosh*		*woshtu*
2nd		*woshgo*		*woshgotu*
3rd		*wosh*		*woshg'tu*
Imperfect Indicative				
1st		*woshgl'*		*woshgl'tu*
2nd		*woshgol'*		*woshgol'tu*
3rd		*woshgl'l'*		*woshgl'l'tu*
Preterit				
1st		*woshglo*		*woshglotu*
2nd		*woshgolo*		*woshgolotu*
3rd		*woshgl'o*		*woshgl'otu*
Future				
1st		*wosh psuta*		*woshtu psuta*
2nd		*wosh psutago*		*woshtu psutago*
3rd		*wosh psutag'*		*woshtu psutag'*
Conditional				
1st		*wosh ēpsuta*		*woshtu ēpsuta*
2nd		*wosh ēpsutago*		*woshtu ēpsutago*
3rd		*wosh ēpsutag'*		*woshtu ēpsutag'*

Present Participle *woshtĕ* Imperative *g'wosh*

Past Participle *woshlo* Gerund *woshl'*

The rising conjugation includes all verbs ending with *wosh* [ ] and *shosh* [ ].

Verb auxiliary inflected forms, Rising conjugation

	Singular		Plural	
[has, have]				
1st Person	⸾	apch	⸾	apchtu
2nd	⸾	apchgo	⸾	apchgotu
3rd	⸾	apch	⸾	apchtu
[having]				
1st	⸾	apchl'	⸾	apchl'tu
2nd	⸾	apchl'go	⸾	apchl'gotu
3rd	⸾	apchl'	⸾	apchl'tu
[had]				
1st	⸾	apchlo	⸾	apchlotu
2nd	⸾	apchlogo	⸾	apchlogotu
3rd	⸾	apchl'o	⸾	apchl'otu
[having had]				
1st	⸾	apachl'	⸾	apachl'tu
2nd	⸾	apachl'go	⸾	apachl'gotu
3rd	⸾	apachl'	⸾	apachl'tu
[had had]				
1st	⸾	apachlo	⸾	apachlotu
2nd	⸾	apachlogo	⸾	apachlogotu
3rd	⸾	apachl'o	⸾	apachl'otu
[shall have, will have]				
1st	⸾	apchp'	⸾	apchp'tu
2nd	⸾	apchp'go	⸾	apchp'gotu
3rd	⸾	apchp'ĕ	⸾	apchp'ĕtu
[would have]				
1st	⸾	ēapchp'	⸾	ēapchp'tu
2nd	⸾	ēapchp'go	⸾	ēapchp'gotu
3rd	⸾	ēapchp'ĕ	⸾	ēapchp'ĕtu

Dictionary entries and "alphabetization"

Entries in the Dvarsh to English dictionary consist of

- a Dvarsh word in Dvarsh characters
- a pronunciation guide in small capitals
- italicized abbreviation of part of speech
- a definition in English.

Entries in the English to Dvarsh dictionary feature

- an English word
- part of speech
- pronunciation guide to the Dvarsh
- the Dvarsh word in Dvarsh characters.

The pronunciation guides approximate phonetic respelling of Dvarsh words in Latin characters. Syllabification is shown. Stressed syllables are in boldface.

Unlike practices current in the world of English, the Dvarsh approach to "alphabetization" assigns different roles to consonants and vowels. This is because vowels are not seen as "letters" in the same sense as consonants. The traditional orders for vowels and consonants interact, but are distinct.

In word lists such as the Dvarsh to English dictionary, words are ordered by the following scheme:

- first by first consonant regardless of whether or not that consonant is preceded by a vowel,
- second by rules of vowel priority,
- third by ordering of consonants.

When comparing two words, at any given position after the first (e.g., the third "letter"), any vowel precedes any consonant. The first consonant of a word, however, determines to which part of the list the word belongs.

Contrary to the general rule for vowel priority, words that begin with vowels are listed according to their first consonant, but following after all words actually beginning with that consonant. The key to the Dvarsh-to-English dictionary is always to search first by the first consonant.

This scheme, as one may suppose, originated among the *hazl*.

The traditional order of consonants lists the twelve falling characters followed by the ten rising characters.

The falling consonants in order, from the top:

⌐	*yĕts*
⌐	*nĕth*
⌐	*fvē*
⌐	*psuta*
⌐	*habv*
⌐	*(h)rash*
⌐	*mo*
⌐	*bvĕta*
⌐	*ch'ch*
⌐	*sos*
⌐	*gabva*
⌐	*aath*

The ten rising consonants in order, from the top:

⌐	*lo*
⌐	*tut*
⌐	*wosh*
⌐	*dza*
⌐	*jaka*
⌐	*ts'na*
⌐	*z'zl*
⌐	*ktho*
⌐	*shosh*
⌐	*dv'n*

The traditional order of vowels:

៰	[*o*]
•	[*a*]
:	[*ē*]
∴	[*ĕ*]
,	[']
៸	[*u*]

Dvarsh to English
Dictionary

⌒ Yets

⌒ [YĔTS] *n.* - shape
⌒₀ [YO] *n.* opening
⌒₀⸲⌇⤴[YO·'ST] *n.* - ditch
⌒₀⌒. [YO·YA] *n.* - spoon
⌒₀⌒⸲⌇.₂ [YO·Y'·MĚSH] *v.* - to transport
⌒₀⌒⌒ [YONTH] *v.* - to form
⌒₀⌇₀ [YO·LO] *n.* - 1. mouth; 2. hole
⌒₀⌇₀⌒. [YO·LOTS·NA] *n.* - well (shaft)
⌒₀⌇.⌒⸳⌒. [YO·LA·GĔ·MA] *n.* - abscess
⌒₀⌇⌇⸳⸲⤴[YOL·MĚT] *n.* - tongue
⌒₀⌇⌇⸳₂. [YOL·WĒ·SHA] *n.* - pocket
⌒₀⌇⌇. [YOL·DZA] *n.* - smile
⌒₀⌇⌇.⤳ [YOL·DZAWSH] *v.* - to smile
⌒₀⤴[YOT] *n.* - piece, part
⌒₀⌇⸳⸳⤳ [YO·TĔTH] *v.* - to break
⌒₀⌇⤳⤳ [YO·W'TH] *v.* - to carve
⌒₀⌇⤳⤶ [YO·DZ'CH] *v.* - to kiss
⌒₀⌇⌒⸳⌇₀ [YO·TS'·NA·LO] *n.* - bay
⌒₀⌇⤳⸲ [YOTS·(H)R'] *n.* - lip
⌒₀⌇⌇⌇₀⌒ [YOK·DVOM] *n.* - kettle
⌒₀⌇₂ [YOSH] *v.* - to pack
⌒₀⌇₂⌇⌇⌇⌇ [YO·SHOK] *n.* - bag
⌒. [YA] *n.* - mold (for shaping or casting)
⌒.⸳⸳⤴[YA·AT] *n.* - berry
⌒.⌒⤳ [YARTH] *v.* - to produce
⌒.⌒. [YA·MA] *n.* - body
⌒.⌒.⌒. [YA·MA·(H)RA] *n.* - motion
⌒.⌒⸳⸳⤳. [YA·MĚ·THA] *n.* - digestion
⌒.⌒⌒⸳⸳₂ [YAM·(H)RĚSH] *v.* - to move
⌒.⌒⌇⸳⸳ [YAM·DĚ] *n.* - flesh
⌒.⌒⌇⸲₂. [YAM·DZU·SHA] *n.* - belly
⌒.⤳ [YATH] *v.* - to mold; to shape
⌒.⌇⸳⸳⌒ [YA·LĚNTH] *v.* - to mix
⌒.⌇⸳ [YA·TA] *n.* - inn
⌒.⌇₀⌒ [YA·DVOM] *n.* - pot, vessel
⌒.⌇₀⌒.⌇ [YA·DVO·MAZL] *n.* - 1. caldron; 2. stewpot
⌒.⌇⤳ [YADTH] *v.* - 1. to bake; 2. to fire (as ceramics)

ᴖ.ᴣᴣₒᴕ[YAD·**THOT**] *n.* - baker

ᴖ.ᴣᴣₒᴕ. [YAD·**THO**·KTHA] *n.* - oven

ᴖ.ᴣᴣ. [**YAD**·THA] *n.* - kiln

ᴖ.ᴣᴣ..ᴣ. [YAD·**THĔ**·THA] *n.* - bakery

ᴖ:ᴗᴣ [YĔLTH] *v.* - to stamp

ᴖ:ᴗ [YĔT] *n.* - point

ᴖ.ᴗᴖ. [YĔM·CHO] *n.* - square

ᴖ.ᴗᴗ. [**YĔM**·TA] *n.* - triangle

ᴖ.ᴗ [YĔBV] *adj.* - that

ᴖ.ᴗᴗ [**YĔ**·BV'M] *adj.* - those

ᴖ.ᴗᴗᴗ. [YĔCH·**LO**·SHA] *n.* - anus

ᴖ.ᴗᴗ. [**YĔCH**·LA] *n.* - 1. excrement; 2. feces

ᴖ.ᴗᴗ. [**YĔS**·TA] *n.* - side

ᴖ.ᴗ [YĔTH] *v.* - to cause

ᴖ.ᴣᴗ. [**YĔTH**·DZA] *n.* - gentleness

ᴖ.ᴗᴗ [**YĔ**·T'CH] *v.* - to defecate

ᴖ.ᴗᴗ [**YĔ**·TSATH] *v.* - to urinate

ᴖ.ᴗᴗᴗ [**YĔTS**·DVOM] *n.* - boat

ᴖ.ᴗ [YĔZL] *n.* - face

ᴖ.ᴗ.ᴗ [**YĔ**·DVOTH] *v.* - to heat

ᴖ.ᴗᴗᴗ. [YĔ·**DVOTH**·DĔ] *n.* - heat

ᴖ.ᴣ.ᴗ. [**YĔD**·FVĔ] *n.* - summer

ᴖ' [Y'] *prep.* - into

ᴖᴗᴗ [**Y'M**·DZ'] *adv.* - well

ᴖᴗᴗᴕ [Y'·**BVOT**] *n.* - forge

ᴖᴗᴗᴣ. [Y'·BVO·**TU**·THA] *n.* - smith

ᴖᴗᴗᴗᴗ [Y'·BVO·**TUK**] *n.* - smithy

ᴖᴗ.ᴣ [**Y'·BVATH**] *v.* - to forge; to fashion

ᴖᴗᴖ. [Y'·**BVU**·FVA] *n.* - genitalia

ᴖᴗᴖ.ᴗ. [Y'·BVU·**FVĔ**·GA] *n.* - vagina

ᴖᴗᴖᴗ. [Y'·BVU·FVU·'·GA] *n.* - penis

ᴖᴗ [Y'CH] *v.* - to improve

ᴖᴗᴗ [**Y'**·S'SH] *v.* to enter

ᴖᴗᴗ. [**Y'·S'**·SHA] *n.* - entrance

ᴖᴗᴗᴗ. [Y'·S'·**SH'**·HA] *n.* - gate

ᴖᴗ [Y'ZL] *adj.* - good

ᴖᴗᴣᴗ. [Y'·**ZUTH**·DĔ] *n.* - kindness

ᴖᴗᴗᴖᴣᴗᴖ [Y'Z·NA·**NĔTH**·NOFV] *exclam.* - "hello;" a greeting

ᴖᴗᴗᴗ [**Y'Z**·WOSH] *v.* - to trust

ﾘﾘﾘﾘﾘ [Y'Z·**WO**·SHA] *n.* - trust

ﾘﾘ [YU] *n.* - drop (fluid)

ﾘﾘﾘ [YUPS] *n.* - fruit

ﾘﾘﾘﾘﾘ [YU·**PĚM**·LOT] *n.* - wine

ﾘﾘﾘﾘﾘ [YU·**P'**·YOT] *n.* - orange (fruit)

ﾘﾘﾘﾘ [**YU**·MĚSH] *v.* - to rub

ﾘﾘﾘ [YU·LÊTH] *v.* - to shame

ﾘﾘﾘﾘ [YU·**TĚ**·DĚ] *n.* - expert

ﾘﾘﾘ [YUSH] *v.* - to fall

ﾘﾘﾘ [**YU**·SHA] *n.* - fall

ﾘﾘﾘﾘ [**YUSH**·L'] *n.* - precipice

ﾘﾘ [YĚZL] *n.* - star

ﾘﾘﾘ [**O**·YOT] *n.* - curve

ﾘﾘﾘﾘ [O·**YĚ**·BVOT] *n.* - degree

ﾘﾘﾘﾘ [**O**·YĚS·TA] *n.* - circle

ﾘﾘﾘﾘﾘ [O·**YĚS**·TANTH] *v.* - to enclose

ﾘﾘﾘﾘﾘ [O·**YĚS·TA**·NA] *n.* - frame

ﾘﾘﾘﾘﾘ [O·**YĚS**·TATH] *v.* - to encircle

ﾘﾘ [A·**Ê**·Y'] *adj.* - out

ﾘﾘﾘﾘﾘ [A·YO·**T'TH**·L'] *adj.* - broken

ﾘﾘﾘﾘﾘ [A·YĚ·**BVO**·(H)RA] *adj.* - responsible

ﾘﾘﾘ [A·**YĚDZ**] *adj.* - precious; dear

ﾘﾘﾘﾘ [A·**Y'M**·DĚ] *adj.* - well

ﾘﾘﾘﾘﾘ [A·**Y'**·**ZUTH**·L'] *adj.* - kind

ﾘﾘﾘﾘ [A·YUSH·**L'**·A] *adj.* - falling

ﾘﾘﾘﾘ [A·**YUSH**·DĚ] *adj.* - steep

ﾘﾘ [**Ê**·Y'] *adv. & prep.* - out

ﾘ Neth

ﾘ [NĚTH] *v.* - to be

ﾘﾘﾘ [NOFV] *adj.* - actual, real

ﾘﾘﾘ [NOM] *n.* - substance

ﾘﾘﾘﾘﾘ [NOM·**TSA**·(H)RA] *n.* - sponge

ﾘﾘﾘ [NOTCH] *v.* - to sleep

ﾘﾘﾘ [**NOT**·CHA] *n.* - sleep

ﾘﾘﾘﾘ [NOT·**CHU**·THA] *n.* - sleeper

ﾘ [NA] *n.* - condition

ﾘﾘﾘ [**NA**·YO] *n.* - tooth

⤳⤳ [**NA·**N'CH] *v.* - to covet

⤳⤳: [**NAN·**FVĒ] *n.* - transcendence; transcendent being

⤳⤳⤳ [**NAN·**FV'**·LU·**THA] *n.* - champion

⤳⤳⤳ [**NAN·**SA**·LĚ·**YA] *n.* - quorum

⤳⤳⤳ [**NAN·S'·**TA] *n.* - ambassador

⤳⤳ [**NANTH**] *v.* - to exist

⤳⤳ [**NAN·**THA] *n.* - entity

⤳⤳ [**NAN·DĚ**] *n.* - existence

⤳⤳ [**NA·MOL·**TA] *n.* - fat (tissue)

⤳⤳ [**NA·**BVUTH] *v.* - to paste

⤳⤳ [**NAS·PĚ**] *n.* - weight

⤳⤳ [**NAS·**PĚRSH] *v.* - to weigh

⤳⤳ [**NASTH**] *v.* - to bite

⤳⤳ [**NAWSH**] *v.* - to happen

⤳⤳ [**NA·**WA] *n.* - event

⤳⤳ [**NA·W'·**MA] *n.* - example

⤳⤳ [**NA·W'·**THOT] *n.* - blade

⤳⤳ [**NA·**JAM] *n.* - physics

⤳⤳ [**NA·**JA**·**TH'**·LO·PĚM**] *n.* - 'pataphysics

⤳⤳ [**NA·**JA**·**TH'**·LO·PĚ·MU·**THA] *n.* - 'pataphysician

⤳⤳ [**NA·**TSA] *n.* - fish

⤳⤳ [**NA·**TSACH] *v.* - to fish

⤳⤳ [**NĚWSH**] *v.* - to hide

⤳⤳ [**NĚ·**BVO] *conj.* - because

⤳⤳ [**NĚ·SPAK·**ZA] *n.* - imp

⤳⤳ [**NĚCH·**TA] *n.* - peace

⤳⤳ [**NĚL·**SONTH] *v.* - to tunnel

⤳⤳ [**NĚWSH**] *v.* - to disguise

⤳⤳ [**NĚ·DZACH·DĚ**] *n.* - lust

⤳⤳ [**NĚ·**DZA**·THUK**] *n.* - qualification

⤳⤳ [**N'·**OT] *n.* - thing

⤳⤳ [**N'·**YĚM] *n.* - comb

⤳⤳ [**N'·**YĚTH] *v.* - to develop

⤳⤳ [**N'PS**] *n.* - bit

⤳⤳ [**N'·**LU] *adv. & prep.* - about

⤳⤳ [**N'K·**SKTHU**·U·L'·O·**SA] *n.* - satellite

⤳⤳ [**NU·P'**] *conj.* - if

⤳⤳ [**NĚWSH**] *v.* - to disguise

⤳⤳ [**NĚ·**DZA] *n.* - simplicity; the simple

~ᴐ⅋ [**NĚ**·DZACH] *v.* - to lust

~ᴐ⅊ [**NĚ**·DZATH] *v.* - to qualify

ₒ~ [ONTH] *v.* - to live

ₒ~ₒ~, [O·**NO**·MA] *n.* - band (small group)

ₒ~, [**O**·NA] *n.* - life

ₒ~ᴗ.. [ON·WĚ] *n.* - nerve (bio.)

.~ₒᴊ⅋ᴊ [A·**NOT**·CHL'] *adj.* - sleeping

.~:ᴗ' [A·**NĚ**·W'] *adj.* - hidden

.~:ᴐ₀, [A·**NĚDZ**·(H)RA] *adj.* - complex

.~..ᴐ [A·**NĚDZ**] *adj.* - loose

.~ₜ~' [A·**NU**·(H)R'] *adj.* - physical

.~ₜᴊ⅋' [A·**NUT**·CH'] *adj.* - possible

.~ᴐ.. [AN·DĚ] *adj.* - simple

:~ [ĚNTH] *v.* - to cease

:~₀ [Ě·NO] *n.* - spirit

:~ₒ~.~ [Ě·**NO**·YAM] *n.* - brain

:~ₒᴂᴂ [Ě·**NOK**] *n.* - spirituality

:~.~ [Ě·NARSH] *v.* - to prostitute

:~.~ᴈₒᴊ [Ě·**NAR**·SHOT] *n.* - prostitute

:~⅊. [ĚN·THA] *n.* - cessation

:~ᴐ' [ĚN·DZ'] *adj.* - stiff

:~ᴐ.~ [ĚN·DZARSH] *v.* - to complicate

:~ᴐ.~. [ĚN·**DZA**·(H)RA] *n.* - complication

'~~..⅊. ['N·**YĚ**·THA] *n.* - development

~ Fvee

~ [FVĚ] *def. art.* - the (also "~:"; plural is always "~:'~")

~₀ [FVO] *numb.* - eight

~ₒ'~ [**FVO**·'NTH] *v.* - to sew

~ₒ'~, [FVO·'·NA] *n.* - stitch

~ₒ'~ᴗ, [FVO·'N·**L**'·A] *n.* - sewing

~ₒ'ᴂ⅋₀ [FVO·'**K**·THO] *n.* - net

~ₒ'ᴈ [**FVO**·'SH] *v.* - to weave

~ₒ'ᴈₒᴊᴊ [FVO·'·**SHOT**] *n.* - weaver

~ₒ'ᴈ. [FVO·'·SHA] *n.* - weave (of fabric)

~ₒ'ᴈ.⅊ᴗ, [FVO·'·SHA·**TH**'·LA] *n.* - sheet

~ₒ'ᴈₜᴗ, [FVO·'·**SHU**·LA] *n.* - garment

~ₒ'ᴈₜᴂ, [FVO·'·**SHU**·KTHA] *n.* - weaving; woven item

[FVO·**'SH**·A] *n.* - fabric

[**FVO**·YA] *n.* - basket

[**FVO**·TU] *numb.* - eighteen

[FVA·**O**·LA] *n.* - glove

[**FVA**·Ē] *numb.* - seven

[FVAPS] *n.* - hand

[**FVA**·PUT] *n.* - finger

[**FVAP**·BVOCH] *v.* - to grip

[FVAMT] *adv., det. & pro.* - each

[**FVA**·GĔ] *n.* - nail, such as fingernail or toenail

[**FVA**·LOPS] *n.* - foot

[FVA·**LOT**] *n.* - toe

[**FVA**·LOSH] *v.* - to walk

[**FVAL**·POSH] *v.* - to step

[FVAL·**PU**·CHĔ] *n.* - stocking

[FVAL·**PU**·TA] *n.* - sock

[**FVA**·WOSH] *v.* - to hallucinate

[**FVAK**·TU] *numb.* - seventeen

[FVASH] *v.* - to run

[FVĒ] *def. art.* - the (also spelled)

[**FVĒ**·'] *numb.* - six

[**FVĒ**·YOM] *n.* - powder

[**FVĒ**·N'TH] *v.* - to isolate

[FVĒ·**N'**·THA] *n.* - singularity

[FVĒ·**N'TH**·DĔ] *n.* - isolation

[**FVĒ**·GARSH] *v.* - to purchase

[FVĒTH] *v.* - to choose

[FVĒ·**THU**·LA] *n.* - selection

[**FVĒ**·SHA] *n.* - direction

[-FVĔ] *suff.* - indicates possession (uncommon use)

[**FVĔ**·NA] *n.* - detail

[**FVĔG**·HA] *n.* - store (retail)

[**FVĔ**·ZA] *n.* - surprise

[**FVĔK**·TU] *numb.* - sixteen

[**FV'**·U] *adj. & pro.* - such

[**FV'**·CHĔ] *adj. & pro.* - most

[FVUM] *numb.* - nine

[**FVUM**·TU] *numb.* - nineteen

[A·**FVO**·NĔ] *adj.* - serious

,ᴏ:ᴏ [**A**·FVĒTS] *adj.* - dry

,ᴏ:ᴏᴐ, [A·FVĒ·TSAR·**L'**·A] *adj.* - arid

,ᴏᴐᴏᴗ [A·**FV'CH**·DĚ] *adj.* - chief

,,ᴏᴦᴐ [Ě·'·FVUM] *numb.* - ninth

ᴦ Psuta

ᴦ [**PSU**·TA] *v.* - verb auxiliary, future tense

ᴦᴏᴏᴦ [**PO**·ONTH] *v.* - to become

ᴦᴏᴐ [POCH] *v.* - to bend

ᴦᴏᴐ:ᴐ [**PO**·CHĚT] *n.* - knee

ᴦᴏᴐ [POTH] *v.* - to start

ᴦᴏᴐᴐ [POLT] *n.* - soap

ᴦ,ᴦ' [**PA**·Y'] *adv.* - far

ᴦ,ᴐ [PACH] *v.* - to investigate; to probe

ᴦ,ᴐᴐᴦᴗᴐ, [PAL·KHU·U·LĚ] *n.* - microphone

ᴦ,ᴗ [PAWSH] *v.* - to clean

ᴦ,ᴗᴏᴐ, [PA·**WOT**·BVA] *n.* - vulture

ᴦ,ᴐ, [**PA**·TSA] *n.* - nipple

ᴦ,ᴐᴦ [**PA**·DV'NTH] *v.* - to design

ᴦ:ᴗ,ᴏ, [PĒ·**WĚ**·(H)RA] *n.* - discovery

ᴦ, [PĚ] *adv.* - still, yet

ᴦ,ᴐ [PĚSH] *v.* - to fold

ᴦ'ᴐᴏᴐ [**P'**·BVOM] *n.* - organization (group)

ᴦ'ᴐᴏᴐ [**P'**·BVOCH] *v.* - to organize

ᴦ'ᴐᴏᴐ, [P'·**BVO**·CHA] *n.* - organization (arrangement)

ᴦ'ᴐ,ᴐ [**P'**·BVĚCH] *v.* - 1. to gear down; 2. to make sustainable;
    3. to optimize; 4. to simplify

ᴦ'ᴐ,ᴐ, [P'·**BVĚ**·CHA] *n.* - simplification

ᴦ'ᴐᴗ,ᴐ [**P'BV**·LĚCH] *v.* - to tune

ᴦ'ᴐᴗ,ᴐᴐᴐ [P'BV·LĚ·**CHUK**] *n.* - musical pitch

ᴦ'ᴐᴦᴏ:ᴦᴗ, [P'K·HU·**(H)RĒN**·GA] *n.* - breeze

ᴦᴦᴐᴐ [PU·**U**·TABV] *conj. & prep.* - until

ᴦᴦᴦ [PUNTH] *v.* - to change

ᴦᴦᴦ, [**PU**·NA] *n.* - change

ᴦᴦᴦ, [**PU**·FVA] *n.* - new

ᴦᴦᴦ [PUPS] *n.* - nation

ᴦᴦᴐ [PUT] *n.* - future, potential

ᴦᴦᴐᴐ [PUTCH] *v. aux.* - may

⌐₁.𝟡. [**PU**·DZA] *n.* - sex

⌐𝟢.ː𝟤𝟢. [**PRĔS**·HA] *n.* - instrument

⌐𝟢ˌ𝟨𝟩 [PRUST] *n.* - waist

⌐𝟤.⌐ [PLANTH] *v.* - to smash

⌐𝟤ₜ𝟡ː𝟤𝟢. [PLU·**WĒL**·(H)RA] *n.* - flute

⌐𝟤ₜ𝟤 [PLUSH] *v.* - to have sex

⌐𝟤ː𝟥 [PWĔTH] *v.* - to dig

⌐𝟤ː𝟥⌐. [**PWĔTH**·YA] *n.* - spade

ˌ⌐⌐ˌ [**APS**·Y'] *adj.* - far

ˌ⌐𝟢ːˌ𝟤ˌ⌐ˌ⌐ₜ𝟤𝟤𝟤 [AP·(H)RĔ·SHA·NA·**NUK**] *adj.* - ontotronic

ˌ⌐𝟨 [APCH] *v. aux.* - have, has

ˌ⌐𝟨𝟤₀ [**APCH**·LO] *v. aux.* - had

ˌ⌐𝟨𝟤ˌ [**APCH**·L'] *v. aux.* - having

ˌ⌐𝟨⌐ˌ [**APCH**·P'] *v. aux.* - will have

ˌ⌐𝟤ˌ [**APS**·L'] *adj. & adv.* - later

ˌ⌐𝟤ˌ𝟤ː [AP·**TĒ**·LĒ] *adj.* - quick

ˌ⌐𝟤ˌ [APS·T'] *adj.* - young

ː⌐ [ĒPS] *adv., conj. & prep.* - before

ː⌐𝟢₀𝟤ˌ [ĒP·**MON**·TA] *n.* - morning

ː⌐𝟤ˌ [**ĒPS**·W'] *adj.* - dirty

ˌ⌐ː ['·PĔ] *conj.* - yet

ₜ⌐𝟢ː [**UPS**·FVĒ] *adj.* - new

⌐ Habv

⌐ [HABV] *n.* - earth, home

⌐₀₀𝟢.⌐ [HO·**O**·MANTH] *v.* - to waver

⌐₀₀𝟢.⌐. [HO·O·**MA**·NA] *n.* - indecision

⌐₀₀𝟢.⌐𝟥. [HO·O·**MAN**·THA] *n.* - human

⌐₀ˌ𝟤𝟤 [HO·'·KTH'] *n.* - purple

⌐₀𝟢.⌐ [**HO**·YAM] *n.* - meat

⌐₀𝟢. [**HO**·NA] *n.* - nature

⌐₀𝟢⌐𝟤₀ [HON·GO] *n.* - mushroom

⌐₀𝟨𝟨𝟢.ˌ𝟤.𝟡. [HOM·SMA·**TĔ**·DZA] *n.* - gorilla

⌐₀𝟨𝟨ˌ𝟢₀𝟨ₜ⌐ [HOCH·GA·**BVO**·CHUM] *n.* - mathematics

⌐₀𝟨𝟨₀𝟤₀𝟨⌐ [HOS·**MO**·LOM] *n.* - family

⌐₀𝟢𝟡. [**HO**·GA] *n.* - plane (geom.)

⌐₀𝟢𝟡.𝟨 [**HO**·GACH] *v.* - to found

⌐₀𝟢𝟡.𝟨𝟢. [HO·**GACH**·MA] *n.* - footing; foundation

ᢛᢛᢛ. [HO·**GA**·KTHA] *n.* - plank

ᢛᢛᢛ [**HOG**·YO] *n.* - door

ᢛᢛᢛ. [HOG·**YO**·TA] *n.* - quality

ᢛᢛᢛ. [**HOG**·MĔCH] *v.* - to be related to

ᢛᢛᢛ. [HOG·MĔ·**CHOK**] *n.* - clan

ᢛᢛᢛ [HOGCH] *v.* - 1. to base ; 2. to root (bot.)

ᢛᢛᢛ. [**HOG**·CHA] *n.* - 1. basis; 2.root

ᢛᢛᢛ. [HOG·**CH'**·MA] *n.* - floor

ᢛᢛᢛ [**HOG**·CHUM] *n.* - relation, kin

ᢛᢛᢛ [**HOG**·SĔK] *n.* - roof

ᢛᢛᢛ. [**HOG**·SKTHA] *n.* - level

ᢛᢛᢛ. [HOG·SKTHANTH] *v.* - to level

ᢛᢛᢛ [HO·**DZUK**] *n.* - happiness

ᢛᢛᢛ. [HO·**JA**·GA] *n.* - sister

ᢛᢛᢛ [**HO**·JĔM] *n.* - sibling

ᢛᢛᢛ. [HO·JU·'·GA] *n.* - brother

ᢛᢛ [HOSH] *v.* - to descend

ᢛᢛ. [**HO**·SHA] *n.* - descent

ᢛᢛ [HODV] *n.* - yellow

ᢛᢛ [**HO**·DVUTH] *v.* - to yellow

ᢛᢛ [HAFV] *adv.* - here

ᢛᢛ. [HA·**FVĒ**·YA] *n.* - location

ᢛᢛ [HABV] *n.* - solid

ᢛᢛ [HA·**BVO**·LOM] *n.* - shoe

ᢛᢛ. [HA·**BVOL**·TA] *n.* - polymer

ᢛᢛ [HA·**BVĒN**·LO] *n.* - coal (min.)

ᢛᢛ [**HA**·BVĒTH] *v.* - to solidify

ᢛᢛ [**HA**·BVĔTS] *n.* - shell

ᢛᢛ. [HA·**BVĔTS**·DZA] *n.* - pearl

ᢛᢛ. [HA·**BV'TS**·NA] *n.* - harbor

ᢛᢛ. [**HABV**·NA] *n.* - rock, stone (material)

ᢛᢛ. [HAB·**DVAR**·SHA] *n.* - the *dvarsh* exile realm

ᢛᢛ. [HA·**CHO**·NA] *n.* - room

ᢛᢛ. [HA·**SĔ**·THA] *n.* - workshop

ᢛᢛ. [HA·SĔ·**TH'**·CHA] *n.* - laboratory

ᢛᢛ [HAG] *n.* - gray

ᢛᢛ. [HA·**GACH**·(H)RA] *n.* - chain

ᢛᢛ. [HA·**GĔS**·TA] *n.* - ring

ᢛᢛ. [HA·GĔS·**TA**·THA] *n.* - torc

ↄ.ↄↄ.ↄ. [HA·GĔ·TA] *n.* - nail (carpentry)

ↄ.ↄ'ↄ [HA·G'·UPS] *n.* - potato

ↄ.ↄↄↄↄ [HAG·HONTH] *v.* - to hook

ↄ.ↄↄ. [HAG·HA] *n.* - iron (metal)

ↄ.ↄↄ. [HAG·LO·A] *n.* - lead (metal)

ↄ.ↄↄ.ↄ. [HAG·LA·(H)RA] *n.* - key

ↄ.ↄↄ. [HAG·ZA] *n.* - steel (metal)

ↄ.ↄↄ [HA·TH'SH] *v.* - to save

ↄ.ↄↄↄↄ [HA·LĔ·HATH] *v.* - to order (arrange)

ↄ.ↄↄ. [HAL·HA] *n.* - order (arrangement)

ↄ.ↄↄ. [HAT·CHA] *n.* - bed

ↄ.ↄↄ [HATZL] *n.* - bread

ↄ.ↄↄↄ. [HA·W'S·TA] *n.* - worm

ↄ.ↄↄ. [HA·W'·THA] *n.* - plow

ↄ.ↄↄↄ [HA·DZĔRSH] *v.* - to store

ↄ.ↄ. [HA·TSA] *n.* - milk

ↄ.ↄↄ. [HA·TSA·(H)RA] *n.* - cheese

ↄ.ↄ [HAZL] *n.* - food

ↄ.ↄↄↄ. [HA·ZATH·RA] *n.* - meal

ↄ.ↄↄↄ [HA·ZĔM] *n.* - fuel

ↄ.ↄↄↄ. [HA·ZĔS·TA] *n.* - throat

ↄ.ↄↄↄ [HA·ZĔTH] *v.* - to feed

ↄ.ↄↄↄ. [HA·Z'·BVU·CHA] *n.* - dependent

ↄ.ↄↄↄ [HA·ZURSH] *v.* - to eat

ↄ.ↄↄ. [HA·ZU·CHA] *n.* - field

ↄ.ↄↄ. [HAZ·YA] *n.* - fork

ↄ.ↄↄↄ [HAZ·W'·OT] *n.* - knife

ↄ.ↄↄ [HA·SHOK] *n.* - stomach

ↄ:ↄ [HĔM] *n.* - dust

ↄ:ↄↄↄ [HĔT·NĔRSH] *v.* - to tire

ↄↄↄ.ↄ [HĔ·NA·CHO] *n.* - cello

ↄↄↄↄ [HĔ·GĔCH] *v.* - to sort

ↄↄ [HĔTH] *v.* - to cook

ↄↄ. [HĔ·DZA] *n.* - land

ↄↄↄ [HĔ·DZĔTH] *v.* - to map

ↄↄↄↄ. [HĔ·DZĔL·SHA] *n.* - country

ↄↄↄↄ [HĔ·DZ'·TOM] *n.* - distance

ↄↄↄↄ. [HĔ·DZ'·TSA] *n.* - island

ↄↄↄ [HĔTS] *adj.* - hot

ﾟ..ﾟ,ﾟ [**HĔ**·TSUNTH] *v.* - to energize

ﾟ..ﾟ,. [**HĔTS**·NA] *n.* - energy

ﾟ..ﾟ [HĔZL] *n.* - sun

ﾟ..ﾟ₆ﾌ [HĔ·**ZOT**] *n.* - dawn

ﾟ..ﾟ,ﾕ [**HĔ**·ZĔTH] *v.* - to gild

ﾟ..ﾟ,ﾟ₆ﾌ [HĔ·Z'·**MOT**] *n.* - galaxy

ﾟ..ﾟ,,ﾌ [HĔ·**ZU**·UL] *adj.* - pink

ﾟ..ﾟ,,ﾌﾟ. [HĔ·ZU·**UL**·DĔ] *n.* - pink

ﾟ..ﾟ,. [**HĔZ**·NA] *n.* - gold (metal)

ﾟ..ﾟ,.ﾌﾟ. [HĔZ·**NAL**·DĔ] *n.* - orange

ﾟ..ﾟ,₆ﾌ [**HĔZ**·HOL] *n.* - bronze (metal)

ﾟ..ﾟ,., [**HĔZ**·**HA**·TA] *n.* - copper (metal)

ﾟ..ﾟ,₆ [**HĔZ**·LO] *n.* - red

ﾟ..ﾟ,₆,ﾕ [HĔZ·**LO**·TUTH] *v.* - 1. to flush; 2. to redden

ﾟ,₆ﾌ [H'·**OT**] *n.* - rock, stone (object)

ﾟ,. [**H'**·A] *n.* - brick

ﾟ,.ﾟ. [H'·**A**·SA] *n.* - street

ﾟﾟ.ﾟ. [H'·**YA**·NA] *n.* - ceramic

ﾟﾟ.ﾟ. [H'·**YA**·GA] *n.* - plate

ﾟﾟ..ﾕﾟ [H'·**YĔTH**·T'] *n.* - 1. sage; 2. Bigfoot, sasquatch, yeti, etc.

ﾟﾟﾟﾟﾟ [**H'**·MUNTH] *v.* - to be decisive

ﾟﾟﾟﾟ₆ﾟ [H'·**MU**·NOM] *n.* - committee

ﾟﾟﾟﾟ. [H'·**MU**·NA] *n.* - decisiveness

ﾟﾟﾟﾟ₆ﾕ. [H'·MUR·**LO**·THA] *n.* - insurance

ﾟﾟﾟﾟﾟ.. [H'Z·**GLA**·A] *n.* - brass (metal)

ﾟﾟﾕ [H'SH] *v.* - to creep

ﾟﾕ. [**HU**·THA] *n.* - friend

ﾟﾕ.ﾟﾟ. [HU·**THAK**·ZA] *n.* - lizard

ﾟﾟ [**HAB**·YĔTS] *n.* - house

ﾟﾟ₆ [**HYO**·LO] *n.* - cave

ﾟﾟ₆ﾟ,ﾕﾟ. [HYO·W'TH·**L'**·A] *n.* - canyon

ﾟﾟﾟﾕ [HAB·YĔ·**BVĔT**·ATH] *v.* - to house

.ﾟ₆ﾟﾟﾟ [A·HO·'·**KTH'**] *adj.* - purple

.ﾟ₆ﾟ [A·**HO**·N'] *adj.* - natural

.ﾟ₆ﾟ [**A**·HOG] *adj.* - flat

.ﾟ₆ﾕ [**A**·HODV] *adj.* - yellow

.ﾟ.ﾟ [**A**·HABV] *adj.* - solid

.ﾟ.ﾟ [**A**·HAG] *adj.* - gray

.ﾟ.ﾟ.ﾟ [A·HA·**DZA**·N'] *adj.* - safe

⸲ﹾﹾ⸲ﹾ [A·HĒT·**NĚR**·L'] *adj.* - tired

⸲ﹾ⸲ﹾ [A·**HĚTS**·DĚ] *adj.* - energetic

⸲ﹾ⸲ﹾ₀ [A·**HĚZ**·LO] *adj.* - red

⸲ﹾ⸲ [A·**H'**·YA] *adj.* - rough

⸲ﹾﹾ⸲ [A·H'·**MU**·NA] *adj.* - decisive

⸲ﹾ ['·HA] *suff.* - -like

⸲ (h)Rash

⸲ [(H)RASH] *v.* - to have

⸲₀ [(H)RO] *adv.* - very

⸲₀⸲ [**(H)RO**·'SH] *v.* - to help

⸲₀⸲⸲⸲⸲ [(H)RO·**BVĚR**·TSA] *n.* - quantum

⸲₀⸲⸲ [(H)RO·**SOT**] *n.* - dancer

⸲₀⸲ [**(H)RO**·SA] *n.* - dance

⸲₀⸲⸲⸲ [(H)RO·S'N·**YO**·LA] *n.* - game (recreation)

⸲₀⸲⸲ [**(H)RO**·S'TH] *v.* - to dance

⸲₀⸲⸲ [**(H)RO**·LASH] *v.* - to regret

⸲₀⸲ [(H)ROT] *n.* - a tenth of a day

⸲₀⸲⸲ [(H)RA·**OT**] *n.* owner

⸲₀⸲ [**(H)RA**·OTH] *v.* - to steal

⸲⸲⸲⸲⸲ [**(H)RAN**·DHONTH] *v.* - to delight

⸲⸲⸲ [**(H)RAP**·SA] *n.* - wrist

⸲⸲⸲⸲ [**(H)RA**·BVOCH] *v.* - to be foolish

⸲⸲⸲⸲⸲ [(H)RA·BVO·**CHOT**] *n.* - fool

⸲⸲⸲⸲ [(H)RA·**BVO**·CHA] *n.* - folly

⸲⸲⸲⸲ [**(H)RA**·SĚTH] *v.* - to earn

⸲⸲⸲⸲ [(H)RA·**THOT**] *n.* - thief

⸲⸲⸲⸲⸲⸲⸲⸲ [(H)RADZ·NĚ·M'K·FVAR·**LAN**·DĚ] *n.* - jouissance

⸲⸲⸲⸲ [**(H)RA**·ZAZL] *n.* - cymbal

⸲⸲⸲₀⸲ [(H)RASH·**LO**·'] *n.* sorrow

⸲⸲⸲⸲ [**(H)RASH**·TU] *n.* - possession

⸲⸲⸲₀⸲ [**(H)RĒ**·LORSH] *v.* - to adopt

⸲⸲⸲⸲⸲⸲ [(H)RĚ·**OS**·PATH] *v.* - to treat

⸲⸲⸲⸲⸲⸲ [(H)RĚ·OS·**PĚ**·THA] *n.* - hospital

⸲⸲⸲⸲ [**(H)RĚ**·OSH] *v.* - to act

⸲⸲⸲⸲ [(H)RĚ·**OSH**·A] *n.* - action

⸲⸲⸲⸲⸲ [**(H)RĚ**·BVOSH] *v.* - 1. to hold; 2. to retain

⸲⸲⸲ [(H)RĚTH] *v.* - to adhere

ᘉ.ᘓ.ᘓ, [(H)RĔ·**LĒSH**·LA] *n.* - crime

ᘉ.ᘓᔌ [(H)RĔTCH] *v.* - to fight

ᘉ.ᘓᔔᘔ [**(H)RĔ**·DZUTH] *v.* - to range

ᘉ.ᘓ [(H)RĔSH] *v.* - to do

ᘉ.ᘓᘓᘓ. [(H)RĔSH·**L**'·DĔ] *n.* - behavior

ᘉᔌᔇ [(H)R'NTH] *v.* - to sour

ᘉᔌᔇ. [**(H)R**'·NA] *n.* - sourness

ᘉᔌᔇᘓ, [**(H)R**'**N**·TSA] *n.* - citrus

ᘉᔌᔇᔇᘓᘓ [(H)R'·**NUK**] *n.* - sobriety

ᘉᔌᘓ, [**(H)R**'·SA] *n.* - 1. earning; 2. profit

ᘉᔌᘓ.ᘔ, [(H)R'·**SĔ**·THA] *n.* - business

ᘉᔌᘔ [(H)R'TH] *v.* - to record

ᘉᔍᔌ [**(H)R**'·T'] *n.* - 1 / 100th of a *(h)rot*

ᘉᔍᔌᘓ, [(H)R'·**T**'·DZA] *n.* - amusement

ᘉᔍᔍ [(H)R'·**T**'·T'] *n.* - 1 / 100th of a *(h)r't'*

ᘉᔍ [(H)RU] *prep.* - through

ᘉᔍᔇ [**(H)RU**·ONTH] *v.* - experience

ᘉᔍᘉ.. [**(H)RU**·BVĔ] *adv. & conj.* - while

ᘉᔍᘓᔌ [**(H)RUS**·P'] *adj.* - tight

ᘉᔍᘓᘓ. [**(H)RUL**·DĔ] *n.* - sadness

ᘉᔍᔍᘓᔇ. [(H)RU·**WO**·YA] *n.* - bottle

ᘉᔍᔍᘓᔇᘓᔌ [(H)RU·**WO**·MOZL] *n.* - quartz

ᘉᔍᔍᘓᘓᘓ [(H)RU·**WOK**] *n.* - glass

ᘉᔍᔍᘓᘓ [**(H)RU**·WOSH] *v.* - to clear

ᘉᔍᔍ, [(H)RU·**W**'·A] *n.* - crystal

ᘉᔍᔍᘓ, [(H)RU·**W**'·DZA] *n.* - diamond (mineral)

ᘉᔍᘓ.ᘓᘓᔍ [(H)RU·**WĔZ**·LO] *n.* - ruby (mineral)

,ᘉ [ARSH] *v.* - to take

,ᘉᔍ [**A**·(H)RO] *adj.* - sober

,ᘉᘓᔌ, [A·**(H)RĔ**·BVU] *adj.* - cheap

,ᘉ.ᘔᔌ [A·**(H)RĔTH**·L'] *adj.* - sticky

,ᘉᔌᔇ. [A·**(H)R**'·NA] *adj.* - sour

,ᘉᔍᔍ [A·**(H)RU**·LO] *adj.* - sad

,ᘉᔍᔍ [A·**(H)RU**·WO] *adj.* - transparent

,ᘉᔍᘓᘓ. [A·(H)RU·**W**'·DĔ] *adj.* - crystalline

,ᘉᘉᔇᘓ. [AR·**BVO**·CHA] *adj.* - foolish

,ᘉᘔᘉᔇᘔ.. [AR·**SOBV**·CHĔ] *adj.* - deep

,ᘉᘔ.ᔍ [**AR**·SĔK] *adj.* - high

,ᘉᔍᔌᘓ. [AR·LU·'·**SA**] *n.* - fretted instrument similar to a cittern

:ᴖ [ĒRSH] *v.* - to lose

:ᴖ..ₐₒ₂ [Ē·(H)RĚ·OSH] *v.* to stand still

:ᴖ..₂ [Ē·(H)RĚSH] *v.* - to undo

:ᴖᴖₒ◡ [ĒR·MOL] *adj.* - intoxicated; drunk

:ᴖᴖᴖ..ᴄ [ĒR·BVYĚTS] *n.* - church; temple

..ᴖᴖᴖₛ.ᴖ:ᴖ [Ě·(H)R'N·SĚ·BVĒRSH] *v.* - to embroider

..ᴖᴖₛ..ᴄᴖ. [ĒR·**BVĚTH**·YA] *n.* - value

ᴄ Mo

ᴄ [MO] *pro.* - he, she, it

ᴄ [MO] *n.* - being

ᴄ [MO] *numb.* - one

ᴄₒₒᴄₒ [MO·**O**·MO] *pro.* - they, them

ᴄₒ.ᴄ.ᴖ [MO·**A**·MANTH] *v.* - to copy

ᴄₒᴖ⟩,ᴖᴖ. [MO·**N'K**·HA] *n.* - template

ᴄₒᴖ⟩ [**MO**·FV'] *n.* - eminence

ᴄₒᴖₒᴖ [**MO**·PONTH] *v.* - to join

ᴄₒᴖ. [**MO**·HA] *n.* - animal

ᴄₒᴖ:ᴖ◡. [MO·**HĒPS**·WA] *n.* - pig

ᴄₒᴖ [MORSH] *v.* - to remove

ᴄₒᴖ. [**MO**·(H)RA] *n.* - object

ᴄₒᴖ..ᴖ.. [MO·**MĚ**·FVĚ] *pro.* - our, ours

ᴄₒᴖ, [**MO**·BVU] *pro.* - who, whom

ᴄₒᴄⁱᴖₒᴖ. [MO·**S'**·**HO**·NA] *n.* - ape

ᴄₒᴄⁱᴖₒᴄ.ᴖ,ᴖᴖ [MO·**S'**·HOS·**PĚK**] *n.* - chimpanzee

ᴄₒᴄⁱᴖₒᴄ◡ [MO·**S'**·**HO**·DZA] *n.* - bonobo

ᴄₒᴄⁱᴖₒᴄ:ᴖ◡ [MO·**S'**·HO·**JĒN**·L'] *n.* - orangutan

ᴄₒᴄ.ᴖ..ᴖᴖ [MOS·**PĚ**·KTHA] *n.* - bear (zool.)

ᴄₒᴄ◡ₒᴖᴖ. [MOS·**MOK**·BVA] *n.* - raven

ᴄₒᴄ◡ₒᴖᴖ:ᴄ. [MOS·MOK·**BVĒ**·CHA] *n.* - crow

ᴄₒᴄ◡. [**MOS**·MA] *n.* - person

ᴄₒᴄ◡:ᴄ. [MOS·**MĒ**·CHA] *n.* - gibbon

ᴄₒ◡ₒ [**MO**·LO] *n.* - 1. residue; 2. spoor; 3. trace; 4. track

ᴄₒ◡◡ [MOLT] *n.* - oil

ᴄₒ◡◡. [**MOL**·TSA] *n.* - butter

ᴄₒ◡, [**MO**·TU] *numb.* - eleven

ᴄₒ◡ [MOWSH] *v.* - to envision

ᴄₒ◡. [**MO**·WA] *n.* - vision

༘ംⒶᑎᲕ. [MO·**JABV**·THA] *n.* - 1. adept; 2. mage; 3. teacher

༘ംᲕᑌᕐᲖ. [MO·**J'T**·(H)RA] *n.* - student

༘ംᲕ᛬ᲖᲙ. [MO·**ZĒTH**·LA] *n.* - violence

༘ംᲕᑎᲖ. [MO·**KTHA**·HA] *n.* - pilot

༘ംᲖᲕᲖ [**MO**·SHOM] *n.* - train

༘ᲕᲕᲖᲖᲖᲖ᛬ᲕᲕ [MA·'K·LAM·BV(H)RO·**SOT**] *n.* - exemplar

༘ᑎᲖᲖ [**MA**·YOM] *n.* - kind

༘ᑎᲕ. [**MAN**·DZA] *n.* - contentment

༘ᲖᲕᵎ [**MA**·(H)R'] *adj.* - inner

༘ᲖᲕᵎᲖᲕᲖᲖ. [MA·(H)R'·**CHAR**·LSA] *n.* - intelligence

༘ᲖᲕᵎᲕ᛬ᑎᲕᲖᲕᲕ᛬ [MA·(H)R'·SHĔP·**HUR**·DĚ] *n.* - tapeworm

༘ᲖᲕᲖᲖ [**MAR**·T'NTH] *v.* - to amplify

༘ᲖᲕᲕᲕᵎᲖᲖ. [MAR·KLU·'·SA] *n.* - guitar

༘᛬᛬ᲖᲕ᛬ [MĒ·Ē·FVĚ] *pro.* - your, yours (sing.)

༘᛬ᲖᲕ. [MĒ·FVA] *pro.* - you (sing.)

༘᛬ᲖᲖᲖ [MĒ·HANTH] *v.* - to settle

༘᛬ᲖᲖᲕᵎᲖ [MĔM·**FVA**·'M] *pro.* - you (plur.)

༘᛬ᲕᲕ. [MĒ·GA] *n.* - metal

༘᛬ᲕᲖ᛬Ზ [**MĒ**·GĒTH] *v.* - to whip

༘᛬᛬᛬ [MĔ·Ē] *adj. & pro.* - hers; his; its

༘᛬᛬ᲖᲖ᛬ [MĔ·FVĚ] *pro.* - my, mine

༘᛬᛬ᲕᲖᲖ [MĔ·GORSH] *v.* - to tax

༘᛬᛬ᲕᵎᲖᲖ. [MĔ·**GA**·(H)RA] *n.* - payment

༘᛬᛬ᲕᵎᲖᲖᲖ. [MĔ·**GAR**·YA] *n.* - money

༘᛬᛬Ვᵎ᛬᛬Ზ. [MĔ·**GĔ**·SA] *n.* - wire

༘᛬᛬ᲕᵎᵎᲖᲖ [MĔ·**G'**·ARSH] *v.* - to sell

༘᛬᛬ᲕᵎᲖᲖᲖ. [MĔ·**G'**·SA] *n.* - ticket

༘᛬᛬Ზ [MĔTH] *v.* - to unite

༘᛬᛬ᲖᲕ᛬ [**MĔTH**·DĔ] *n.* - unity

༘ᵎᲖᲖ᛬Ზ [M'·FVĒNTH] *v.* - to stand apart

༘ᵎᲖᲖ᛬Ზ. [M'·**FVĒ**·NA] *n.* - 1. one apart; 2. outlier

༘ᵎᲖᲖ. [M'·HA] *adv. & pro.* - same

༘ᵎᲖᲖᲖ [M'·HANTH] *v.* - to equal

༘ᵎᲖᲖᲕ [M'·HAWSH] *v.* - to match

༘ᵎᲖᲕᲖᲖᲖᲖᲖ [M'·MO·**MU**·MU] *adj. & pro.* - many, much

༘ᵎᲖ᛬᛬Ზ᛬ [M'·**MĒ**·FVĚ] *pro.* - your, yours (plur.)

༘ᵎᲖ᛬᛬ᲖᲖ [M'·MĔRSH] *v.* - to process

༘ᵎᲖ᛬᛬ᲖᲖ. [M'·**MĔ**·(H)RA] *n.* - process

༘ᵎᲖ᛬᛬ᲖᲖ [M'·MĔSH] *v.* - to shake

ᘇ᠍ᡞᢔᡒᢇ [**M'TH**·LOM] *n.* - village

ᘇ᠍ᡞᢔᡒᡒᢕᢩ [M'TH·LO·**MO**·TA] *n.* - villager

ᘇ᠍ᡞᢔᡔᡒᢩ [M'TH·L'·**MA**·TA] *n.* - town

ᘇ᠍ᡞᢔᡔᡒᢩᢩᢗᠹ [M'TH·L'·MA·**TĔ**·DZA] *n.* - city

ᘇ᠍ᡞᡒᢩᢩᠹ [M'K·(H)RĔ·'·DĚ] *n.* - effect pedal

ᘇ᠍ᡞᡒ [M'SH] *v.* - to blanket

ᘇ᠍ᡞᡒᢩᢇ [M'·**SHĒ**·NA] *n.* - opposite

ᘇᢇᢩ [**MU**·YA] *n.* - box

ᘇᢇᢩᢩᠹ [MU·YA·**TĔ**·DZA] *n.* - chest (furn.)

ᘇᢇᢩᢞᢩ [MU·**YAK**·LA] *n.* - drawer

ᘇᢈᢔᡒᢇᠹ [**MUM**·G(H)ROT] *n.* - prose

ᘇᢈᢔ [MUMTH] *v.* - to connect

ᘇᢈᢔᡒᢇ [MUM·**THOM**] *n.* - network

ᘇᢈᢔᢩ [**MUM**·THA] *n.* - connection

ᘇᢈᡒᢇᠻ [MUCH·**L'**·O] *adj., adv. & pro.* - enough

ᘇᢈᢩᢩᠻ [**MU**·GĔRSH] *v.* - 1. to disrobe; 2. to undress

ᘇᢈᢩᢩᢇᡞ [MU·**GĚ**·FVUNTH] *v.* - to clothe

ᘇᢈᢩᢩᡞᢇᠹ [MU·**GĚFV**·NOT] *n.* - clothing

ᘇᢈᢩᢩᢩ [MU·**GĚ**·SA] *n.* - cloth

ᘇᢈᢩᢖ [**MU**·THĒTH] *v.* - to beat

ᘇᢈᠹ [MUDZ] *n.* - wolf

ᘇᢈᠹᢞᢩᢩ [MU·DZA·TS'·**HA**·TA] *n.* - orca

ᘇᢈᢩᢩ [**MU**·SHĔSH] *v.* - to touch

ᘇᢈᢩᢩᢩ [MU·**SHĔ**·SHA] *n.* - touch

ᘇᢇ [**MO**·FVĒ] *pro.* - I, me

ᘇᢇᢇ [MO·**MO**·FVĒ] *pro.* - we, us

ᘇᢩᢇᢩ [**MWA**·FVĒ] *n.* - autumn; fall (season)

ᘇᠹ [**MO**·DZA] *n.* - 1. companion; 2. mate; 3. partner

ᢇᢇᢕ [**O**·MO] *pro. & n.* - all

ᢇᢇᢕᢇᢩ [O·**MO**·FVĒ] *pro.* - everybody, everyone

ᢇᢇᢕᢇ [**O**·MORSH] *v.* - to vacate

ᢇᢇᢕᢇᢔ [O·**MO**·MUTH] *v.* - 1. to draw together; 2. to gather

ᢇᢇᢕᢇᢔᢔᠹ [O·MO·MUTH·**LO**·A] *n.* - 1. assembly; 2. gathering

ᢇᢇᢕᢔ [**O**·MOTH] *n.* - to encounter

ᢇᢕᢔ [OMTH] *v.* - to meet

ᢇᢕᢩᢔ [**OM**·WATH] *v.* - to harvest

ᢇᢕᢩᢔᢩ [OM·**WATH**·A] *n.* - harvest

ᢇᢕᢩᢖᢩ [OM·**ZĚ**·THA] *n.* - destruction

ᢩᢇᢕᢇ [A·**MO**·FV'] *adj.* - whole

ᔥᦞᏃᣴᎫᦵ [A·MO·**ZĚ**·TH'L] *adj.* - violent

ᔥᦵᦲᣵᏃᣳ᠂ [A·**MAN**·DĚ] *adj.* - content

ᔥᦵᏃᦥ᠂ [A·**M'**·HA] *adj.* - same

ᔥᦵᏍ᠄ [**AM**·FVĚ] *adj.* - 1. only; 2. single

ᔥᦵᏍᦥᦲᦲᏍᣲ [AM·**BV(H)RO**·S'] *adj.* - unique

ᔥᦵᏃᣲ [**AM**·DZ'] *adj.* - full

᠄ᦥᦲ[Ě·MO] *numb.* - zero

᠄ᦥᦲᦲ [Ě·**MO**·O] *pro.* - no one, nobody

᠄ᦥᦲᦲᣱᣱ [Ě·MO·**MU**·MU] *adj. & pro.* - few

᠄ᦥᣱᣳᣴᦥᣲ [Ě·MU·**GĚ**·FV'] *adj.* - naked

᠄ᦥᣳᦵᏃᏃ᠂ [ĚM·**SO**·KTHA] *n.* - silence

᠄ᦴᦵᦥᦲᣵᣴᎫ [Ě·LO·**MO**·MUTH] *v.* - to disperse

᠄᠄ᣲᦥᦲ [Ě·'·MO] *numb.* - first

᠄᠄ᣲᦥ᠄ [Ě·'·MĚ] *n.* - hero

ᦥ Bveta

ᦥ [**BVĚ**·TA] *n.* - 1. embrace, hug; 2. pledge

ᦥᦲᣲ [**BVO**·'] *adj.* - rigid

ᦥᦲᣲᦥᣳᣴᎫ [BVO·'·**GĚS**] *n.* - card

ᦥᦲᣵᏃ [**BVO**·'SH] *v.* - 1. to bear; 2. to give birth

ᦥᦲᣱ [BVONTH] *v.* - to bond

ᦥᦲᦲ [BVORSH] *v.* - to owe

ᦥᦲᣴ [BVOM] *n.* - belief

ᦥᦲᣱᦲᣵᎫᏃ᠂ [BVOM·FVO·**L'**·KTHA] *n.* - religion

ᦥᦲᣵᎫᣴᎫ [**BVOM**·TUTH] *v.* - to believe

ᦥᦲᣵᦲᦲᎫ [**BVO**·BVOTH] *v.* - to weld

ᦥᦲᣴᣴ [BVOCH] *v.* - 1. to depend; 2. to rely

ᦥᦲᣴᣴᏃᦲᦲᣱᣳ᠂ [BVOCH·SMO·**ON**·DĚ] *n.* - self-reliance

ᦥᦲᦲᏃ᠂ [**BVO**·GA] *n.* - wall

ᦥᦲᦲᏃᣱ [**BVO**·GANTH] *v.* - to obstruct

ᦥᦲᎫᏃ [BVOLM] *n.* - divinity

ᦥᦲᎫᏃᣳᏃ᠂ [BVOL·**MA**·GA] *n.* - goddess

ᦥᦲᎫᣱᣲᏃ᠂ [BVOL·MU·'·GA] *n.* - god

ᦥᦲᎫ [BVOT] *n.* - unit

ᦥᦲᎫᦥᏃ [**BVO**·TOM] *n.* - scale

ᦥᦲᎫᦥᦴ [**BVO**·TOWSH] *v.* - to rate

ᦥᦲᦲᏃ [BVOK] *n.* - south

ᦥᣳ [BVA] *numb.* - two

[**BVA**·ATH] *v.* - 1. to get; 2. to obtain

[BVA·A·L'] *adv.* - please

[BVANH] *adv. & conj.* - now

[BVA·**NA**·TA] *n.* - news

[BVAFV] *n.* - time

[**BVA**·FVOM] *adv.* - 1. always; 2. forever

[**BVA**·FVU] *adv.* - then

[BVA·**FVU**·THA] *n.* - clock

[**BVAFV**·TACH] *v.* - to time

[BVAFV·**TA**·CHA] *n.* - occasion

[**BVA**·MOLT] *n.* - wax

[**BVAM**·BVAPS] *adv.* - twice

[BVAMT] *det.* - every

[BVACH] *v.* - to request

[BVA·**SĔ**·THOT] *n.* - bicycle

[**BVAG**·JĔK] *n.* - hat

[BVATH] *v.* - 1. to distribute; 2. to strew

[BVATH·**RAL**·DĔ] *n.* - standard

[BVATH·**L'**·DĔ] *n.* - generosity

[**BVA**·TA] *n.* - amount

[**BVA**·TACH] *v.* - to count

[BVA·**TA**·CHA] *n.* - sum, tally, total

[BVA·TA·CHA·**TAZL**] *n.* - calendar

[BVA·**TAT**] *n.* - fowl

[**BVA**·TU] *numb.* - twelve

[**BVAT**·YOT] *n.* - number

[BVAT·YĔ·**O**·SHA] *n.* - arithmetic

[BVAT·**YU**·LA] *n.* - receipt

[BVA·**W'**·THOM] *n.* - scissors

[BVA·**W'**·THA] *n.* - half

[BVAK·Z'·**NĔ**·'TH] *v.* - to vaccinate

[BVĔPS] *adv.* - early

[BVÊMTH] *v.* - to parallel

[BVĔPSH] *v.* - to pledge

[BVĔRSH] *v.* - to keep

[**BVĔ**·(H)R'SH] *v.* - to swear

[BVĔCH] *v.* - 1. to reveal; 2. to show; 3. to tell

[**BVĔ**·CHA] *n.* - account

[BVĔ·**CHA**·TA] *n.* - story

ᠵ᠁ᡣᢀ. [**BVĔCH**·GA] *n.* - statement

ᠵ᠁ᡣᢀ᠁ᢁ. [BVĔCH·**DĔ**·NA] *n.* - fiction

ᠵ᠁� [BVĔTH] *v.* - to forgive

ᠵ᠁ᢠᢀ. [**BVĔTH**·BVA] *n.* - mercy

ᠵ᠁᠍ᢞᢇ[BVĔ·**TA**·AT] *n.* - hip

ᠵ᠁ᢞᢀ [**BVĔ**·TARSH] *v.* - 1. to embrace; 2. to hug

ᠵ᠁ᢞᢠᢀ. [BVĔT·**ATH**·RA] *n.* - 1. portion; 2. share

ᠵ᠁ᢛᢀ [**BVĔ**·WOTH] *v.* - 1. to broadcast; 2. to publish

ᠵ᠁ᢛᢀᢀ. [BVĔ·**WĔTH**·NA] *n.* - scroll

ᠵ᠁ᢞᢀ [**BVĔ**·DZANTH] *v.* - to allow

ᠵ᠁ᢛᢀ [**BVĔ**·ZONTH] *v.* - to polish

ᠵ᠁ᢞᢠ [**BVĔ**·ZATH] *v.* - to roll

ᠵ᠁ᢞᢠ. [BVĔ·**ZA**·THA] *n.* - roll

ᠵ᠁ᢞᢀ [**BVĔ**·Z'NTH] *v.* - to photograph

ᠵ᠁ᢞᢀ. [**BVĔZ**·NA] *n.* - photograph

ᠵ᠁ᢞᢀᢀᢞ [BVĔZ·NAH·**YOT**] *n.* - X ray (image)

ᠵ᠁ᢞᢠᢀᢞ [BVĔZ·**SĔ**·YOT] *n.* - camera

ᠵ᠁ᢞ [BVĔSH] *v.* - to come

ᠵ᠁ᢞ. [BVĔ·**SHO**·A] *n.* - effect

ᠵ᠁ᢞᢞ [**BVĔ**·SHOSH] *v.* - to tryst

ᠵ᠁ᢞᢞᢞ [BVĔ·**SHOSH**·L'] *n.* - tryst

ᠵ᠁ᢞᢀ. [BV'·**ĔS**·KHA] *n.* - glide

ᠵ᠁ᢞᢀᢞ [BV'·**ĔS**·KHASH] *v.* - to glide

ᠵᢞ [BV'TH] *v.* - 1. to abandon; 2. to deposit; 3. to leave behind

ᠵᢞᢀᢞ [BV'·TSA·**TO**·MO] *numb.* - twenty-one

ᠵᢞᢞ [BV'·**TSA**·TU] *numb.* - twenty

ᠵᢞᢀ [**BVUM**] *adj., adv. & pro.* - this

ᠵᢞᢀᢞ [**BVU**·M'M] *adj., adv. & pro.* - these

ᠵᢞᢀ. [**BVUG**·SA] *n.* - skirt

ᠵᢀᢞᢞᢀ. [BVRA·MO·**N'K**·HA] *n.* - agent

ᠵᢀᢀ. [**BVRA**·MA] *n.* - role

ᠵᢀᢀ [BVRM] *n.* - godchild

ᢀᢞ [**BVĔT**·ATH] *v.* - to give

ᢀᢞᢀ [BVĔT·**ATH**·RASH] *v.* - to share

.ᢀᢞᢀᢞ. [A·BVATH·**RAL**·DZA] *adj.* - standard

.ᢀᢞᢞ. [A·BVATH·**L'**·A] *adj.* - generous

.ᢀᢞᢞ [A·BVA·**Z'**·T'] *adj.* - regular

.ᢀᢞᢞ [A·**BVĔ**·P'] *adj.* - early

.ᢀᢞ [A·BV'] *adj.* - long

:ᘯᣞᢣ [Ē·**BVO**·'SH] *v.* - to abort

:ᘯᣞᢦ [Ē·BVONTH] *v.* - to separate

:ᘯᢊ [Ē·BVAFV] *adv.* - never

:ᘯᣞ⟑⟩ [Ē·**BVĒ**·Z'] *adj.* - special

⸪ᣞᘯᣞ [Ĕ·'·BVA] *numb.* - second

⸪ᘯᣞ⸪ [Ĕ·BVĔ] *adv.* - again

⸪ᘯᣞᢣ [Ĕ·BVOSH] *v.* - to return

⸪ᘯᣞᢣ⸴ [Ĕ·**BVO**·SHA] *n.* - return

⸪ᘯᣞ⸴ [Ĕ·BVU] *adv. & pro.* - what

⟩ᘯᣞᢦ ['·BVURSH] *v. aux.* - must

⟩ᘯᣞᢊ [U·BVAFV] *adv. & conj.* - when

⟩ᘯᢦ⸪ [UBV·MĔ] *adv.* - ever

ᢣ Ch'ch

ᢣ [CH'CH] *v.* - 1. to desire; 2. to seek; 3. to want

ᢣᣞ [CHO] *numb.* - four

ᢣᣞᣞᢣ [**CHO**·OTH] *v.* - to understand

ᢣᣞᣞᢣ⸴ [CHO·**O**·THA] *n.* - concept

ᢣᣞᣞᢣᢣ⸪ [CHO·**OTH**·DĔ] *n.* - understanding

ᢣᣞᢣ⟨ [**CHO**·TU] *numb.* - fourteen

ᢣᣞᢣᢣ⸴ [CHO·**W'**·THA] *n.* - fourth

ᢣ⸴ [CHA] *n.* - goal, aim

ᢣ⸴ᢦ [CHANTH] *v.* - to guess

ᢣ⸴ᣞᣞᢣ [**CHA**·HOCH] *v.* - to hurl

ᢣ⸴ᣞᢣ⸴ [**CHAR**·LSA] *n.* - world

ᢣ⸴ᣞᢣ⸴ [CHA·**BVO**·TA] *n.* - law

ᢣ⸴ᣞ⟩ [**CHA**·BV'] *n.* - rule

ᢣ⸴ᢣ [CHACH] *v.* - to pitch, to throw

ᢣ⸴ᢣ⸴ [**CHA**·SA] *n.* - purpose

ᢣ⸴ᢣ [CHATH] *v.* - to inspire

ᢣ⸴ᢣᢣ⸪ [**CHATH**·DĔ] *n.* - inspiration

ᢣ⸴ᢣᢣ [CHA·W'SH] *v.* - to adjust

ᢣ⸴⟨⸴ [**CHA**·ZA] *n.* - jewel

ᢣ⸪ᢣ [**CHĒ**·'CH] *v.* - to kick

ᢣ⸪ᢣᣞᢣᢣ [CHĒ·'·**CHOT**] *n.* - kicker

ᢣ⸪ᢣ⸴ [**CHĒ**·'·CHA] *n.* - kick

ᢣ⸪⟨⸴ [CHĒ·'·TSA] *n.* - coffee

ᢣ⸪ [CHĔ] *adv. & pro.* - more

64

ᘞᘏ [CHĔMPS] *n.* - mound

ᘞᘏ [CHĔMTH] *v.* - to pile

ᘞ [CHĔG] *n.* - 1. hill; 2. upland

ᘞᘏ [CHĔ·GOK] *n.* - mountain

ᘞᘏ [CHĔG·NA] *n.* - mesa

ᘞᘏ [CHĔ·TSU·LA] *n.* - coat

ᘞᘏ [CHĔ·TSUK] *n.* - warmth

ᘞ [CHĔZL] *adj.* - old

ᘞ [CH'] *prep.* - 1. for; 2. in favor of

ᘞ [CH'·CHA] *n.* - search

ᘞ [CH'·SĔTH] *v.* - to experiment

ᘞ [CH'·SĔ·THA] *n.* - experiment

ᘞ [CH'·TUTH] *v.* - to crave

ᘞ [CH'CH·L'] *n.* - seeking

ᘞ [CHU·THAT] *n.* - farm

ᘞ [CHUL] *adv.* - so

ᘞ [CHRĔSH] *v.* - to repeat

ᘞ [A·CHĔZ·(H)RO] *adj.* - ancient

ᘞ [ACH·RO·N'] *adj.* - common

ᘞ [ACH·R'] *adj.* - frequent

ᘞ [Ē·CHĔ] *adv. & pro.* - less

ᘞ [Ē·CH'T] *prep.* - against

ᘞ [Ĕ·CHĔTS] *adj.* - warm

ᘞ [U·CHO·NA] *n.* - space

ᘞ [U·CHOK] *n.* - "outer" space

ᘞ [U·CH'] *adv. & prep.* - above

ᘞ Sos

ᘞ [SOS] *n.* - path, way

ᘞ [SO·YĔBV] *n.* - chin

ᘞ [SONTH] *v.* - to evolve

ᘞ [SON·DĔ] *n.* - evolution

ᘞ [SOBV] *adj., adv. & prep.* - down

ᘞ [SO·BVĒCH] *v.* - to protest

ᘞ [SOBV·GA] *n.* - floor

ᘞ [SOCH] *v.* - to listen

ᘞ [SOS·NODZ] *n.* - 1. Nod's Way; 2. rectitude

ᘞ [SOS·PĔKCH] *v.* - to shout

[**SO**·LASH] *v.* - to fart
[SO·**TA**·(H)RA] *n.* - tendency
[**SO**·TSASH] *v.* - to drain
[**SO**·TS'] *n.* - creek
[**SOTS**·TO] *n.* - river
[SOTS·**TOK**·CHO] *n.* - bayou
[SOK] *n.* - sound
[SO·**KTHO**·LASH] *v.* - to brag
[SO·KTHO·**LU**·THA] *n.* - braggart
[**SO**·KTHADZ] *n.* - music
[SOK·**YO**·LA] *n.* - voice
[SOK·**YO**·LĒWSH] *v.* - to whisper
[SOK·**HU**·THAM] *n.* - harmony
[SOK·(H)RO·**BVĔR**·TĔ] *n.* - drone (sound)
[**SOK**·(H)RUSH] *v.* - to whistle
[**SOK**·LASH] *v.* - to embellish
[SOK·**LU**·THA] *n.* - hobbit
[**SOK**·W'TH] *v.* - to scream
[SOSH] *v.* - to follow
[SO·**SHO**·YOT] *n.* - stage (developmental)
[**SO**·SHOSH] *v.* - to travel
[SO·**SHO**·SHA] *n.* - journey
[SOSH·**YA**·TA] *n.* - station
[SA] *n.* - road
[**SA**·OCH] *v.* - to turn
[**SAN**·TANTH] *v.* - to explore
[SAN·**TA**·NA] *n.* - exploration
[**SA**·BVĔCH] *v.* - to screw
[SA·BVĔ·**CHOT**] *n.* - screwdriver
[SA·**BVĔ**·CHA] *n.* - screw
[**SA**·TSUSH] *v.* - to swim
[SA·TSU·**SHOT**] *n.* - swimmer
[SA·**TSU**·SHA] *n.* - swim
[SA·TSUSH·**T'**·TA] *n.* - swimming place (pool, hole, etc.)
[**SA**·KTHO] *n.* - bridge
[**SA**·KTHUSH] *v.* - to wander
[SA·KTHU·**SHOT**] *n.* - wanderer
[SA·KTHUSH·**T'**·TA] *n.* - vastness
[SĒ·**THO**·YA] *n.* - wheel

༾:ॐ. **[SĒK·HA]** *n.* - mute

༾:ॐ **[SĔ·YOT]** *n.* - apparatus

༾:ॐ. **[SĔ·FVA]** *n.* - ant

༾:ॐ **[SĒTH]** *v.* - to work

༾:ॐ. **[SĔ·THA]** *n.* - work

༾:ॐ **[SĒTH·YO·SHUK·YA]** *n.* - technology

༾:ॐ. **[SĒTH·YA]** *n.* - tool

༾:ॐ **[SĒTH·LOM]** *n.* - guild

༾:ॐ. **[SĒTH·LU·THA]** *n.* - servant

༾:ॐ **[SĒTH·SHOT]** *n.* - cart

༾:ॐ. **[SĔ·LU·THA]** *n.* - worker

༾:ॐ. **[SĒTS·DVA]** *n.* - power

༾:ॐ **[SĒTS·DVA·LOM]** *n.* - union

༾:ॐ **[SĔK]** *adj., adv. & prep.* - up

༾:ॐ **[SĔK·YĒS·TOT]** *n.* - arch

༾:ॐ **[SĔK·YUTH]** *v.* - to wind

༾:ॐ **[SĔK·(H)ROSH]** *v.* - to support

༾:ॐ **[SĔK·CHĒTH]** *v.* - to lift

༾:ॐ. **[SĔK·CHU·THA]** *n.* - porter

༾:ॐ **[SĒSH]** *v.* - jump

༾:ॐ **[S'·YUSH]** *v.* - to slope

༾:ॐ **[S'·PURSH]** *v.* - to credit

༾:ॐ. **[S'·PU·(H)RA]** *n.* - credit

༾:ॐ. **[S'·GĔ·JA]** *n.* - idea

༾:ॐ **[S'·G']** *adj.* - intrinsic

༾:ॐ **[S'·KTH']** *n.* - ideal

༾:ॐ **[S'·KTH'S·MO·ON·DĔ]** *n.* - the archetype of one's self

༾:ॐ **[SU·P'CH]** *v.* - to plan

༾:ॐ. **[SU·P'·CHO·THA]** *n.* - structure

༾:ॐ. **[SUP·CHO·NA]** *n.* - office

༾:ॐ. **[SU·THA]** *n.* - machine

༾:ॐ. **[SU·THĔTS·DVA]** *n.* - engine

༾:ॐ **[SNORTS]** *n.* - brandy

༾:ॐ **[SPO·YUCH]** *v.* - to err

༾:ॐ. **[SPO·YU·CHA]** *n.* - error

༾:ॐ **[SPOCH]** *v.* - to spin

༾:ॐ **[SPO·CHOT]** *n.* - spinner

༾:ॐ **[SPO·CHA·TĔDZ]** *n.* - yarn (fiber)

༾:ॐ **[SPO·CHĔ·DZ'K]** *n.* - cord

ॐᗱᏋᏋ᠂ᨦ [**SPO**·CH'K] *n.* - thread

ॐᗱᏋᏋ᠂ᨦᨦ [SPO·**CHUK**] *n.* - string

ॐᗱᏋᏋᏋ᠄ [**SPOCH**·TĚ] *adj.* - 1. thick; 2. wide

ॐᗱᏋᨦᨦᡕ [**SPO**·KTH'T] *conj.* - between

ॐᗱ᠂ᢙ᠂ [**SPA**·NA] *n.* - insect

ॐᗱ᠂ᢙᢙ᠄ᢲ [**SPAN**·GĚS] *n.* - silk

ॐᗱ᠂ᢙᢙ᠄ᨦ᠂ [**SPAN**·**GĚ**·LA] *n.* - slip (undergarment)

ॐᗱ᠂ᢙ [SPAPS] *n.* - grain

ॐᗱ᠂ᢙ᠄᠄ᢙᢙᨦᡕ [SPA·**PĚRM**·LOT] *n.* - beer

ॐᗱ᠂ᢲ᠄᠄ᨦ᠂ [SPA·**CHĚ**·DZA] *n.* - viola

ॐᗱ᠂ᢲ [SPATH] *v.* - 1. to heal; 2. to recover

ॐᗱ᠂ᢲᨦ᠄ [SPATH·**L'**·A] *n.* - recovery

ॐᗱ᠂ᢲᨦ᠄ [**SPATH**· DĚ] *n.* - health

ॐᗱ᠂ᨦᨦᨦᣥ [**SPADZ**·WOSH] *v.* - to care

ॐᗱ᠂ᨦᢲᨦ [**SPAZ**·CHO] *n.* - violin

ॐᗱ᠂ᨦᨦ᠄᠄ᡕ [**SPAK**·LĚT] *n.* - goat

ॐᗱ᠂ᨦᨦ᠄ᢙ᠄ [SPAK·**DZA**·(H)RA] *n.* - verse

ॐᗱ᠂ᨦᨦ [SPAKZL] *adj.* - little

ॐᗱ᠄᠄ᨦ [SPĚK] *adj.* - big; large

ॐᗱ᠄᠄ᨦᨦ᠄ [**SPĚK**·TA] *adj.* - heavy

ॐᗱᡕᨦᢲ᠄ [**SPUL**·CHA] *n.* - advertisement

ॐᢙᏋᏋᢙ [**SMO**·ONTH] *v.* - to individuate

ॐᢙᏋᏋᢙᨦᨦᨦ [SMO·O·**NOK**] *n.* - 1. individuality; 2. self

ॐᢙᏋᏋᢙᢲ᠄ [SMO·O·**NO**·TA] *n.* - clone

ॐᢙᏋᏋᢙᢲ᠄ [SMO·**ON**·DĚ] *n.* - selfhood

ॐᢙᏋᏋᡕ [**SMO**·OT] *n.* - 1. identity; 2. persona

ॐᢙᏋᏋᢙᡕ [**SMO**·NOT] *n.* - 1. center; 2. core

ॐᢙᏋᢙᡕ᠄ᨦ [**SMO**·NUSH] *v.* - to automate

ॐᢙᏋᢙᢲᨦ᠄ [**SMOM**·TA] *n.* - society

ॐᢙᏋᢲ᠄ᨦᨦ᠄ [SMO·**SA**·TA] *n.* - nomad

ॐᢙᏋᨦᢲᢙ᠄ [SMO·**TA**·GA] *n.* - woman

ॐᢙᏋᨦᢙᢙ᠄ [SMO·TU·'·GA] *n.* - man

ॐᢙᨦᢲ [**SMA**·ĚTH] *v.* - to enforce

ॐᢙᨦᢲ᠄ [**SMĚ**·CHA] *n.* - monkey

ॐᢙᡕᢙᡕ [**SMU**·PUT] *n.* - thumb

ॐᢙᡕᨦᨦᣥ [**SMU**·JĚSH] *v.* - to manifest

ॐᢙᡕᨦ [SMUSH] *v.* - to spread

ॐᨦᡕᢙᢙᢙ [**STĚ**·FVĚNTH] *v.* - to advise

ॐᨦᨦᢲ [SWĚTH] *v.* - to taste

⤳ [SWĔTZL] *n.* - cake

⤳ [SWĔ·**DZA**·TSA] *n.* - honey

⤳ [SWĔ·**DZU**·THA] *n.* - bee

⤳ [**SWĔ**·TSUK] *n.* - jelly

⤳ [**SW'**·OT] *n.* - salt

⤳ [SWUK] *n.* - sugar

⤳ [**SKTHO**·'RSH] *v.* - 1. to accept; 2. to receive

⤳ [**SKTHO**·GA] *n.* - shelf

⤳ [SKTHA·**(H)RĒTS**·NA] *n.* - gin

⤳ [**SKTHA**·(H)R'CH] *v.* - to stink

⤳ [SKTHARTH] *v.* - to smell

⤳ [SKTHART] *n.* - 1. aroma; 2. odor

⤳ [**SKTHAR**·TOTH] *v.* - to disgust

⤳ [SKTHURSH] *v.* - to hear

⤳ [OSK] *prep.* - over

⤳ [A·**SO**·'BV] *adj.* - low

⤳ [A·**SO**·TĔDZ] *adj.* - loud

⤳ [A·SA·**KTHUSH**·TA] *adj.* - vast

⤳ [A·SĒK·L'] *adj.* - mute

⤳ [A·SĔK·**YO**·T'] *adj.* - round

⤳ [A·**S'**·KTH'] *adj.* - ideal

⤳ [ASPS] *adj.* - 1. narrow; 2. small

⤳ [AS·POT·**WA**·NA] *adj.* - general

⤳ [AS·PO·**KTH'**·TA] *adj.* - 1. average; 2. middle value

⤳ [AS·**PAN**·G'] *adj.* - smooth

⤳ [AS·**MON**·TA] *adj.* - middle

⤳ [AS·**MON**·SHLU] *adj.* - automatic

⤳ [AS·**WĒ**·GA] *adj.* - bitter

⤳ [AS·**WĒG**·TSA] *n.* - alkali

⤳ [**AS**·WĔDZ] *adj.* - sweet

⤳ [ĒS·**PATH**·DĔ] *n.* - illness

⤳ [ĒS·**PĔK**·T'] *adj.* - light (weight)

⤳ [ĒST] *adv.* - not

⤳ Gabva

⤳ [**GA**·BVA] *n.* - plant

⤳ [GO·**'**·NU] *n.* - left (direction)

⤳ [GOPS] *n.* - seed

〰 [**GO**·PO] *n.* - child

〰 [**GO**·**PA**·GA] *n.* - daughter

〰 [**GO**·PU·'·GA] *n.* - son

〰 [GORSH] *v.* - to think

〰 [**GO**·(H)RA] *n.* - thought

〰 [**GOR**·POSH] *v.* - to reason

〰 [**GOR**·PĚ·SHA] *n.* - reason

〰 [GOM] *adj.* - robust

〰 [GOS·KTHA·**(H)ROK**] *n.* - herb

〰 [GOS·**KTHA**·(H)RA] *n.* - mint (herb)

〰 [GOTH] *v.* - 1. to penetrate; 2. to pierce

〰 [GO·**LO**·PUCH] *v.* - to repair

〰 [GO·LO·**PU**·CHA] *n.* - repair

〰 [GOT] *n.* - baby

〰 [GODZ] *n.* - cannabis, hemp

〰 [**GODZ**·MA] *n.* - domesticated plant

〰 [**GO**·ZUL] *adj.* - light-colored

〰 [**GOZ**·DĚ] *n.* - pallor

〰 [GA] *n.* - snack

〰 [**GA**·ATH] *v.* - to toil

〰 [GARSH] *v.* - 1. to meddle; 2. to tamper

〰 [GA·**(H)R'K**·HĚNTH] *v.* - to intervene

〰 [**GA**·BVOCH] *v.* - to measure

〰 [**GA**·BVATH] *v.* - 1. to begin; 2. to plant; 3. to sow

〰 [GA·**BVA**·THA] *n.* - beginning

〰 [**GA**·BV'ST] n. - grass

〰 [**GA**·GOPS] *n.* - forest

〰 [**GA**·JOTH] *v.* - to lucubrate

〰 [GAZL] *n.* - silver (color)

〰 [**GAZ**·HA] *n.* - silver (metal)

〰 [**GA**·KTHO] *n.* - tree

〰 [GA·**KTHO**·MA] *n.* - wood (material)

〰 [GA·**KTH'S**·TA] *n.* - rod

〰 [**GAK**·MO·'] *n.* - grove

〰 [**GAK**·LA] *n.* - stick

〰 [GĚ·**MO**·HA] *n.* - cat (domestic)

〰 [GĚ·**MOT**] *n.* - feline

〰 [GĚ·MĚK] *n.* - sickness

〰 [GĚ·MĚSH] *v.* - to sicken

〜:〜〜 [GĔ·MURSH] *v.* - to doubt

〜:〜〜. [GĒM·BVA] *n.* - disease

〜:ろ〜〜〜 [GĒ·**THOK**] *n.* - evil

〜:〜〜〜 [GĔ·**LA**·MUDZ] n. - fox

〜:〜〜' [GĔ·N'] *n.* - right (direction)

〜:〜 [GĔRSH] *v.* - to will

〜:〜〜.3. [GĔ·**RU**·THA] *n.* - theorist

〜:〜〜〜〜〜 [GĔR·SYOT] *n.* - hypothesis

〜:〜〜〜〜〜2 [GĔR·SYOSH] *v.* - to hypothesize

〜:〜〜3 [GĔRTH] *v.* - to theorize

〜:〜〜3. [GĔR·THA] *n.* - theory

〜:〜3 [GĔS] *n.* - fiber

〜:〜3〜.3 [GĔS·PATH] *v.* - to therapize

〜:〜3〜.3. [GĔS·**PA**·THA] *n.* - therapy

〜:〜3〜〜 [GĔS·LĔT] *n.* - sheep

〜:〜〜〜3 [GĔ·G'TH] *v.* - 1. to govern; 2. to manage

〜:〜〜3. [GĔ·**GU**·THA] *n.* - manager

〜:〜. [GĔ·TA] *n.* - horn

〜:〜 [GĔJ] *n.* - head

〜:〜:〜 [GĔ·JĔM] *n.* - hair (collective)

〜:〜:〜3 [GĔ·JĔS] *n.* - hair (individual)

〜:〜〜〜 [GĔ·J'NTH] *v.* - to lead

〜:〜〜〜3. [GĔ·J'·**NU**·THA] *n.* - leader

〜:〜〜〜 [GĔ·**TSA**·TU] *numb.* - thousand

〜:〜〜 [GĔZL] *n.* - wool

〜〜〜〜〜 [G(H)RO·FVOM] *n.* - list

〜〜〜〜〜〜 [G(H)RO·**FVO**·MOWSH] *v.* - to list

〜〜〜〜:. [G(H)ROM·FVĔ] *n.* - name

〜〜〜〜:.2 [G(H)ROM·FVĔSH] *v.* - to name

〜〜〜〜,3 [G(H)ROM·BVACH] *v.* - to price

〜〜〜〜 [G(H)ROT] *n.* - word

〜〜..2 [G(H)RĔSH] *v.* - to slip

〜〜.. [**GLA**·A] *n.* - back

〜〜..〜 [**GLA**·ARSH] *v.* - to answer

〜〜〜. [**GLA**·LA] *n.* - bottom

〜〜〜〜3〜〜〜〜〜 [GLA·LA·THOM·**TU**·LOK] *n.* - bass guitar

〜〜:〜〜〜3. [GLĔN·LU·'·SA] *n.* - ukulele

〜〜:3 [GLĔCH] *v.* - to age

〜〜〜 [O·'**G**·NU] *adj.* - left (direction)

,~ [AG] *adj.* - female

,~̨₀₂. [A·**GO**·ZĚ] *adj.* - pale

,~. [**A**·GA] *n.* - female

,~:₃₀♪₃. [A·GĚ·MO·**T'**·HA] adj. - feline

,~:₃. [A·**GĚ**·MA] *adj.* - sick

,~:₃₀₂₂. [A·GĚ·**THO**·KTHA] *adj.* - evil

,~̨.⌐ [**A**·GĚT] *adj.* - short

,~⌐⁓ [**AG**·N'] *adj.* - right (direction)

,~⌐.. [A·**GLA**·A] *adj.* - back

,~⌐.⌐. [A·**GLA**·LA] *adj.* - bottom

:~̨₀ [Ě·GO] *adj.* - neuter

:~̨₀⌐ [Ě·GOM] *adj.* - 1. frail; 2. weak

:~̨₀₃ [Ě·GOTH] *v.* - to neuter

:~̨: [Ě·GĚ] *adj.* - neutral

,⌐⁓ [**U**·'G] *adj.* - male

,⌐⁓. [**U**·'G·A] *n.* - male

₃ Aath

₃ [**A**·ATH] *v.* - to make, to build

₃₀.⌐ [**THO**·ADZ] *n.* - improvisation

₃₀⁓₀₂₂₂ [THO·**MOK**] *n.* - court

₃₀⁓₃.₃ [THO·**M'**·MĚSH] *v.* - 1. to court; 2. to recruit

₃₀⁓↗⌐. [THOM·**TU**·LA] *n.* - obesity

₃₀⁓. [**THO**·GA] *n.* - table

₃₀⁓:.₅. [THO·**GĚ**·CHA] *n.* - tray

₃₀⌐ [THOT] *n.* - arm

₃₀↗₀↗↗ [THO·**TOT**] *n.* - elbow

₃.⁓₀₃ [**THA**·YOTH] *v.* - to hammer

₃.⁓₀↗↗ [THA·**YOT**] *n.* - hammer

₃.₅:⌐ [**THA**·BVĚSH] *v.* - to lock

₃.₅.₃ [**THA**·SĚTH] *v.* - to use

₃.₅₃₀⁓ [THAS·**TH'**·OM] *n.* - industry

₃.⁓ [THAG] *adj.* - nonsynthetic

₃.↗. [**THA**·TA] *n.* - artifact

₃.↗.₅. [THA·**TA**·CHA] *n.* - operation

₃.↗↗. [THA·**T'**·TA] *adj.* - 1. artifactual; 2. artificial

₃.₂₂₀⁓. [**THA**·KTHO·MA] *n.* - foliage

₃.₂₂₀⌐ [**THA**·KTHOT] *n.* - leaf

[**THĒ**·NOTH] *v.* - to divide
[**THĒN**·THOK] *n.* - division
[THĒSH] *v.* - to brake
[THĔ·**BVO**·LA] *n.* - boot
[**THĔ**·SOTH] *v.* - to drive
[THĔTH] *v.* - to start
[THĔ·**SHOT**] *n.* - vehicle
[**TH'N**·GOTH] *v.* - to guide
[TH'N·**GO**·KTHĔK] *n.* - landmark
[TH'N·**GA**·GA] *n.* - mother
[TH'N·**GA**·GASH] *v.* - to mother
[TH'N·**G'**·UPS] *n.* - apple
[TH'N·GU·'·GA] *n.* - father
[TH'N·**GUK**] *n.* - parent
[**TH'N**·GUSH] *v.* - to parent
[TH'·**BVĔSH**] *v.*- to defend
[TH'L] *adj.* - thin
[TH'·LO·**FVA**·SHA] *n.* - competition
[TH'·**LOPS**] *adv. & prep.* - beyond
[**TH'**·LOSH] *v.* - to stretch
[**THUN**·WA] *n.* - picture
[THUMTH] *v.* - to drum
[**THU**·WONTH] *v.* - to imagine
[**THU**·ZĒTH] *v.* - to hit
[THUSH] *v.* - to send
[**THRA**·ATH] *v.* - to win
[THRĔSH] *v.* - to rule
[THRM] *n.* - 1. a species of small, empathic hominid; 2. an individual of this species; 3. elf
[THRMTH] *v.* - *(archaic)* approx. "to make to have wholeness"
[THRDZ] *n.* - ecstasy
[THL'] *n.* - building
[THWOMTH] *v.* - to print
[O·**TH'**·OT] *n.* - art
[O·TH'·**U**·THA] *n.* - artist
[**OTH**·YAK] *n.* - feather
[A·**THOM**·TUL] *adj.* - fat; overweight
[A·**THAN**·Y'] *adj.* - sharp
[**A**·THĔT] *adj.* - tall

,ߩ,ߪߪ, [A·TH'·**LOSH**·L'] *adj.* - elastic

,ߩ,ߧ;ߝߪ, [A·TH'·LĒ·**GO**·M'] *adj.* - delicate

,ߩ,ߦߪߝ,ߪ, [A·THU·WO·**N**'·HA] *adj.* - imaginary

,ߩߦߝ,ߝ, [ATH·LO·**BVA**·N'] *adj.* - modern

:ߩ [ĒTH] *v.* - to kill

,ߩ,ߝ [**U**·THANTH] *v.* - to force

,ߩ,ߝߝߪߦ, [U·THAN·**YO**·LO] *n.* - needle

,ߩ,ߩߝ:ߝ [U·**THAK**·YĒNTH] *v.* - to twist

,ߩ:,ߪ,ߝ [U·**THĔ**·DZANTH] *v.* - to satisfy

,ߩ:,ߩ:,ߦ,ߦ [U·THĔ·**DVĔ**·TSARSH] *v.* - to outrage

ߦ **Lo**

ߦ [LO] *n.* - shadow

    plural, ߦ,ߝ [**LO**·'M]

ߦߪ [LO] *v. aux.* - indicates preterit tense

ߦߪ,ߪ [**LO**·ASH] *v.* - to spoil

ߦߪ, [**LO**·'] *prep.* - by

ߦߪ,ߝ, [LO·'·MU] *prep.* - beside; besides; in addition to

ߦߪ,ߩ [**LO**·'TH] *v.* - to foul

ߦߪ,ߪ [**LO**·'SH] *v.* - to pass

ߦߪ,ߪߪ: [LO·'**SH**·DĔ] *n.* - passage

ߦߪߝ [LOM] *n.* - group

ߦߪߧ, [**LO**·BV'] *adj.* - hard

ߦߪߧ,ߩߦ [**LO**·BV'ST] *n.* - rail

ߦߪߪ [LOCH] *v.* - to order (command)

ߦߪߩ: [**LO**·SĔ] *adv.* - over

ߦߪߩߦߧ,ߪ [LOS·**HO**·BV'CH] *v.* - to protect

ߦߪߩ [LOTH] *v.* - to elapse

ߦߪߩߝߪ [**LOTH**·GO] *n.* - year

ߦߪߦ,ߪ [**LO**·L'SH] *v.* - to retreat

ߦߪߦ,ߪ, [LO·**L**'·SHA] *n.* - retreat

ߦߪߦ,ߪ [**LO**·WASH] *v.* - to watch

ߦߪߦ [LODZ] *n.* - trouble

ߦߪߦ,ߦ:ߝ, [LO·J'·**LĒ**·NA] *n.* - discussion

ߦߪߦ,ߩ [**LO**·TSATH] *v.* - to reek

ߦߪߦߪߧ, [LO·**SHO**·BVA] *n.* - curtain

ߦߪߪ, [**LO**·SHA] *n.* - opinion

ߦߪߪߧ,ߩߦ, [LOSH·BV'·**CHO**·TA] *n.* - shield

ᔑᓭᣔᣔᕼ [LA·HA·**GUK**] *n.* - utensil

ᔑᣔᓭᣔᕱᣔ᠍ᣔ [LAR·HA·**BV(H)RAK·N'**] *n.* - clarinet

ᔑᣔᣔ [**LA**·MUDZ] *n.* - dog

ᔑᣔᓭᣔ [LA·**BVA**·TA] *n.* - chicken

ᔑᣔᣔ [**LA**·TĔDZ] *n.* - danger

ᔑᣔᣔ [**LAT**·ZUCH] *v.* - to fear

ᔑᣔ [**LASH**] *v.* - to close

ᔑᣔᣔ [**LASH**·TA] *n.* - button

ᔑᣔᓭ [**LĒ**·ORSH] *v.* - to cry

ᔑᣔᓭᣔ [**LĒ**·MOSH] *v.* - to continue

ᔑᣔᓭᣔ [LĒ·**MOSH**·PA] *n.* - posterity

ᔑᣔᓭᣔ [LĒ·**MOSH**·DĔ] *n.* - continuity

ᔑᣔᓭᣔ [**LĒCH**·L'] *adv. & prep.* - under

ᔑᣔᓭᣔ [LĒCH·**TSU**·(H)RA] *n.* - cushion

ᔑᣔᓭ [**LĒTH**] *v.* - to fail

ᔑᣔᓭᣔ [**LĒ**·TH'SH] *v.* - to deflect

ᔑᣔ [**LĒDZ**] *n.* - duration

ᔑᣔᣔ [LĒ·DZANTH] *v.* - to last

ᔑᣔᣔ [**LĒ**·DZUTH] *v.* - to protract; to extend

ᔑᣔᣔᓭ [LĒ·**DZUTH**·PA] *n.* - eternity

ᔑᣔᣔᓭ [LĒ·**DZUT**·YA] *n.* - infinity

ᔑᣔᓭ [**LĒSH**·NA] *n.* - badness

ᔑᣔ [**LĔ**] *pref.* - indicates non-specificity, e.g. "some" in "somewhere"

ᔑᣔᓭᣔ [LĔ·**NĔ**·TA] *n.* - sphincter

ᔑᣔᓭ [**LĔ**·HA] *n.* - place

ᔑᣔᓭᣔᓭ [LĔ·**HAR**·YOT] *n.* - property

ᔑᣔᓭᣔ [**LĔ**·HATH] *v.* - to put

ᔑᣔᓭᣔ [LĔ·**H'**·OT] *n.* - mineral

ᔑᣔᓭᣔ [LĔ·**(H)R'**·T'] *n.* - moment

ᔑᣔᓭ [LĔM] *pro.* - some

ᔑᣔᓭ [**LĔ**·MO] *n.* - 1. somebody; 2. someone

ᔑᣔᓭᣔ [LĔ·**LA**·HABV] *n.* - somewhere

ᔑᣔᓭᣔ [LĔ·**WO**·HA] *n.* - position

ᔑᣔᓭᣔ [**LĔ**·TSOSH] *v.* - to sweat

ᔑᣔᓭᣔ [L'·**A**·SHATH] *v.* - to crush

ᔑᣔᓭ [**LUM**·HA] *n.* - rat

ᔑᣔ [**LU**·LA] *n.* - shade

ᔑᣔᓭᣔ [LU·LAK·**YU**·LA] *n.* - umbrella

ᔑᣔᓭ [**LU**·DVĒRSH] *v.* - to hate

  ,ↄↄ [A·**LOTH**·GO] *adj.* - yearly, annual

  ,ↄ, [A·**LĒ**·N'] *adj.* - certain (specific unnamed)

  ,ↄ:ↄↄ, [A·LĒ·**HO**·TA] *adj.* - private

  ,ↄ:ↄ.ↄ. [A·LĒ·**CHĚ**·CHĚ] *adj.* - lesser

  ,ↄ:ↄ, [A·**LĒ**·CH'] *adj.* - under

  ,ↄ:ↄↄ,ↄ, [A·LĒS·**PA**·TH'] *adj.* - ill

  ,ↄ:ↄↄ [A·**LĒ**·LO] *adj.* - poor

  ,ↄ:ↄↄↄ, [A·LĒ·**TO**·TH'] *adj.* - dead

  ,ↄ:ↄↄↄ [A·**LĒ**·WOT] *adj.* - secret

  ,ↄ:ↄ.ↄↄ. [A·LĒ·**DZUTH**·PA] *adj.* - eternal

  ,ↄ:ↄↄↄↄↄↄↄↄ, [A·LĒK·NOT·**CHL'**·A] *adj.* - dozing

  ,ↄ:ↄↄ, [A·**LĒSH**·L'] *adj.* - bad

  ,ↄ:.ↄ.ↄↄ, [A·LĒ·**HAN**·L'] *adj.* - fixed

  ,ↄ:.ↄ [A·**LĚM**] *adj.* - some

  ,ↄ:.ↄↄↄↄↄↄ. [A·LĚM·**SO**·KTHA] *adj.* - silent

  ,ↄ,ↄↄ [A·**L'S**·TO] *adj.* - ready

  ,ↄↄↄↄ.ↄ. [A·LUBV·**CHĚ**·NA] *adj.* - political

  ,ↄↄↄↄ [A·**LU**·Z'G] *adj.* - forward

  :ↄↄↄ [Ē·**LO**·'SH] *v.* - to wait

  :ↄↄↄↄ. [Ē·LO·'**SH**·DĚ] *n.* - waiting

  :ↄↄↄↄ [Ē·**LO**·WASH] *v.* - to ignore

  :ↄ:ↄↄↄ [Ē·LĒ·**MĚSH**] *v.* - to alter

  :ↄ:ↄ, [Ē·**LĒ**·TU] *adj.* - fickle

  :ↄ:ↄↄ [Ē·**LĒ**·TUNTH] *v.* - to be fickle

  ,ↄ. ['·LĚ] *adv., det. & pro.* - any

  ,ↄↄↄ, ['**L**·SHL'] *adv. & prep.* - off

ↄ Tut

ↄ [TUT] *n.* - sprout

ↄↄↄↄ [**TO**·YOTH] *v.* - to branch

ↄↄↄ.ↄↄ.ↄↄ. [TO·MAS·**FVAN**·GA] *n.* - synthesis

ↄↄↄ.ↄↄ.ↄↄↄ [TO·MAS·**FVAN**·G'TH] *v.* - to synthesize

ↄↄↄ.ↄↄ.ↄↄↄↄ. [TO·MAS·FVAN·**GU**·THA] *n.* - synthesizer

ↄↄↄↄ:.ↄ.ↄ. [TOM·WĒ·LĚ·(H)RA] *n.* - trumpet

ↄↄↄↄ:.ↄↄ,ↄↄ [TOM·DĚ·'·**BV'**·DZUNTH] *v.* - to generate

ↄↄↄ [TOTH] *v.* - to be born

ↄↄↄ. [**TO**·THA] *n.* - birth

ↄↄↄ, [**TO**·W'] *n.* - green

ᴊᵒᵧ, [**TO**·TSA] *n.* - tea

ᴊ, [TA] *numb.* - three

ᴊ,,ᴊ [**TA**·AT] *n.* - leg

ᴊᵧ⌒ [TANTH] *v.* - to adorn

ᴊᵧ⌒ᵧ⤳ [**TA**·N'CH] *v.* - to need

ᴊᵧᵩ⌒ᵧ [**TA**·(H)R'NTH] *v.* - 1. to cherish; 2. to progress

ᴊᵧᵩᵧᵧ, [TA·**(H)R'**·NA] *n.* - progress

ᴊᵧᵩᵧ⌒ᵤᴊ [TA·**(H)R'N**·YOT] *n.* - sweetheart

ᴊᵧᵩᵧᵯᵧᵤ,, [TA·**(H)R'N**·DĚ] *n.* - progression

ᴊᵧᵩᵧᵧᵧ⤳ [TARCH] *v.* - to influence

ᴊᵧᵧᵻ⌒, [TA·**MU**·YA] *n.* - parcel

ᴊᵧ⤳ [TACH] *v.* - to control

ᴊᵧᵧᵧ, [**TA**·GA] *n.* - girl

ᴊᵧᵤ₀ [**TA**·LO] *n.* - night

ᴊᵧᵤₒᵧᵧᵤᴊᴊ [**TA**·LOBV·**CHOT**] *n.* - mosquito

ᴊᵧᵤₒᵤ,ᵧ [**TA**·**LO**·JĚM] *n.* - mystery

ᴊᵧᵤᵧᵧᵤᵤᵤᵤ [**TA**·LĚM·**SOK**] *n.* - owl

ᴊᵧᵤᵤᵧᵧᵤᵧᵧ [TAL·**TA**·GOPS] *n.* - glade

ᴊᵧᵤᵤᵧ,, [**TAL**·TĚ] *n.* - meadow

ᴊᵧᵤₜ [**TA**·TU] *numb.* - thirteen

ᴊᵧᵤᵤ,,ᵧ [TAT·LĚM] *n.* - pants (garment); trousers

ᴊᵧᵤᵧᵦ, [TA·**W'**·THA] *n.* - third (portion)

ᴊᵧᵤ [TAZL] *n.* - day

ᴊᵧᵤₑᵧ [**TA**·ZĚPS] *n.* - yesterday

ᴊᵧᵤₜᵧ [**TA**·ZUM] *n.* - today

ᴊᵧᵤᵤ,,ᴊ [**TAZ**·LĚT] *n.* - dusk

ᴊᵧᵤᵤᵧₜ [TAZL·**TSA**·TU] *n.* - period of ten days

ᴊᵧᵩₒᵧ [**TA**·SHOPS] *adv.* - tomorrow

ᴊᵧᵩₒᵧ, [**TA**·**SHO**·PA] *n.* - tomorrow

ᴊᵧᵩₒᵧ [**TA**·DVOM] *n.* - bulb

ᴊᵧ⌒ [TĚNTH] *v.* - to slice

ᴊᵧᵤₒᵧᵧ, [TĚ·**WON**·YA] *n.* - poison

ᴊᵧᵤₒᵧᵧ, [TĚ·**WON**·CHA] *n.* - liquor

ᴊᵧᵤₒᵤᵤᵧ, [TĚ·WO·**ZĚ**·NA] *n.* - whiskey

ᴊᵧₒᵤᵤᵩ [TĚ·OKSH] *v.* - to rush; to hurry

ᴊᵧₒᵤᵤᵩ, [TĚ·**OK**·SHA] *n.* - haste; hurry

ᴊᵧᵧᵧ [TĚ·'NTH] *v.* - 1. to decorate; 2. to apply makeup

ᴊᵧᵧ, [**TĚ**·HA] *n.* - size

ᴊᵧᵤₒᵧ [**TĚ**·LOM] *n.* - herd

〤〤 [TĔ·DZORSH] *v.* - to respect

〤〤 [TĔ·DZA·LĔT] *n.* - cow

〤〤 [TĔD·SHOT] *n.* - truck

〤〤 [T'·GĔT] *n.* - stem

〤〤 [T'·TUNCH] *v.* - to yearn

〤〤 [TU·'·GA] *n.* - boy

〤〤 [TU·NOCH·NA] *n.* - hunger

〤〤 [TUNCH] *v.* - to hunger

〤〤 [TUG] *n.* - neck

〤〤 [TUGS·TUL] *n.* - collar

〤〤 [TUTH] *v.* - to grow

〤〤 [TU·THOT] *n.* - a thing grown or growing; a growth

〤〤 [TU·THA·TĔ·DĔ] *n.* - expansion

〤〤 [TUT·FVĔ] *n.* - spring (season)

〤〤 [TUZL] *n.* - egg

〤〤 [TU·Z'TH] *v.* - to freshen, to refresh

〤〤 [TU·Z'TH·DĔ] *n.* - renewal

〤〤 [TU·Z'L] *n.* - daybreak

〤〤 [TWOS·WUK] *n.* - rum

〤〤 [TWĔZ·LO] *n.* - brown

〤〤 [O·TA] *conj. & prep.* - 1. and; 2. plus

〤〤 [O·TATH] *v.* - to add

〤〤 [OT·YUTH] *v.* - to increase

〤〤 [A·TO·W'] *adj.* - green

〤〤 [A·TAN·CHL'] *adj.* - necessary

〤〤 [A·TARN·L'] *adj.* - progressive

〤〤 [A·TA·ZA] *adj.* - daily

〤〤 [A·TA·Z'·TA·Z'] *adj.* - normal

〤〤 [A·TĔTS·L'] *adj.* - feeble

〤〤 [A·TĔDZ] *adj.* - great

〤〤 [A·TĔ·DZOR·CHĔM·THL'·A] *adj.* - venerable

〤〤 [A·TĔDZ·CHĔ] *adj.* - greater

〤〤 [A·TU·THAM·DZ'] *adj.* - fertile

〤〤 [A·TUZL] *adj.* - fresh

〤〤 [A·TU·Z'TH·L'] *adj.* - freshing

〤〤 [Ĕ·TOTH] *v.* - to die

〤〤 [Ĕ·TOTH·NA] *n.* - death

〤〤 [Ĕ·TA] *conj.* - but

〤〤 [Ĕ·'·TA] *numb.* - third

,ᴊ ['T] *conj.* - so
,ᴊ,ᴊ ['·TUT] *n.* - thigh

ꙡ Wosh

ꙡ [WOSH] *v.* - to see
ꙡₒᴖ [WONTH] *v.* - to be seen
ꙡₒᴖ. [WO·NA] *n.* - 1. that which can be observed; 2. matter
ꙡₒᴖₒᴊ [WON·YOT] *n.* - chemical
ꙡₒᴖ�ᴊ. [WON·**BVA**·TA] *n.* - quotient
ꙡₒᴖ⩽ [WONCH] *v.* - to wish
ꙡₒᴖ⩽ₜꙩꙩ [WON·**CHUK**] *n.* - wish
ꙡₒᴖꙅₒᴊ. [WON·**THO**·TA] *n.* - image
ꙡₒᴖ. [WO·FVA] *n.* - canvas
ꙡₒᴖᴊ. [WOP·TA] *n.* - rice
ꙡₒᴖᴖ [WO·HANTH] *v.* - to look
ꙡₒᴖ [WOM] *n.* - mass
ꙡₒᴖₒꙍ [WO·MOZL] *n.* - white
ꙡₒᴖᴖₒꙍ [WOM·GOZL] *n.* - cotton
ꙡₒᴊₜꙩꙩ [WO·**TUK**] *n.* - dream
ꙡₒᴊ⩽ [WOTCH] *v.* - to dream
ꙡₒᴊ⩽ₜꙅ.ᴖₒᴊ⩽. [WOT·CHU·THA·**NOT**·CHA] *n.* - hypnarch
ꙡₒᴊ⩽ₜꙅ.ᴖ. [WOT·CHU·**THA**·GA] *n.* - queen
ꙡₒꙅ. [WO·SHA] *n.* - eye
ꙡ.. [WA·A] *n.* - 1. sign; 2. marking
ꙡ..⩽ [WA·ACH] *v.* - to hope
ꙡ..⩽ₜꙩꙩ [WA·A·**CHUK**] *n.* - hope
ꙡ.꙯ꙍₒ [WA·'**K**·GO] *n.* - bark (bot.)
ꙡ.ᴖₒᴖ. [WA·**YO**·FVA] *n.* - leather
ꙡ.ᴖ. [WA·YA] *n.* - skin
ꙡ.ᴖ⁚ᴖ [WA·YĚNTH] *v.* - to materialize
ꙡ.ᴖ⁚ᴖ. [WA·YĚ·NA] *n.* - surface
ꙡ.ᴖ⁚ᴖꙡ⁚ [WA·**YĚN**·DĚ] *n.* - material
ꙡ.ᴖₜꙍ [WA·NUK] *n.* - fact
ꙡ.ꙅₒꙍ [WA·SOBV] *n.* - vocation
ꙡ.ꙅ⁚⩽ [WA·SĚTH] *v.* - to cover
ꙡ.ꙅ⁚ꙍ [WA·SĚK] *n.* - top
ꙡ.ꙅᴖ⁚⩽. [WAS·**GĚ**·SA] *n.* - rope
ꙡ.⩽ [WATH] *v.* - to seem

ひ,ろ,ひ,へ [WA·**TH'**·MĚNTH] *v.* - to flicker

ひ:へ [WĒPS] *conj.* - unless

ひ:ひひ:へ, [WĒK·**(H)RĒ**·NA] *n.* - eyesore

ひ,,ぐへ♂ [WĚCH·YOT] *n.* - representative

ひ,,ろ,ぐ [WĚ·THACH] *v.* - to offer

ひ,へ,,ぐ♂, [W'·**YĚS**·TA] *n.* - tube

ひ,へ,へ [**W'**·P'NTH] *v.* - to test

ひ,へ,♡, [W'·**HA**·GA] *n.* - pin

ひ,ぐo♂, [W'·**SO**·TA] *n.* - angle

ひ,ぐ♂ [W'ST] *n.* - line

ひ,ぐ♂♂ [**W'S**·TOT] *n.* - tail

ひ,ぐ♂,ひひ, [W'S·**TAK**·ZA] *n.* - snake

ひ,ぐ♂:ろ, [W'S·**TĒ**·THA] *n.* - gun

ひ,ぐ♂ゃへ, [W'S·**TU**·(H)RA] *n.* - pipe

ひ,ぐ♂ゃ♂ [**W'**·STUL] *n.* - band (decorative or mechanical)

ひ,♡,,ろ, [W'·**GĚ**·SA] *n.* - strand (fiber)

ひ,ろ [W'TH] *v.* - to cut

ひ,ひoひ,ろ [W'·**WO**·ZĚTH] *v.* - 1. to glisten; 2. to glitter

ひ,ひoへ [**W'**·WOSH] *v.* - to blink

ひ,ひoへ, [W'·**WO**·SHA] *n.* - blink

ひゃへ,,ろ [**WU**·YĚTH] *v.* - to appear

ひゃへ,ぐ [**WU**·Y'CH] *v.* - to expect

ひゃへひ,, [**WUR**·DĚ] *n.* - attention

ひゃぐゃへ [**WU**·S'RSH] *v.* - to chance

ひゃぐへo♂ [**WUS**·YOT] *n.* - die (singular of "dice")

ひゃぐo♂ろ, [WUS·**(H)RU**·THA] *n.* - plenipotentiary

ひゃぐひ [WUSK] *n.* - chance

ひゃひ,, [**WU**·DĚ] *n.* - performance

ひへoへ, [**W(H)RO**·MA] *n.* - sand

,:ひoへ, [A·Ê·**WO**·NA] *adj.* - 1. unseen; 2. unnoticed

,ひoへ, [A·**WO**·NA] *adj.* - seen, observed

,ひoへへ,ぐひ,,ひ, [A·WON·YAS·**WĚ**·DZA] *adj.* - saccharine

,ひoへゃひ [A·**WO**·MUZL] *adj.* - white

,ひ,ひひ, [A·**WAT**·DZ'] *adj.* - important

,ひ:ひへ: [A·**WĒK**·(H)RĒ] *adj.* - ugly

,ひ,ぐ, [A·**W'**·S'] *adj.* - straight

,ひゃぐ, [A·**WU**·SA] *adj.* - chance

,:ひ [ÊWSH] *v.* - to mask

,:ひoへ [Ê·WONTH] *v.* - to be unseen

80

꞉ᔓᏒ. [Ê·**WO**·NA] *n.* - that which is unseen

꞉ᔓᏒ.ᔓ. [Ê·WO·**NA**·THA] *n.* - ogre

꞉ᔓᎧ [Ê·WOT] *n.* - secret

꞉ᔓ. [Ê·WA] *n.* - mask

꞉ᔓ.Ꮢ꞉.Ꮢ [Ê·**WA**·YÊNTH] *v.* - to dematerialize

꞉ᔓᏒ꞉.ᔓ [Ê·**WU**·YÊTH] *v.* - to disappear

.꞉ᔓ. [Ê·'·WA] *n.* - comparison

ᔓ Dza

ᔓ [DZA] *n.* - joy

ᔓᏔᔓ [DZO·OTH] *v.* - to laugh

ᔓᏔᔓᏒ꞉ [DZO·**OTH**·DĔ] *n.* - laughter

ᔓᏔᏒ [DZOCH] *v.* - to play

ᔓᏔᏒᏔᏒ. [DZO·**CHO**·GA] *n.* - stage (theatrical)

ᔓᏔᏒ꞉Ꮢ [DZO·CHÊNTH] *v.* - to trick

ᔓᏔᏒᏔᏔᎧ [DZO·G(H)ROT] *n.* - quip

ᔓᏔᔓ.ᏒᏒ. [DZO·**ZAR**·NA] *n.* - humor

ᔓ.. [DZA·A] *numb.* - five

ᔓ..Ꮢ [DZA·ACH] *v.* - to sing

ᔓ.Ꮢ꞉.ᔓ [DZA·YÊTH] *v.* - to draw

ᔓ.Ꮢ [DZANTH] *v.* - to free

ᔓ.ᏒᏒ. [DZA·NA] *n.* - an autonomous being

ᔓ.Ꮢ.ᔓ [DZA·NADZ] *n.* - freedom

ᔓ.ᏒᏒ꞉.ᔓ.ᔓ [DZAN·**BVĔT**·ATH] *v.* - to be free

ᔓ.Ꮢ [DZARSH] *v.* - to prosper

ᔓ.ᏒᏔᏒ [DZA·(H)RONTH] *v.* - to boast

ᔓ.Ꮢᔓ [DZARTH] *v.* - to orgasm

ᔓ.ᏒᔓᏒᏒ.. [DZAR·**TH'**·CHĔ] *n.* - orgasm

ᔓ.ᏒᏒᏒᏒᏒ [DZAM·GURSH] *v.* - to reward

ᔓ.Ꮢ꞉.ᔓᔓ.. [DZA·**BVĔTH**·DĔ] *n.* - pleasure

ᔓ.ᏒᔓᏔᏒ [DZABV·KTHOCH] *v.* - to comfort

ᔓ.ᏒᏔᎧᎧ [DZA·**CHOT**] *n.* - singer

ᔓ.Ꮞ; [DZA·TU] *numb.* - fifteen

ᔓ.ᔓ.. [DZA·DĔ] *n.* - song

ᔓ.ᔓ.Ꮢ [DZA·ZANTH] *v.* - to yodel

ᔓ.ᔓ.ᏒᏔᎧᎧ [DZA·ZA·**NOT**] *n.* - yodeler

ᔓ.ᔓ.ᏒᏒ. [DZA·**ZA**·NA] *n.* - 1. *homo neanderthalensis;* 2. troll

ᔓ.. [DĔ] *suff.* - suffix indicating state or condition; -hood

ᔓ,ᔓ [DĔ·'·LĒ] *n.* - 1. gist; 2. quintessence

ᔓ,ᔓ, [DĔ·NA] *n.* - ornament

ᔓ,ᔓ,ᔓ [DĔ·BV'DZ] *exclam.* - welcome!

ᔓ,ᔓ,ᔓ,ᔓ, [DĔ·BV'D·HLU·'·SA] *n.* - banjo

ᔓ,ᔓ,ᔓ [DĔ·BV'DZCH] *v.* - to welcome

ᔓ,ᔓ,ᔓ [DĔ·LA·(H)RO·SA] *n.* - instinct

ᔓ,ᔓ,ᔓ [DĔL·TĒNTH] *v.* - to infect

ᔓ,ᔓ,ᔓ, [DĔ·W'·GA] *n.* - flower

ᔓ,ᔓ,ᔓ [DĔ·W'K] *n.* - beauty

ᔓ,ᔓ,ᔓ,ᔓ [DĔ·W'·KTH'TH] *v.* - beautify

ᔓ,ᔓ [DZ'TH] *v.* - to fuck

ᔓ,ᔓ,ᔓ [DZU·BVĔCH] *v.* - to collectivize

ᔓ,ᔓ,ᔓ, [DZU·BVĔ·CHA] *n.* - collective

ᔓ,ᔓ [DZUTH] *v.* - 1. to complete; 2. to end; 3. to finish

ᔓ,ᔓ,ᔓ [DZU·THOT] *n.* - entirety

ᔓ,ᔓ, [DZU·THA] *n.* - end

ᔓ,ᔓ,ᔓ [DZU·THA·HA] *n.* - completion

ᔓ,ᔓ,ᔓ,ᔓ [DZU·THA·BVĔCH] *v.* - to persevere

ᔓ,ᔓ,ᔓ,ᔓ, [DZU·THA·BVĔ·CHA] *n.* - perseverance

ᔓ,ᔓ,ᔓ,ᔓ, [DZUTH·LOP·YA] *n.* - beyond

ᔓ,ᔓ [DZUT] *interj.* - all purpose affirmative exclamation

ᔓ,ᔓ,ᔓ [DZU·TUTH] *v.* - 1. to enjoy; 2. to like

ᔓ,ᔓ,ᔓ,ᔓ,ᔓ, [DHON·LU·U·ZA] *n.* - harp

ᔓ,ᔓ,ᔓ, [DHU·GA] *n.* - plug

ᔓ,ᔓ,ᔓ,ᔓ,ᔓ, [DHUG·LĔ·NĔ·TA] *n.* - hemorrhoid

ᔓ,ᔓ [DZA·MO] *n.* - gift, treasure

ᔓ,ᔓ,ᔓ [DZA·BVĔT·ATH] *v.* - to please, to pleasure

ᔓ,ᔓ,ᔓ [DZWOSH] *v.* - to love

ᔓ,ᔓ,ᔓ,ᔓ [DZWO·SHOT] *n.* - lover

ᔓ,ᔓ,ᔓ, [DZWO·SHA] *n.* - love

,ᔓ [ADZ] *adj.* - joyous

,ᔓ,ᔓ,ᔓ [A·DZA·NOTZL] *adv.* - freely

,ᔓ,ᔓ [A·DZA·N'] *adj.* - free

,ᔓ,ᔓ,ᔓ, [A·DZĔ·W'·KTH'] *adj.* - beautiful

,ᔓ,ᔓ,ᔓ [A·DZUTH·LO] *adj.* - complete

,ᔓ,ᔓ,ᔓ,ᔓ, [A·DZUTH·LOP·Y'] *adj.* - farther

,ᔓ,ᔓ,ᔓ,ᔓ [A·DZU·THOT] *adj.* - entire

,ᔓ [ĒDZ] *n.* - indifference

:,ᔓ,ᔓ,ᔓ [Ē·DZA·YĔTH] *v.* - to erase

꞉ꞈ꞉ꞈ. [Ē·DZUTH·PA] *n.* - waste

ꞈ Jaka

ꞈ [JA·KA] *n.* - 1. knowledge; 2. lore; 3. science

ꞈꞈ.ꞈ꞉ [JO·AN·THĒ] *suff.* - meta-

ꞈꞈꞈ [JO·'NTH] *v.* - to arrive

ꞈꞈꞈ. [JO·'·NA] *n.* - arrival

ꞈꞈꞈꞈ [JO·SOSH] *v.* - to study

ꞈꞈꞈ [JOL] *adj.* - right (correct)

ꞈꞈꞈ꞉ [JO·LĔ·'] *adv.* - correctly

ꞈꞈꞈ [JOWSH] *v.* - to perceive

ꞈꞈꞈ [JOK] *n.* - magic

ꞈꞈꞈꞈꞈꞈꞈꞈꞈ. [JOK·M'·HO·CHO·A·NU·THA] *n.* - metamathemage

ꞈꞈꞈꞈꞈꞈꞈꞈ꞉ [JOK·M'·HO·CHO·AN·THĒ] *n.* - metamathemagics

ꞈ꞉꞉ [JA·ATH] *v.* - to quote

ꞈ꞉ꞈ꞉ꞈ [JA·'·GĔM] *n.* - brush

ꞈ꞉ꞈꞈ. [JA·'L·WA] *n.* - pencil

ꞈ꞉ꞈ [JA·'WSH] *v.* - to sketch

ꞈꞈꞈꞈ [JA·YOZL] *n.* - chalk

ꞈꞈ. [JA·YA] *n.* - pen

ꞈꞈ꞉ꞈ. [JA·YĔ·GA] *n.* - paper

ꞈꞈ꞉꞉ [JA·YĔTH] *v.* - to write

ꞈꞈ꞉꞉ꞈ [JA·YĔTH·L'] *n.* - writing

ꞈꞈ꞉꞉ꞈ [JA·YĔ·LU] *n.* - 1. the set of characters of the Dvarsh writing system; 2. any alphabet, syllabary or similar set of characters used for writing.

ꞈꞈꞈ [JA·NO] *n.* - truth

ꞈꞈꞈꞈ [JA·MO·'NTH] *v.* - 1. to agree; 2. to conform

ꞈꞈꞈꞈ꞉ [JA·MO·'·DĔ] *n.* - consensus

ꞈꞈꞈꞈ [JAM·NO] *n.* - contract

ꞈꞈꞈꞈꞈ [JAM·NORSH] *v.* - to contract (legal)

ꞈꞈꞈꞈꞈꞈ꞉ [JAM·NO·(H)RO·TA] *n.* - 1. household; 2. marriage

ꞈꞈꞈꞈꞈꞈ. [JAM·NO·(H)RA] *n.* - obligation

ꞈꞈ.꞉ [JA·BVATH] *v.* - to teach

ꞈ꞉ [JACH] *v.* - to ask

ꞈꞈ꞉ [JA·GĔ] *n.* - note

ꞈꞈꞈꞈ [JA·GU·UM] *n.* - garden

ꞈꞈ꞉꞉ [JA·W'TH] *v.* - to analyze

ꞈꞈꞈꞈ [JA·ZOM] *n.* - book

ᴐ.ᴐ⌐ℨ [JA·Z'TH] *v.* - to find

ᴐ.ᴐⱼᴐ [JA·Z'ZL] *n.* - archaic 121 character syllabary; source of the modern Dvarsh consonants.

ᴐ.ᴐ₊ᶜ [JA·ZUCH] *v.* - to feel

ᴐ.ᴐⱼₐᴊ [JAZ·YĔTS] *n.* - library

ᴐ.ᴐₒᴊ [JA·KTHOT] *n.* - page

ᴐⱼ⌐ₒ [JĒ·NO] *n.* - wisdom

ᴐⱼⱼⱼᴐⱼᴐ. [JĔ·NĔ·BVĒ·BVA] *n.* - empathy

ᴐⱼᴐⱼᴐⱼⱼᶜₒᴐⱼₒᴊ [JĔ·GAK·MA·**SOK**·YOT] *n.* - xylophone

ᴐⱼℨᴊₒᴊ. [JĔTH·**LO**·TA] *n.* - essay

ᴐⱼⱼℨ [JĔ·WATH] *v.* - to mark

ᴐⱼⱼ₊⌐ [J'·HUNTH] *v.* - to judge

ᴐⱼⱼ [J'RSH] *v.* - to know

ᴐⱼᴊ⌐. [J'**T**·HA] *n.* - school

ᴐⱼᴊ⌐.ᶜⱼ [J'T·**HA**·CHĔ] *n.* - college

ᴐⱼᴊ⌐. [J'**T**·(H)RA] *n.* - education

ᴐⱼᴊᶜⱼℨ [J'**T**·SĔTH] *v.* - to train

ᴐⱼᴊ⌐.ℨ [J'**TS**·(H)RASH] *v.* - to learn

ᴐⱼᴐⱼᴐⱼ [J'·**KTH'**·KTH'] *n.* - intuition

ᴐⱼᴐⱼᴐⱼ⌐ₒᴊᴊ [J'·KTH'·KTH'·**MOT**] *n.* - intuit

ᴐⱼᴐⱼᴐⱼ⌐ₒⱼ [J'·KTH'·KTH'·**BVO'**] *n.* - simpleton

ᴐⱼᴐⱼᴐⱼᴐⱼ.ℨ [J'·KTH'·**KTH'TS**·(H)RASH] *v.* - to intuit

ᴐ₊⌐ⱼᶜ [JU·N'CH] *v.* - to question

ᴐ₊ℨ. [JU·THA] *n.* - authority

ᴐ₊ℨ [JUSH] *aux. v.* - can; to be able to

ᴐ₊ᴊₒⱼ [JU·WORSH] *v.* - to view

ᴐ₊ᴊ.ℨ [JU·WASH] *v.* - to contemplate

ᴐⱼ [JA·(H)RASH] *v.* - to know

ᴐᴊ⌐ [JA·TUPS] *n.* - prelude

ₒᴐ.ᴊⱼ⌐ₒ [O·JA·**LĔ**·NO] *n.* - 1. idiom; 2. language

ₒᴐᴊⱼ⌐ [OJ·LĔNTH] *v.* - to talk

.ᴐⱼⱼ [A·**JA**·N'] *adj.* - true

.ᴐⱼ⌐ᴐ₊ⱼ [A·JAN·JU·(H)R'] *adj.* - certain; sure

.ᴐⱼⱼⱼ⌐ₒⱼ [A·JAM·**NO**·(H)R'] *adj.* - 1. contracted; 2. "married"

.ᴐⱼⱼᴊⱼ [A·JĔN·L'] *adj.* - wise

.ᴐⱼᶜⱼ.ℨ [A·J'S·**PA**·THA] *adj.* - medical

.ᴐ₊ⱼᴊⱼ [A·**JUSH**·L'] *adj.* - able

⸱ᴐₒⱼ⌐ [Ē·JO·'NTH] *v.* - 1. to fail to arrive; 2. to fall short

⸱ᴐₒᴊ [Ē·JOWSH] *v.* - 1. to miss; 2. to overlook

:ᴏ.⌒ₒ [Ė·JA·NO] *adj.* - false
:ᴏ.⌒ᴖ, [Ė·JA·NĚ·'] *adv.* - falsely
:ᴏ;ᴗᴗ, [Ė·JĒZ·L'] *adj.* - strange
:ᴏᴗ [ĖJL] *adj.* - wrong

♂ Ts'na

♂ [TS'·NA] *n.* - water
♂ₒₒᴗ [TSO·OL] *n.* - humidity
♂ₒ⌒.ᴧᴧ [TSO·YAM] *n.* - muscle
♂ₒ⌒ [TSONTH] *v.* - to flow
♂ₒ⌒. [TSO·NA] *n.* - liquid
♂ₒ⌒ᴏ.. [TSON· DĚ] *n.* - flow
♂ₒ⋖ [TSOCH] *v.* - to thirst
♂ₒ⋖ᴏ.. [TSOCH·DĚ] *n.* - thirst
♂ₒᴗᴗₒ⋖⋖ [TSOL·TOS] *n.* - current
♂ₒᴗ⌒ₜᴗ [TSOL·PUT] *n.* - charm
♂ₒᴗᴗ. [TSOL·TA] *n.* - fluid
♂ₒᴗᴗ. [TSOL·SHA] *n.* - bucket
♂ₒᴏ. [TSO·TSA] *n.* - flood
♂ₒᴏ.ᴗ [TSO·TSAWSH] *v.* - to bathe
♂ₒᴏ.ᴗ. [TSO·TSA·WA] *n.* - bath
ᴏ.⌒⌒,⋖ [TSAPS·Y'TH] *v.* - to limit
ᴏ.⌒ [TSARSH] *v.* - to drink
ᴏ.⌒. [TSA·(H)RA] *n.* - beverage
ᴏ.⌒,ᴨ [TSA·BV'SH] *v.* - to cup
ᴏ.⌒⌒. [TSABV·YA] *n.* - cup
ᴏ.ᴧₜ [TSA·TU] *numb.* - ten
ᴏ.ᴏ.ᴧₜ [TSA·TSA·TU] *numb.* - hundred
ᴏ.ᴨ.⌒,ᴏ.⌒ [TSA·SHA·BV'·DZANTH] *v.* - to disrupt
ᴏ.ᴨ.⌒,ᴏ.⌒. [TSA·SHA·BV'·DZA·NA] *n.* - disruption
ᴏ.ᴨ. [TSA·DVA] *n.* - strength
ᴏ.ᴨ..⋖ [TSA·DVĚTH] *v.* - to do the apparently impossible
ᴏ;⋖ [TSĖTH] *v.* - to freeze
ᴏ;ᴗ [TSĖT] *n.* - ice
ᴏ;ᴗ,⋖ [TSĖ·T'TH] *v.* - to ice
ᴏ;ᴗ⌒.. [TSĖT·FVĚ] *n.* - winter
ᴏ;ᴏ.⌒. [TSĖ·JA·NA] *n.* - alcohol
ᴏ..⌒ₒ [TSĚ·YO] *n.* - wound

ও঻ৡ [TSĔPS] *n.* - north

ও঻ৡৢ৽ [TSĔ·(H)ROSH] *v.* - to boil

ও঻ৡৢৡৢ [TSĔ·TA·**CHO**·MA] *n.* - ship

ও঻ৢ [TSĔJ] *n.* - blood

ও঻ৢৡ' [TSĔJ·Y'] *n.* - artery

ও঻ৢৡৢ [TSĔJ·**Y'**·T'] *n.* - capillary

ও঻ৢৢৡ'. [TSĔJ·**S'**·A] *n.* - vein

ৡৢৡৢ. [TS'·**YUK**·NA] *n.* - paint

ৡৢ [TS'NTH] *v.* - to pool

ৡৢৢ [**TS'**·NOT] *n.* - lake

ৡৢৢ. [TS'·**NA**·ZA] *n.* - soup

ৡৢৡ. [**TS'N**·YA] *n.* - pond

ৡৢৡ [TS'NCH] *v.* - to pump

ৡৢৢ঻ [**TS'N**·DĔ] *n.* - pool

ৡৢৡৢ. [**TS'N**·KTHA] *n.* - cloud

ৡৢৢ.ৡ [**TS'**·FVASH] *v.* - to stream

ৡৢৡ.ৡ. [TS'·**FVA**·SHA] *n.* - stream

ৡৢৢৢৡ. [TS'·**HOS**·MA] *n.* - dolphin

ৡৢ.ৡ঻ [TS'·**HA**·YĔ] *n.* - ocean

ৡৢ.ৢৢৢ [TS'·**HA**·HOT] *n.* - whale

ৡৢ.ৢৡ [TS'·**HA**·T'] *n.* - sea

ৡৢ.ৢৡৢ.ৡৢ [TS'·HA·**T'**·JAK] *n.* - repository

ৡৢ.ৢৡৢৡৡ. [TS'·HA·**T'K**·BVA] *n.* - gull

ৡৢৢৢ [**TS'**·MOT] *n.* - ondine, undine

ৡৢৢৢৡ. [TS'·**GO**·GA] *n.* - waterlily

ৡৢৡ. [**TS'**·GA] *n.* - lotus

ৡৢৢ [**TSU**·'SH] *v.* - to pour

ৡৢৢৡ. [TSU·**U**·GA] *n.* - cane (bot.)

ৡৢৢ [TSUNTH] *v.* - to melt

ৡৢৢ' [**TSU**·(H)R'] *adj.* - soft

ৡৢৢৢৢ [**TSUL**·TOK] *n.* - seat

ৡৢৢ.ৡ [**TSU**·ZANTH] *v.* - to shock

ৡৢৢৡ. [**TSUZ**·NA] *n.* - electricity

ৡৢৢৡ. [**TSU**·KTHA] *n.* - gel

ৡৢৢৢৢৡ [**TSUK**·TOCH] *v.* - to sit

ৡৢৢৢ [TS(H)R'ST] *n.* - edge

.ৡৢৢ [A·**TSO**·OL] *adj.* - humid

.ৡৢৢৡৢৢৢ [A·TSOL·**PUT**·L'] *adj.* - charming

.ৡৢৢৢৢ [A·**TSOL**·T'] *adj.* - fluid

.ᴕ.ᴣ.ᴕ. [A·TSA·**DVA**·TA] *adj.* - strong

.ᴕ.ᴣᴣ [A·**TSĒTH**·T'] *adj.* - cold

.ᴕ.ᴄᴖ [A·**TSĔ**·FV'] *adj.* - wet

.ᴕᴖᴕᴣ [UTS·**P'**·T'] *adv.* - quite

ᴕ Z'zl

ᴕ [Z'ZL] *n.* - light

ᴕᴄᴖᴄᴕᴕ [ZO·**YOT**] *n.* - bone

ᴕᴄᴖ [ZOM] *n.* - east

ᴕᴄᴖᴖ. [**ZO**·BVA] *n.* - gem

ᴕᴄᴕ [ZOT] *adv. & det.* - no

ᴕᴄᴕᴕᴄᴖᴕᴣ, [ZOT·**KTHOL**·THA] *n.* - thunder

ᴕᴄᴖ.ᴕ. [ZO·**TSA**·TU] *numb.* - million

ᴕᴄᴣ.ᴖ. [ZO·**THA**·GA] *n.* - ray (as of light)

ᴕᴄᴣ.ᴖ.ᴄᴖᴄᴖᴕᴕ [ZO·**THA**·GAH·**YOT**] *n.* - X ray (radiation)

ᴕᴄᴣ.ᴖ.ᴕᴖ. [ZO·**THA**·**GU**·KTHA] *n.* - radiation

ᴕᴄᴕᴣ. [**ZOL**·THA] *n.* - noise

ᴕᴄᴣ [**ZA**·OTH] *v.* - to beam

ᴕᴄᴣ. [ZA·**O**·THA] *n.* - beam

ᴕ.ᴖᴖ [**ZA**·ANTH] *v.* - to glow

ᴕ.ᴖᴕ. [ZA·**AN**·DĔ] *n.* - glow

ᴕᴖᴄᴕ [**ZA**·HOL] *n.* - zinc (metal)

ᴕᴖᴖ [ZARNTH] *v.* - to say

ᴕᴖᴖᴖᴖ [**ZAR**·BVĔCH] *v.* - to present

ᴕᴖᴕᴖ. [**ZAR**·**DZA**·(H)RA] *n.* - poetry

ᴕᴖ [ZAM] *n.* - lamp

ᴕᴖᴄᴕᴕ. [ZA·**MOL**·TA] *n.* - candle

ᴕᴖᴕ [**ZA**·M'] *adj.* - sudden

ᴕᴖᴣ [ZAMTH] *v.* - burst

ᴕᴖᴕ. [ZAM·DĔ] *n.* - brightness

ᴕᴖ [ZABV] *n.* - 1. embryo; 2. fetus

ᴕᴖᴖ [**ZA**·BVANTH] *v.* - to be pregnant

ᴕᴖᴖᴕ. [ZA·**BVAN**·DĔ] *n.* - pregnancy

ᴕᴖᴕᴣ [**ZA**·BVĔTH] *v.* - to become pregnant

ᴕᴕᴕᴖᴖ [**ZAG**·LARNTH] *v.* - to reply

ᴕᴕᴖ [ZA·**ZĒNTH**] *v.* - to dim

ᴕᴕᴖ. [ZA·**ZĒ**·NA] *n.* - twilight

ᴕᴕ [ZASH] *v.* - to dart

ᴅ:ᴩ [ZĒNTH] *v.* - to darken

ᴅ:ᴩᴐ. [ZĒN·DĚ] *n.* - darkness

ᴅ:ᴩᴊₒ [ZĒN·LO] *n.* - black

ᴅ:ᴣ [ZĒTH] *v.* - 1. to damage; 2. to harm; 3. to hurt

ᴅ:ᴣ.ᴐ. [ZĒ·**THA**·DZA] *n.* - cruelty

ᴅ:ᴣᴩᴏ [ZĒ·THURSH] *v.* - to punish

ᴅ:ᴣᴩᴏᴊ. [ZĒ·**THUR**·LA] *n.* - punishment

ᴅ:ᴣᴩ.. [ZĒTH·CHĚ] *n.* - blemish

ᴅ:ᴣᴐ. [ZĒTH·DĚ] *n.* - 1. damage; 2. injury

ᴅ:ᴊ [ZĒL] *n.* - war

ᴅ:ᴊₒᴩ [ZĒ·LOM] *n.* - army

ᴅ:ᴊ. [ZĒ·LA] *n.* - west

ᴅ:ᴊᴊ. [ZĒL·TSA] *n.* - ink

ᴅ:ᴩᴩ [ZĒ·T'RSH] *v.* - to crack

ᴅ:ᴩᴏ. [ZĒT·HA] *n.* - adversary

ᴅ..ᴣ,ᴐ [ZĚ·TH'SH] *v.* - to reflect

ᴅ..ᴣᴐₒᴊ [ZĚTH·SHOT] *n.* - mirror

ᴅᴩᴊₒᴦ [Z'N·TOCH] *v.* - to nap

ᴅᴩᴏₒ [Z'·HO] *n.* - tin (metal)

ᴅᴩᴏ [Z'RSH] *v.* - to read

ᴅᴩᴦ [Z'CH] *v.* - 1. to meditate; 2. to ponder

ᴅᴩᴏ.ᴊ [Z'·GAWSH] *v.* - to suggest

ᴅᴩᴏ.ᴊ. [Z'·**GA**·WA] *n.* - suggestion

ᴅᴩᴏᴊ.. [Z'G·**LA**·A] *n.* - front

ᴅᴩᴦ [Z'·T] *adv.* - even

ᴅᴩᴦᴏ [Z'·T'RSH] *v.* - to balance

ᴅᴩᴊᴊ.. [Z'T·DĚ] *n.* - balance

ᴅᴩᴦ [ZUCH] *v.* - to open

ᴅᴩᴦᴏₒ [**ZUCH**·GO] *n.* - innocence

ᴅᴩᴦᴐ. [**ZUCH**·DZA] *n.* - courage

ᴅᴩᴣ [ZUTH] *v.* - to wash

ᴅᴩᴊ..ᴣ [ZU·LĚTH] *v.* - to wave

ᴅᴩᴩᴏ..ᴣ [ZU·**L'**·MĚTH] *v.* - to flutter

ᴅᴩᴊₒᴣ [ZU·TOTH] *v.* - to respond

ᴅᴩᴊₒₒ. [ZUT·**(H)RO**·SHA] *n.* - reaction

ᴅᴩᴐᴐ [ZUK] *n.* - color

ᴅᴩᴐᴐᴩᴣ [**ZU**·KTHUTH] *v.* - to color

.ᴅᴩᴐ. [A·**ZAM**·DZA] *adj.* - bright

.ᴅ:ᴩᴊₒᴦ [A·ZĒN·**LO**·] *adj.* - black

,ꝛ:ꝛ,ꝛ, [A·ZĒ·**THA**·DZ'] *adj.* - cruel

,ꝛ:ꝛₒ₅, [A·ZĒL·**BVO**·CHA] *adj.* - military

,ꝛ,ꝛꝛ, [A·**Z'G**·LA] *adj.* - front

,ꝛₜꝛ, [A·**ZU**·TA] *adj.* - public

:ꝛ,ꝛ [Ē·ZASH] *v.* - to shut

:ꝛ:ꝛ [Ē·ZĒTH] *v.* - to mend

:ꝛ,ꝛ [Ē·Z'RSH] *v.* - to reject

,ꝛ,₅ꝛ, ['·**Z'CH**·L'] *adv.* - on

,ꝛꝛₒ ['**Z**·LO] *n.* - moon

,ꝛꝛₒ₅ ['**Z**·LORSH] *v.* - to howl

,ꝛꝛₒꝛ['**Z**·LOT] *n.* - lunar cycle; lunar month

ₜꝛ,ꝛꝛ, [U·**Z'G**·LA] *adv.* - forward

ꝛ Ktho

ꝛ [KTHO] *n.* - sky

ꝛₒ₅, [**KTHO**·NA] *n.* - gas

ꝛₒ₅ꝛ, [**KTHON**·TSA] *n.* - steam

ꝛₒ₅ₒꝛ[**KTHO**·FVOT] *n.* - wing

ꝛₒ₅, [**KTHO**·FVA] *n.* - 1. fly; 2. any flying insect

ꝛₒ₅,ꝛₜꝛₒ₅,ꝛ, [KTHO·FVA·ZU·L'·**MĔ**·THA] *n.* - butterfly

ꝛₒ₅ꝛ [KTHOMTH] *v.* - to cough

ꝛₒ₅ₒ₅ [**KTHO**·BVOM] *n.* - flock

ꝛₒ₅, [**KTHO**·BVA] *n.* - bird

ꝛₒ₅,₅,₅, [KTHO·BVA·**CHA**·SA] *n.* - wren

ꝛₒ₅,ꝛ, [KTHO·**BVA**·TA] *n.* - songbird

ꝛₒ₅₅ₒꝛꝛ[KTHOBV·**CHOT**] *n.* - raptor

ꝛₒ₅ [KTHOCH] *v.* - to rest

ꝛₒ₅ₒ₅, [KTHO·**CHO**·YA] *n.* - stillness

ꝛₒ₅ₒꝛꝛ, [KTHO·**CHOK**·TA] *n.* - quiet

ꝛₒ₅ꝛ, [**KTHOCH**·TA] *n.* - rest

ꝛₒꝛₜ₅ [**KTHO**·JUCH] *v.* - to sense

ꝛₒ₅ꝛ [KTHOSH] *v.* - to sneeze

ꝛₒ₅ꝛ₅ꝛ [**KTHO**·SHOSH] *v.* - to fly

ꝛₒ₅ꝛ₅ₒ [**KTHOSH**·NO] *n.* - flight

ꝛₒ₅ꝛꝛ, [**KTHOSH**·TA] *n.* - sneeze

ꝛₜ₅ [KTHABV] *n.* - blue (color)

ꝛₜ₅ₒ₅, [KTHA·**BVO**·BVA] *n.* - jay

ꝛₜ₅:ꝛ [**KTHA**·BVĒZL] *n.* - violet (color)

ഗ,ുഃ [**KTHA**·THO] *n.* - chest (anat.)

ഗ,ഗ, [**KTHAT**·W'] *n.* - blue-green (color)

ഗ,ൂ [KTHASH] *v.* - to blow

ഗ,ൂു. [**KTHASH**·TA] *n.* - wind

ഗ,ൂഹം [**KTHASH**·TYO] *n.* - window

ഗ,ൂഹൂ. [KTHASH·**T'**·SHA] *n.* - flag

ഗ.ു' [**KTHĔ**·'] *adv. & det.* - 1. yes; 2. okay

ഗ.ു:ഹ [**KTHĔ**·YĔT] *prep.* - among

ഗ.ു [KTHĔFV] *adv.* - there

ഗ.ുഹൂ [**KTHĔ**·FVOSH] *v.* - 1. to cross; 2. to transit

ഗ.ുഹൂു, [KTHĔ·**FVO**·SHL'] *n.* - 1. crossing; 2. transit

ഗ.ുഹഗ.ഹ [KTHĔ·**L'**·ZARNTH] *v.* - to approve

ഗ.ുൂ [KTHĔSH] *v.* - to ascend; to rise

ഗ,ുഹൂ. [KTH'·TH'N·**GU**·THA] *n.* - boss

ഗ,ഗ, [**KTH'**·KTH'] *n.* - subjectivity

ഗ,ൂ. [**KTHUSH**·LA] *n.* - shirt

ഗ,ൂ [KYUSH] *v.* - to rain

ഗഹഹ.ഹൂ [KHON·FVA·**BVU**·UL] *n.* - 1. confabulation; 2. the meta-mathemage collective

ഗഹ.ൂ. [**KHAR**·LA] *n.* - melody

ഗഹ.ഹഗ.ഹൂ. [KHA·**L'N**·KHĔ·**N'**·DĔ] *n.* - cumulo-nimbus cloud

ഗഹ.ഹഹ. [**KHĔN**·**YO**·NA] *n.* - eagle

ഗഹ.ഹഹ [**KHĔN**·YUNTH] *v.* - to soar

ഗഹ.ഹൂ. [KHĔ·**(H)R'**·LA] *n.* - aerie

ഗഹ.ഹഹ [**KHĔ**·BV'NTH] *v.* - to launch

ഗഹ.ൂഹൂ. [KH'·**DZAR**·LO] *exclam.* - thank you

ഗഹൂഗ.ഹൂ. [KH'M·SKTHU·U·L'·**OS**·HA] *n.* - constellation

ഗഹ:ഹ. [**K(H)RĔ**·NA] *n.* - pain

ഗഹൂ [KRUT] *conj. & prep.* - than

ഗൂ.ഹൂ.ൂ. [KLA·**(H)RA**·LU·**WĔ**·ZA] *n.* - piano

ഗൂ.ൂഹൂ [KLA·**TĔ**·(H)ROM] *n.* - percussion

ഗൂ.ൂ [KWĔCH] *n.* - a board game played by the Dvarsh

ഗൂ.ൂ [KWĔCH] *v.* - to daydream

ഹഗ [OK] *n.* - ear

ഹഗഹ [**O**·KTHONTH] *v.* - to breathe

ഹഗഹ. [O·**KTHO**·NA] *n.* - breath

ഹഗ:ഹ [**OK**·NĔNTH] *v.* - to smoke

ഹഗ:ൂ. [OK·**NĔ**·ZA] *n.* - smoke

ഹഗഹ.ഹൂ [OK·**HA**·NUL] *n.* - peak

ᴏⵌᴗ.ᴗ. [OK·**GA**·MA] *n.* - cork

ᴏⵌᴣ₀ⵌ [**OK**·THOM] *n.* - weather

ᴏⵌᴗ₆ⵌ [**OK**·TSOM] *n.* - mist

ᴏⵌᴗ [OKSH] *v.* - to sail

ᴏⵌᴗᴗ. [**OK**·SHGA] *n.* - sail

,ⵌ₆ᴄ₀, [A·KTHO·**CHO**·'] *adj.* - still

,ⵌ₆ᴄⵌ, [A·**KTHOCH**·KTH'] *adj.* - quiet

,ⵌ,ᴗᴗ [A·**KTHABV**·L'] *adj.* - blue (color)

,ⵌ,ᴗ:ⵌ₆ [A·KTHA·**BVĒZ**·LO] *adj.* - violet (color)

,ⵌ,ᴗᴗ [A·**KTHAT**·W'] *adj.* - blue-green (color)

,ⵌ,.ᴗᴗ [A·**KTHĔSH**·L'] *adj.* - rising

,ⵌᴣ₀ [**AK**·THO] *n.* - air

,ⵌᴣ₀ᴗ [AK·**THO**·LA] *n.* - nose

:ⵌ₆ᴄ [**Ē**·KTHOCH] *v.* - to awake

:ⵌᴗ₆ᴗ [**ĒK**·NOTCH] *v.* - to doze

,ⵌ:. [**U**·KTHĔ] *adv. & prep.* - across

ᴗ Shosh

ᴗ [SHOSH] *v.* - to go

ᴗ₆ⵌ [SHOPS] *conj./prep.* - after

ᴗ₆ⵌᴗ [**SHOP**·L'] *adv.* - late

ᴗ₆ᴄ₀ᴗ [**SHO**·MOT] *n.* - horse

ᴗ₆ᴗ,ᴄ [**SHO**·BVUCH] *v.* - to hang

ᴗ₆ᴄ [SHOCH] *v.* - to pull

ᴗ₆ᴄᴗ,ⵌ. [**SHOCH**·L'·DĔ] *n.* - attraction

ᴗ₆ⵌ [SHOK] *adv.* - why

ᴗ₆ⵌ₆ᴗ₆ⵌ [**SHO**·KTHO·LOM] *n.* - company

ᴗ₆ⵌ₆ᴗ [**SHO**·KTHOSH] *v.* - 1. to exchange; 2. to trade

ᴗ₆ⵌᴗ,ᴗ [**SHOK**·P'SH] *v.* - 1. to bargain; 2. to negotiate

ᴗ₆ⵌ. [**SHOK**·HA] *n.* - market

ᴗ₆ⵌᴗ,ᴗ [**SHOK**·MASH] *v.* - to argue

ᴗ₆ⵌᴗ:.ᴗ [**SHOK**·LĔSH] *v.* - to market

ᴗ₆ᴗᴗ,ⵌ [SHO·**SHO**·SH'M] *n.* - rhythm

ᴗ,ᴗᴄ [**SHA**·FVURSH] *v.* - to tie (as a knot)

ᴗ,ᴗᴗ:.ᴗ [**SHAFV**·(H)RĔTS] *n.* - prison

ᴗ,ᴗⵌᴄ. [SHAFV·**KTHU**·(H)RA] *n.* - knot

ᴗ,ᴗ [SHABV] *n.* - heart

ᴗ,ᴗ₆ᴄ [**SHA**·BVOCH] *v.* - 1. to be aware; 2. to consider

෧ᆻᆼᅇ [SHA·**BVO**·CH'] *n.* - mind

෧ᆻᆼᇰᇰ [SHA·**BVĔSH**] *v.*- to attack

෧ᆻᆼᇰᆻᇰᆻ [SHA·BV'·**DZA**·NA] *n.* - the wild, wildness

෧ᆻᆼᇰᆻᇰᇰ [SHA·BV'·**DZANTH**·DĔ] *n.* - wilderness

෧ᆻᆼᇰᇰᇰ [SHABV·**CH'**·DĔ] *n.* - consciousness

෧ᇰ [SHATH] *v.* - to push

෧ᇰᇰᇰ [SHA·**THĔSH**] *v.* - to defeat

෧ᇰᆻᇰᇰ [SHA·**THUK**] *n.* - quest

෧ᇰᇰᇰ [**SHAL**·KTHA] *n.* - dress (garment)

෧ᇰᇰᇰᇰ [**SHA**·KTHĔFV] *n.* - emptiness

෧ᇰᇰᇰᆼ [**SHAK**·YO] *n.* - bowl

෧ᇰᇰᇰᆻᇰ [**SHAK**·YĔ·DZA] *n.* - basin

෧ᇰᇰᇰᇰ [SHA·**KTHĔ**·YA] *n.* - hollow

෧ᇰᇰ [SHĔNTH] *v.* - 1. to idle; 2. to laze

෧ᇰᇰᆼᇱ [**SHĔ**·NOT] *n.* - other

෧ᇰᇰᇰᆼᇰ [SHĔN·**FVO**·SHA] *n.* - linen

෧ᇰᇰᇰᇰ [**SHĔN**·DĔ] *n.* - idleness

෧ᇰᇰᆻᇰᇰᇰ [SHĔ·N'·**LOK**·DĔ] *n.* - differential

෧ᇰᇰᇰᇰ [SHĔNSH] *v.* - to differ

෧ᇰᇰᇰᇰᇰᇰ [SHĔP·**HUR**·DĔ] *n.* - parasite

෧ᇰᇰᇰᇰᇱᇱ [SHĔTH·L'·**OT**] *n.* - letter (epistle)

෧ᇰᇱ [SHĔTS] *adv.* - how

෧ᇰᇰᇰ [SH'BVCH] *v.* - to interest

෧ᇰᇰᇱᇱ [**SH'**·SHOT] *n.* - car

෧ᇰᇰ [SHUNTH] *v.* - to attempt

෧ᇰᇰᇰᇰ [SHU·**PUK**] *n.* - system

෧ᇰᇰᇰᇰ [**SHU**·BVĔCH] *v.* - to guard

෧ᇰᇰᇰᇰᇱᇱ [SHU·BVĔ·**CHOT**] *n.* - guardian

෧ᇰᇰᇰᇰᇰ [SHU·**BVĔ**·CHA] *n.* - guard

෧ᇰᇰᇰ [**SHU**·SHĔ] *prep.* - toward

෧ᇰᇰᇰᇰᇰ [SHNA·'·**DĔRSH**] *v.* - to tailor

෧ᇰᇰᇱ [**SHLO**·A] *n.* - past

෧ᇰᇰᇰᇰᇱ [**SHLO**·**CHA**·TA] *n.* - history

෧ᇰᇰᇰᇰᇰ [**SHLO**·KTHĔFV] *n.* - oblivion

෧ᇰᇰᇰᇰᇰ [**SHLOK**·FVA] *n.* - memory

෧ᇰᇰᇰᇰᇰᇰ [**SHLOK**·FVASH] *v.* - to remember

෧ᇰᇰᇰᇰᇰᇰᇰ [**SHLOK**·**LU**·THA] *n.* - 1. aide; 2. assistant

෧ᇰᇰᇰ [SHLASH] *v.* - to slow

෧ᇰᇰᇰᇱ [A·SHO·**BVA**·TA] *adj.* - hanging

,ϨₒϨₒϨᵎ⌐' [A·SHO·SHO·**SH'**·M'] *adj.* - rhythmic

,Ϩₒ⌐ [A·SHAFV] *adv. & conj.* - where

,ϨₒᗡᵎϨₒ⌐, [A·SHA·BV'·**DZA**·NA] *adj.* - wild

,Ϩₒᗡᗡ' [A·**SHABV**·CH'] *adj.* - conscious

,ϨₒϿᗡ⌐' [A·**SHAK**·Y'] *adj.* - hollow

,Ϩₒ�⌐. [A·**SHĔ**·NA] *adj.* - lazy

,ϨₒᵎϿϨ. [A·**SHĔN**·DĔ] *adj.* - idle

,Ϩₒᵎᵎ⌐' [A·**SHĔ**·N'] *adj.* - different

,Ϩᵎᗡ. [A·**SH'**·SA] *adj.* - probable

,Ϩᵑᗡ' [ASH·PL'] *adj.* - late

:ᗡ [ĔSH] *v.* - to stop

:ᗡₒϿϿᵎᗡ [Ĕ·**SHLO**·KTH'SH] *v.* - to forget

'ᗡᗡₜ ['SH·LU] *adv. & prep.* - near

ₜᗡₒᵑ [U·SHAPS] *adv.* - almost

ₜᗡᵎ [U·SHĔ] *prep.* - to

ₜᗡᵑₒᵑᵎ [USH·**MO**·MĔ] *adv.* - together

ₜᗡᗡₒᗨ [USH·**LACH**] *v.* - to approach

ₜᗡᗡ' [USH·L'] *adj.* - near

ₜᗡᗨₒᵑᗨ [USH·**ZARCH**] *v.* - to introduce

ₜᗡᗨₒᵑᗨₒᗡᗡᗡ [USH·ZAR·**CHOK**] *n.* - introduction

ᗡ Dv'n

ᗡ [DV'N] *n.* - fire

ᗡₒᗨ [DVOBV] *n.* - debt

ᗡₒᗡₜᗡ [**DVO**·TSASH] *v.* - to mourn

ᗡₒᗡᗡ. [**DVO**·KTHA] *n.* - bell

ᗡₒᗡᗡₒᗡ [**DVO**·KTHASH] *v.* - 1. to peal; 2. to ring out

ᗡₒᵑ [DVARSH] *n.* - 1. a species of small, robust hominid closely related to humans; 2. ethnonym of the *dvarsh* people; 3. their common language; 4. an individual of this species

ᗡₒᵑ [DVAPS] *n.* - nut

ᗡₒᵑᵎᗡ [**DVA**·(H)R'SH] *v.* - to relish

ᗡₒᵑₜ [**DVA**·BVU] *adj. & pro.* - which (sing.)

ᗡₒᵑᵑ. [**DVABV**·NA] *n.* - coal; ember

ᗡᵎᗞ [DVATH] *v.* - 1. to ignite; 2. to make fire; 3. to turn on

ᗡᵎᗡᵑ. [DVA·**L'**·PA] *n.* - match (igniter)

ᗡᵎᵑ [DVĔNTH] *v.* - to snow

ᗡᵎᗨ [DVĔBV] *n.* - rage

ᗡᵎᗨᗨ [DVĔBVCH] *v.* - to rage

⏤ [**DVĔ**·TSARSH] *v.* - to anger

⏤ [**DVĔTS**·(H)RA] *n.* - anger

⏤ [**DVĔTS**·(H)RATH] *v.* - to become angry

⏤ [DV'NTH] *v.* - to create

⏤ [DV'·**NĔ**·YA] *n.* - apprentice

⏤ [**DV'N**·THA] *n.* - dragon

⏤ [DV'N·THA·**NĒ**·W'] *n.* -modesty

⏤ [**DV'N**·DĔ] *n.* - creation

⏤ [DV'·**GĔ**·JA] *n.* - impulse

⏤ [DV'·**W'**·GA] *n.* - flame

⏤ [DV'·**JAL**·THA] *n.* - invention

⏤ [**DVU**·TSA] *n.* - acid

⏤ [DVUSH] *v.* - to suck

⏤ [DV(H)RASH] *v.* - to burn

⏤ [**DV(H)RU**·THANTH] *v.* - to sting

⏤ [**O**·DVOM] *n.* - ball

⏤ [A·DVAR·**SH'**·HA] *n.* - (bio.) approx. "dvarshlike beings;" in *dvarsh* taxonomy, a genus similar but not congruent to *"homo"* in human nomenclature.

⏤ [A·**DVĒBV**·CHĔ] *adj.* - eager

⏤ [A·**DVĔTS**·(H)ROTZL] *adv.* - angrily

⏤ [A·**DVĔTS**·(H)RA] *adj.* - angry

Other

⏤ [**O**·O] *conj.* - or

⏤ [**O**·A] *prep.* - of, from

⏤ [**O**·'] *prep.* - with, at

⏤ [**A**·A] *art.* - a, an

⏤ [Ĕ·'] *prep.* - as, like

⏤ ['·A] *prep.* - in, on

English to Dvarsh
Dictionary

A

a, an, *art.* - [A·A] ..
abandon, *v.* - [BV'TH] ⌢⸴ᘔ
able, *adj.* - [A·**JUSH**·L'] ,ᴐₜᘔᴐ⸴
abort, *v.* - [Ĕ·**BVO**·'SH] :⸝ᴐᵒ⸴ᘔ
about, *adv. & prep.* - [**N'**·LU] ⸝⸴ᴐₜ
above, *adv. & prep.* - [**U**·CH'] ₜᙠ⸴
abscess, *n.* - [YO·LA·**GĒ**·MA] ⸝ᴐᴐ⸴ᙠ:⸝.
accept, *v.* - [**SKTHO**·'RSH] ᙠᴐᴐᵒ⸴⸝
account, *n.* - [**BVĔ**·CHA] ⸝:ᙠ.
acid, *n.* - [**DVU**·TSA] ᘔₜᴐ.
across, *adv. & prep.* - [**U**·KTHĔ] ₜᴐᴐ:
act, *v.* - [(**H**)**RĔ**·OSH] ⸝:ᵒᴐ
action, *n.* - [(H)RĔ·**OSH**·A] ⸝:ᵒᴐ.
actual, *adj.* - [NOFV] ⸝ᵒ⸝
add, *v.* - [**O**·TATH] ᵒᴐᴔᘔ
adept, *n.* - [MO·**JABV**·THA] ⸝ᵒᴐ.⸝ᘔ.
adhere, *v.* - [(H)RĔTH] ⸝:ᘔ
adjust, *v.* - [**CHA**·W'SH] ᙠᴐᴔᴐ
adopt, *v.* - [(**H**)**RĒ**·LORSH] ⸝:ᴐᵒ⸝
adorn, *v.* - [TANTH] ᴐ⸝
advarsh'ha, *n.* - [A·DVAR·**SH'**·HA] ,ᘔₜᴐᴔ⸝.
adversary, *n.* - [**ZĒT**·HA] ᴐ:ᴔ⸝.
advertisement, *n.* - [**SPUL**·CHA] ᙠᴔₜᴔᙠ.
advise, *v.* - [**STĔ**·FVĔNTH] ᙠᴐ:⸝:⸝
aerie, *n.* - [KHĔ·(**H**)**R'**·LA] ᴔᴔ⸝:ᴐᴐᴐ.
after, *conj. & prep.* - [SHOPS] ᘔᵒ⸝
again, *adv.* - [Ĕ·BVĔ] .⸝:
against, *prep.* - [Ĕ·CH'T] :ᙠᴔᴐ
age, *v.* - [GLĔCH] ᴐᴐ:ᙠ
agent, *n.* - [BVRA·MO·**N'K**·HA] ⸝⸝.⸝ᵒ⸝⸴ᴐᴐ⸝.
agree, *v.* - [JA·**MO**·'NTH] ᴐ.⸝ᵒ⸝
aide, *n.* - [SHLOK·**LU**·THA] ᴔᴐᵒᴐᴐₜᘔ.
aim, *n.* - [CHA] ᙠ.
air, *n.* - [**AK**·THO] ,ᴐᴔᘔᵒ
alcohol, *n.* - [TSĔ·**JA**·NA] ᴐ:ᴐ.⸝.
alkali, *n.* - [AS·**WĔG**·TSA] ,ᙠᴐ:ᴐᴐᴐ.
all, *pro. & n.* - [**O**·MO] ᵒ⸝ᵒ

allow, *v.* - [**BVĚ**·DZANTH] ᵔ᛫ᵒᵔ᛭

almost, *adv.* - [**U**·SHAPS] ᵗᵔ᛫ᵔ

alphabet, *n.* - [JA·**YĚ**·LU] ᵒᵔ᛫ᵔᵗ

alter, *v.* - [Ě·LĚ·MĚSH] ᵗᵔᵔ᛫ᵔ

always, *adv.* - [**BVA**·FVOM] ᵔ᛫ᵔᵔ

ambassador, *n.* - [NAN·**S'**·TA] ᵔᵔᵔᵔ᛫

among, *prep.* - [**KTHĚ**·YĚT] ᵔᵔ᛫ᵔᵔᵔ

amount, *n.* - [**BVA**·TA] ᵔ᛫ᵔ

amplify, *v.* - [**MAR**·T'NTH] ᵔᵔᵔᵔ

amusement, *n.* - [(H)R'·**T'**·DZA] ᵔᵔᵔ᛫

analyze, *v.* - [JA·W'TH] ᵒᵔᵔᵔ

ancient, *adj.* - [A·**CHĚZ**·(H)RO] ᵗᵔ᛫ᵔᵔᵒ

and, *conj.* - [**O**·TA] ᵒᵔᵗ

anger, *n.* - [**DVĚTS**·(H)RA] ᵔ᛫ᵔᵔᵔ

anger, *v.* - [**DVĚ**·TSARSH] ᵔ᛫ᵔᵔᵔ

angle, *n.* - [W'·**SO**·TA] ᵔᵔᵔᵔᵗ

angrily, *adv.* - [A·**DVĚTS**·(H)ROTZL] ᵗᵔ᛫ᵔᵔᵔᵔ

angry, *adj.* - [A·**DVĚTS**·(H)RA] ᵗᵔ᛫ᵔᵔᵔ

angry, to become, *v.* - [**DVĚTS**·(H)RATH] ᵔ᛫ᵔᵔ᛫ᵔ

animal, *n.* - [**MO**·HA] ᵔᵒᵔᵗ

annual, *adj.* - [A·**LOTH**·GO] ᵔᵒᵔᵔᵒ

answer, *v.* - [**GLA**·ARSH] ᵔᵔ᛫᛫ᵔ

ant, *n.* - [**SĚ**·FVA] ᵔ᛫ᵔᵗ

anus, *n.* - [YĚCH·**LO**·SHA] ᵔ᛫ᵔᵒᵔᵗ

any, *adv., det. & pro.* - ['·LĚ] ᵔᵔ᛫

ape, *n.* - [MO·**S'**·**HO**·NA] ᵔᵒᵔᵔᵒᵔᵗ

apparatus, *n.* - [**SĚ**·YOT] ᵔ᛫ᵔᵒᵔ

appear, *v.* - [**WU**·YĚTH] ᵔᵔ᛫ᵔ

apple, *n.* - [TH'N·**G'**·UPS] ᵔᵔᵔᵔᵔᵔ

apprentice, *n.* - [DV'·**NĚ**·YA] ᵔᵔ᛫ᵔᵗ

approach, *v.* - [**USH**·LACH] ᵗᵔᵔ᛫ᵔ

approve, *v.* - [**KTHĚ**·**L'**·ZARNTH] ᵔᵔ᛫ᵔᵔᵔᵔᵔ

arch, *n.* - [**SĚK**·**YĚS**·TOT] ᵔ᛫ᵔᵔᵔ᛫ᵔᵔᵔ

archetype, *n.* - [**S'**·KTH'S·MO·**ON**·DĚ] ᵔᵔᵔᵔᵔᵒᵒᵔᵔ᛫᛫

argue, *v.* - [**SHOK**·MASH] ᵔᵒᵔᵔᵔᵔ

arid, *adj.* - [A·FVĚ·TSAR·**L'**·A] ᵔᵔ᛫ᵔᵒᵔᵔᵔ

arithmetic, *n.* - [BVAT·YĚ·**O**·SHA] ᵔ᛫ᵔᵔ᛫᛫ᵒᵔᵗ

arm, *n.* - [THOT] ᵔᵒᵔ

army, *n.* - [ZĚ·LOM] ᵔ᛫ᵔᵒᵔ

aroma, *n.* - [SKTHART] ᔇᒉ᠊ᔐ

arrival, *n.* - [JO·'·NA] ᔐᦓ᠊

arrive, *v.* - [JO·'NTH] ᔐᦓᦓ

art, *n.* - [O·**TH'**·OT] ᦓᕽᦓᒉ

artery, *n.* - [TSĔJ·Y'] ᒉᦂᔐᦓ'

artifact, *n.* - [**THA**·TA] ᕽᦓᕽ

artifactual, *adj.* - [THA·**T'**·TA] ᕽᦓᒉᒉᕽ

artificial, *adj.* - [THA·**T'**·TA] ᕽᦓᒉᒉᕽ

artist, *n.* - [O·TH'·U·THA] ᦓᕽᦓᕽ

as, *prep.* - [Ĕ·'] ᦓᕽ

ascend, *v.* - [KTHĔSH] ᒉᒉᦂᔐ

ask, *v.* - [JACH] ᔐᦓ

assembly, *n.* - [O·MO·MUTH·LO·A] ᦓᔐᦓᒉᦓᕽᦓᦓ

assistant, *n.* - [SHLOK·LU·THA] ᒉᦓᔐᒉᒉᦓᕽ

at, *prep.* - [O·'] ᦓᦓ

attack, *v.*- [SHA·**BVĔSH**] ᒉᦓᕽᒉᒉ

attempt, *v.* - [SHUNTH] ᒉᦓᦓ

attention, *n.* - [**WUR**·DĔ] ᔐᦓᦓᕽ

attraction, *n.* - [SHOCH·**L'**·DĔ] ᒉᦓᦓᒉᒉᦓᕽ

authority, *n.* - [JU·THA] ᔐᦓᕽ

automate, *v.* - [**SMO**·NUSH] ᔇᔐᦓᦓᒉ

automatic, *adj.* - [AS·**MON**·SHLU] ᔇᔐᦓᦓᒉᦓ

autonomous being, *n.* - [**DZA**·NA] ᔐᦓᦓ

autumn, *n.* - [**MWA**·FVĔ] ᔐᦓᦓᕽ

average, *adj.* - [AS·PO·**KTH'**·TA] ᔇᔐᦓᦓᒉᒉ

awake, *v.* - [Ē·KTHOCH] ᕽᔐᦓᔐ

aware, to be, *v.* - [**SHA**·BVOCH] ᒉᦓᔐᦓ

B

baby, *n.* - [GOT] ᔐᦓᒉ

back, *adj.* - [A·**GLA**·A] ᦓᔐᦓᕽ

back, *n.* - [**GLA**·A] ᔐᦓᕽ

bad, *adj.* - [A·**LĒSH**·L'] ᦓᦂᔐᒉ'

badness, *n.* - [**LĒSH**·NA] ᦓᦂᔐᦓ

bag, *n.* - [YO·**SHOK**] ᦓᦓᒉᔐᒉᒉ

bake, *v.* - [YADTH] ᦓᦓᕽ

baker, *n.* - [YAD·**THOT**] ᦓᦓᕽᦓᒉ

bakery, *n.* - [YAD·**THĔ**·THA] ᦓᦓᕽᦂᕽ

balance, *n.* - [**Z'T**·DĔ] ᔐᦓᒉᦂ

99

balance, *v.* - [**Z'**·T'RSH] ⟋⟋⟋⟋

ball, *n.* - [**O**·DVOM] ⟋⟋⟋

band (small group), *n.* - [O·**NO**·MA] ⟋⟋⟋.

band (decorative or mechanical), *n.* - [W'·STUL] ⟋⟋⟋⟋

banjo, *n.* - [DĚ·BV'D·HLU·'·SA] ⟋⟋⟋⟋⟋⟋.

bargain, *v.* - [**SHOK**·P'SH] ⟋⟋⟋⟋⟋

bark (bot.), *n.* - [WA·**'K**·GO] ⟋⟋⟋⟋⟋

base, *v.* - [HOGCH] ⟋⟋⟋⟋

basin, *n.* - [SHAK·**YĚ**·DZA] ⟋⟋⟋⟋.

basis, *n.* - [**HOG**·CHA] ⟋⟋⟋.

basket, *n.* - [**FVO**·YA] ⟋⟋.

bass guitar, *n.* - [GLA·LA·THOM·**TU**·LOK] ⟋⟋⟋⟋⟋⟋⟋⟋

bath, *n.* - [**TSO**·TSA·WA] ⟋⟋⟋.

bathe, *v.* - [**TSO**·TSAWSH] ⟋⟋⟋

bay, *n.* - [YO·TS'·**NA**·LO] ⟋⟋⟋⟋.

bayou, *n.* - [SOTS·**TOK**·CHO] ⟋⟋⟋⟋⟋⟋

be, *v.* - [NĚTH] ⟋

beam, *n.* - [ZA·**O**·THA] ⟋⟋⟋.

beam, *v.* - [**ZA**·OTH] ⟋⟋⟋

bear (zool.), *n.* - [MOS·**PĚ**·KTHA] ⟋⟋⟋⟋⟋.

bear, *v.* - [**BVO**·'SH] ⟋⟋⟋

beat, *v.* - [**MU**·THĒTH] ⟋⟋⟋

beautiful, *adj.* - [A·DZĚ·**W'**·KTH'] ⟋⟋⟋⟋

beautify, *v.* - [DĚ·**W'**·KTH'TH] ⟋⟋⟋⟋

beauty, *n.* - [**DĚ**·W'K] ⟋⟋⟋

because, *conj.* - [**NĚ**·BVO] ⟋⟋⟋

become, *v.* - [**PO**·ONTH] ⟋⟋⟋

bed, *n.* - [**HAT**·CHA] ⟋⟋⟋.

bee, *n.* - [SWĚ·**DZU**·THA] ⟋⟋⟋⟋.

beer, *n.* - [SPA·**PĚRM**·LOT] ⟋⟋⟋⟋⟋⟋

before, *conj./prep.* - [ĚPS] ⟋⟋

begin, *v.* - [**GA**·BVATH] ⟋⟋⟋

beginning, *n.* - [GA·**BVA**·THA] ⟋⟋⟋.

behavior, *n.* - [(H)RĚSH·**L'**·DĚ] ⟋⟋⟋⟋⟋

being, *n.* - [MO] ⟋

belief, *n.* - [BVOM] ⟋⟋⟋

believe, *v.* - [**BVOM**·TUTH] ⟋⟋⟋⟋

bell, *n.* - [**DVO**·KTHA] ⟋⟋⟋.

belly, *n.* - [YAM·**DZU**·SHA] ⟋⟋⟋⟋.

100

bend, *v.* - [POCH] ⌒₆⌒

berry, *n.* - [YA·AT] ⌒.. ⌒

beside; besides, *prep.* - [LO·'M] ⌒₆'⌒

between, *conj.* - [SPO·KTH'T] ⌒⌒₆∂∂.⌒

beverage, *n.* - [TSA·(H)RA] ∂.⌒.

beyond, *adv. & prep.* - [TH'·LOPS] ⌐,⌒₆⌒⌒

beyond, *n.* - [DZUTH·LOP·YA] ∂₊⌐⌒₆⌒⌒.

bicycle, *n.* - [BVA·SĔ·THOT] ⌒.⌒:⌐₆⌒

big, *adj.* - [SPĔK] ⌒⌒:.∂∂

Bigfoot, *n.* - [H'·YĔTH·T'] ⌒'⌒:.⌐⌒'

bird, *n.* - [KTHO·BVA] ∂∂₆⌒.

birth, *n.* - [TO·THA] ⌒₆⌐.

bit, *n.* - [N'PS] ⌒'⌒

bite, *v.* - [NASTH] ⌒.⌐⌐

bitter, *adj.* - [AS·WĒ·GA] .⌐∪:∂.

black, *adj.* - [A·ZĒN·LO·'] .∂:⌒∂₆'

black, *n.* - [ZĒN·LO] ∂:⌒∂₆

blade, *n.* - [NA·W'·THOT] ⌒.∪'⌐₆⌒

blanket, *v.* - [M'SH] ⌒'∂

blemish, *n.* - [ZĒTH·CHĚ] ∂:⌐⌒:.

blink, *n.* - [W'·WO·SHA] ∪'∂₆∂.

blink, *v.* - [W'·WOSH] ∪'∂₆∂

blood, *n.* - [TSĔJ] ∂:.∂

blow, *v.* - [KTHASH] ∂∂.∂

blue (color), *adj.* - [A·KTHABV·L'] .∂∂.⌒∂'

blue (color), *n.* - [KTHABV] ∂∂.⌒

blue-green (color), *adj.* - [A·KTHAT·W'] .∂∂.∪∪'

blue-green (color), *n.* - [KTHAT·W'] ∂∂.∪∪'

boast, *v.* - [DZA·(H)RONTH] ∂.⌒₆⌒

boat, *n.* - [YĔTS·DVOM] ⌒:.∂∂₆⌒

body, *n.* - [YA·MA] ⌒.⌒.

boil, *v.* - [TSĔ·(H)ROSH] ∂:.⌒₆∂

bond, *v.* - [BVONTH] ⌒₆⌒

bone, *n.* - [ZO·YOT] ∂₆⌒₆∪∪

bonobo, *n.* - [MO·S'·HO·DZA] ⌒₆⌐'⌒₆∂.

book, *n.* - [JA·ZOM] ∂.∂₆⌒

boot, *n.* - [THĔ·BVO·LA] ⌐:.⌒₆∪.

born (to be), *v.* - [TOTH] ⌒₆⌐

boss, *n.* - [KTH'·TH'N·GU·THA] ∂∂'⌐'⌒⌒⌐₊⌐.

bottle, *n.* - [(H)RU·**WO**·YA] ༄.

bottom, *adj.* - [A·**GLA**·LA] ༄.

bottom, *n.* - [**GLA**·LA] ༄.

bowl, *n.* - [**SHAK**·YO] ༄

box, *n.* - [**MU**·YA] ༄.

boy, *n.* - [TU·'·GA] ༄.

brag, *v.* - [SO·**KTHO**·LASH] ༄

braggart, *n.* - [SO·KTHO·**LU**·THA] ༄.

brain, *n.* - [Ê·**NO**·YAM] ༄.

brake, *v.* - [THÊSH] ༄

branch, *v.* - [**TO**·YOTH] ༄

brandy, *n.* - [SNORTS] ༄

brass (metal), *n.* - [H'Z·**GLA**·A] ༄..

bread, *n.* - [HATZL] ༄

break, *v.* - [**YO**·TÊTH] ༄

breath, *n.* - [O·**KTHO**·NA] ༄.

breathe, *v.* - [O·KTHONTH] ༄

breeze, *n.* - [P'K·HU·**(H)RÊN**·GA] ༄.

brick, *n.* - [H'·A] ༄.

bridge, *n.* - [**SA**·KTHO] ༄

bright, *adj.* - [A·**ZAM**·DZA] ༄.

brightness, *n.* - [ZAM·DĔ] ༄.

broadcast, *v.* - [**BVĔ**·WOTH] ༄

broken, *adj.* - [A·YO·**T'TH**·L'] ༄

bronze (metal), *n.* - [**HĔZ**·HOL] ༄

brother, *n.* - [HO·JU·'·GA] ༄.

brown, *n.* - [**TWĔZ**·LO] ༄

brush, *n.* - [JA·'·GĔM] ༄

bucket, *n.* - [**TSOL**·SHA] ༄.

build, *v.* - [**A**·ATH] ༄

building, *n.* - [THL'] ༄

bulb, *n.* - [**TA**·DVOM] ༄

burn, *v.* - [DV(H)RASH] ༄

burst, *v.* - [ZAMTH] ༄

business, *n.* - [(H)R'·**SĔ**·THA] ༄.

but, *conj.* - [Ê·TA] ༄.

butter, *n.* - [**MOL**·TSA] ༄.

butterfly, *n.* - [KO·FVA·ZU·L'·**MĔ**·THA] ༄.

button, *n.* - [**LASH**·TA] ༄.

by, *prep.* - [**LO·'**] ౨౬'

C

cake, *n.* - [SWĔTZL] ౨౨ᵢ౨౨

caldron, *n.* - [YA·**DVO**·MAZL] ౬ᵢ౨౬ᵢ౨

calendar, *n.* - [BVA·TA·CHA·**TAZL**] ౬ᵢౢ౬ᵢ౨౨

camera, *n.* - [BVĔZ·**SĔ**·YOT] ౬ᵢ౨౬ᵢ౬ᵒౢ౨

can, *aux. v.* - [JUSH] ౨ₜ౨

candle, *n.* - [ZA·**MOL**·TA] ౨ᵢ౬ᵒ౨౨ᵢ

cane (bot.), *n.* - [TSU·**U**·GA] ౨ₜₜ౬ᵢ

cannabis, *n.* - [GODZ] ౬ᵒ౨

canvas, *n.* - [**WO**·FVA] ౨ᵦ౬ᵢ

canyon, *n.* - [HYO·W'TH·**L'**·A] ౬౬ᵒ౨ᵢ౨౨ᵢ

capillary, *n.* - [TSĔJ·**Y'**·T'] ౨ᵢ౨౬ᵢ౨ᵨ

car, *n.* - [SH'·**SHOT**] ౨ᵢ౨ᵦ౨౨

card, *n.* - [BVO·'·GĔS] ౬ᵒ౨౨ᵢౢౢ

care, *v.* - [**SPADZ**·WOSH] ౨౬ᵢ౨౨ᵦ౨

cart, *n.* - [**SĔTH**·SHOT] ౨ᵢౢ౨ᵦ౨

carve, *v.* - [**YO**·W'TH] ౬ᵒ౨ᵢౢ

cat (domestic), *n.* - [GĔ·**MO**·HA] ౬ᵢౢ౬ᵒ౬ᵢ

cause, *v.* - [YĔTH] ౬ᵢౢౢ

cave, *n.* - [**HYO**·LO] ౬౬ᵒ౨ᵦ

cease, *v.* - [ĔNTH] ᵢ౬

cello, *n.* - [HĔ·**NA**·CHO] ౬ᵢ౬ᵢౢ౬ᵦ

center, *n.* - [**SMO**·NOT] ౨౬ᵒ౬ᵒ౨

ceramic, *n.* - [H'·**YA**·NA] ౬ᵢ౬ᵢ౬ᵢ

certain (specific unnamed), *adj.* - [A·**LĔ**·N'] ᵢ౨ᵢ౬'

certain (sure), *adj.* - [A·JAN·**JU**·(H)R'] ᵢ౨ᵢ౬౬ᵢ౬ᵒ౬'

cessation, *n.* - [**ĔN**·THA] ᵢ౬ౢ ᵢ

chain, *n.* - [HA·**GACH**·(H)RA] ౬ᵢ౬ᵢ౬ᵒ ᵢ

chalk, *n.* - [JA·YOZL] ౨ᵢ౬ᵦ౨

champion, *n.* - [NAN·FV'·**LU**·THA] ౬ᵢ౬౬ᵢ౨ₜ౬ᵢ

chance, *adj.* - [A·**WU**·SA] ᵢ౨ₜౢ ᵢ

chance, *n.* - [WUSK] ౨ₜౢ౨౨

chance, *v.* - [**WU**·S'RSH] ౨ₜౢ౨ᵦ

change, *n.* - [**PU**·NA] ౬ₜ౬ᵢ

change, *v.* - [PUNTH] ౬ₜ౬

charm, *n.* - [**TSOL**·PUT] ౨ᵦ౨౬ₜ౨

charming, *adj.* - [A·TSOL·**PUT**·L'] ᵢ౨ᵦ౨౬ₜ౨౨'

cheap, *adj.* - [A·**(H)RĒ**·BVU]

cheese, *n.* - [HA·**TSA**·(H)RA]

chemical, *n.* - [**WON**·YOT]

cherish, *v.* - [**TA**·(H)R'NTH]

chest (anat.), *n.* - [**KTHA**·THO]

chest (furn.), *n.* - [MU·YA·**TĚ**·DZA]

chicken, *n.* - [LA·**BVA**·TA]

chief, *adj.* - [A·**FV'CH**·DĚ]

child, *n.* - [**GO**·PO]

chimpanzee, *n.* - [MO·S'·**HOS**·PĚK]

chin, *n.* - [**SO**·YĚBV]

choose, *v.* - [FVĒTH]

church, *n.* - [**ĒR**·BVYĚTS]

circle, *n.* - [O·**YĚS**·TA]

citrus, *n.* - [**(H)R'N**·TSA]

city, *n.* - [M'TH·L'·MA·**TĚ**·DZA]

clan, *n.* - [HOG·MĚ·**CHOK**]

clarinet, *n.* - [LAR·HA·**BV(H)RAK**·N']

clean, *v.* - [PAWSH]

clear, *v.* - [**(H)RU**·WOSH]

clock, *n.* - [BVA·**FVU**·THA]

clone, *n.* - [SMO·O·**NO**·TA]

close, *v.* - [LASH]

cloth, *n.* - [MU·**GĚ**·SA]

clothe, *v.* - [MU·**GĚ**·FVUNTH]

clothing, *n.* - [MU·**GĚFV**·NOT]

cloud, *n.* - [**TS'N**·KTHA]

coal, *n.* - [**DVABV**·NA]

coal (min.), *n.* - [HA·**BVĒN**·LO]

coat, *n.* - [CHĚ·**TSU**·LA]

coffee, *n.* - [CHĒ·'·TSA]

cold, *adj.* - [A·**TSĒTH**·T']

collar, *n.* - [**TUGS**·TUL]

collective, *n.* - [DZU·**BVĚ**·CHA]

collectivize, *v.* - [**DZU**·BVĚCH]

college, *n.* - [J'T·**HA**·CHĚ]

color, *n.* - [ZUK]

color, *v.* - [**ZU**·KTHUTH]

comb, *n.* - [**N'**·YĚM]

come, *v.* - [BVĔSH] ᔇ.ᔈ

comfort, *v.* - [**DZABV**·KTHOCH] ᔈᔇᔇᔈ

committee, *n.* - [H'·**MU**·NOM] ᔇᔇᔇᔈᔇ

common, *adj.* - [ACH·**RO**·N'] ᔇᔈᔇᔇ'

companion, *n.* - [**MO**·DZA] ᔇᔈ

company, *n.* - [SHO·**KTHO**·LOM] ᔈᔇᔈᔇᔈᔇᔇ

comparison, *n.* - [Ĕ·'·WA] ᔈᔇ.

competition, *n.* - [TH'·LO·**FVA**·SHA] ᔈᔈᔇᔇ.ᔈ.

complete, *adj.* - [A·**DZUTH**·LO] .ᔈᔈᔈ

complete, *v.* - [DZUTH] ᔈᔈ

completion, *n.* - [DZU·**THA**·HA] ᔈᔈ.ᔇ.

complex, *adj.* - [A·**NĒDZ**·(H)RA] .ᔇ:ᔈᔇ.

complicate, *v.* - [ĒN·DZARSH] :ᔇᔈᔇ.

complication, *n.* - [ĒN·**DZA**·(H)RA] :ᔇᔈᔇ.

concept, *n.* - [CHO·**O**·THA] ᔈᔇᔈ.

condition, *n.* - [NA] ᔇ.

confabulation, *n.* - [KHON·FVA·**BVU**·UL] ᔈᔈᔇᔇᔇᔈᔇᔈᔇ

conform, *v.* - [JA·**MO**·'NTH] ᔈᔇᔇᔇ

connect, *v.* - [MUMTH] ᔇᔈᔈ

connection, *n.* - [**MUM**·THA] ᔇᔈᔈ.

conscious, *adj.* - [A·**SHABV**·CH'] .ᔈᔇᔈ'

consciousness, *n.* - [SHABV·**CH'**·DĔ] ᔈᔇᔈᔈ.

consensus, *n.* - [JA·MO·'·DĔ] ᔈᔇᔇᔈᔈ

consider, *v.* - [**SHA**·BVOCH] ᔈᔇᔇᔈ

constellation, *n.* - [KH'M·SKTHU·U·L'·**OS**·HA] ᔈᔈᔇᔈᔈᔈᔇᔈᔈᔈ.

contemplate, *v.* - [JU·WASH] ᔈᔈᔈ

content, *adj.* - [A·**MAN**·DĔ] .ᔇᔇᔈᔈ

contentment, *n.* - [**MAN**·DZA] ᔇᔇᔈ.

continue, *v.* - [LĒ·MOSH] ᔈ:ᔇᔈ

continuity, *n.* - [LĒ·**MOSH**·DĔ] ᔈ:ᔇᔈᔈᔈ

contract, *n.* - [**JAM**·NO] ᔈᔇᔇ

contract (legal), *v.* - [**JAM**·NORSH] ᔈᔇᔇᔈ

contracted, *adj.* - [A·JAM·**NO**·(H)R'] .ᔈᔇᔇᔈ'

control, *v.* - [TACH] ᔈᔈ

cook, *v.* - [HĔTH] ᔇ.ᔈ

copper (metal) *n.* - [HĔZ·**HA**·TA] ᔇ.ᔈᔇ.ᔈ.

copy, *v.* - [MO·**A**·MANTH] ᔈᔇ.ᔇᔇ

cord, *n.* - [SPO·**CHĔ**·DZ'K] ᔈᔇᔈ.ᔈᔈᔈ

core, *n.* - [**SMO**·NOT] ᔈᔈᔇᔇᔈ

cork, *n.* - [OK·**GA**·MA] ୶ஜఎ౨.ఇ.

correctly, *adv.* - [JO·**LĔ**·'] ఎఎ౨.౿'

cotton, *n.* - [**WOM**·GOZL] ౫౬ஜఞ౿౨

cough, *v.* - [KTHOMTH] ஜஜ౬ఇ

count, *v.* - [**BVA**·TACH] ౬.౿.ఇ

country, *n.* - [HĔ·**DZĔL**·SHA] ఇ.౿.ఎ.౨౨.

courage, *n.* - [**ZUCH**·DZA] ౿౼ఇఎ.

court, *n.* - [THO·**MOK**] ఇ౬ఞ౬ஜஜ

court, *v.* - [THO·**M'**·MĔSH] ఇ౬ఞ'ఇ.౨

cover, *v.* - [**WA**·SĔTH] ౫.ఇ.ఇ

covet, *v.* - [**NA**·N'CH] ఇ.ఞ'ఇ

cow, *n.* - [TĔ·**DZA**·LĔT] ఎ.౿.ఎ.ఞ .

crack, *v.* - [**ZĔ**·T'RSH] ౿౼౬ఞఎ

crave, *v.* - [**CH'**·TUTH] ఇ౼౼ఇ

create, *v.* - [DV'NTH] ౼ఞ

creation, *n.* - [**DV'N**·DĔ] ౼ఞఎ.

credit, *n.* - [S'·**PU**·(H)RA] ఇఞఞఎ.

credit, *v.* - [S'·**PURSH**] ఇఞఞఎ

creek, *n.* - [**SO**·TS'] ఇ౬ఎ౼

creep, *v.* - [H'SH] ఞఞ౨

crime, *n.* - [(H)RĔ·**LĔSH**·LA] ఇ.ఎ౼౿.

cross, *v.* - [**KTHĔ**·FVOSH] ஜ౼ఞ౬౨

crossing, *n.* - [KTHĔ·**FVO**·SHL'] ஜ౼ఞఞ౬౼౼

crow, *n.* - [MOS·MOK·**BVĔ**·CHA] ఞ౬౿౬ఞஜஜ౼ఇ.

cruel, *adj.* - [A·ZĔ·**THA**·DZ'] ౼ఇ౼ఎ'

cruelty, *n.* - [ZĔ·**THA**·DZA] ౿౼ఇ౼ఎ.

crush, *v.* - [L'·**A**·SHATH] ౼ఞఇఇ

cry, *v.* - [**LĔ**·ORSH] ౼౼ஜఞ

crystal, *n.* - [(H)RU·**W'**·A] ఇఞఎ.

crystalline, *adj.* - [A·(H)RU·**W'**·DĔ] ఇఞఎ౼ఎ.

cumulo-nimbus cloud, *n.* - [KHA·**L'N**·KHĔ·**N'**·DĔ] ஜఞ౼ఇ౼ஜஜ౼ఞ౼ఎ.

cup, *n.* - [**TSABV**·YA] ఞఇఞ.

cup, *v.* - [**TSA**·BV'SH] ఞఇఞ౼౨

current, *n.* - [TSOL·**TOS**] ఎ౬ఞఞ౬ఞఇ

curtain, *n.* - [LO·**SHO**·BVA] ఎ౬ఞ౬ఞ.

curve, *n.* - [**O**·YOT] ౬ఞ౬ఞ

cushion, *n.* - [LĔCH·**TSU**·(H)RA] ఎ౼ఇ౿ఞ౬.

cut, *v.* - [W'TH] ఎ౼ఇ

cymbal, *n.* - [(**H)RA**·ZAZL] ఇఎఎ

D

daily, *adj.* - [A·**TA**·ZA] ⌐⌐.

damage, *n.* - [**ZĒTH**·DĚ] ⌐⌐⌐.

damage, *v.* - [ZĒTH] ⌐⌐

dance, *n.* - [(H)**RO**·SA] ⌐⌐.

dance, *v.* - [(H)**RO**·S'TH] ⌐⌐⌐

dancer, *n.* - [(H)RO·**SOT**] ⌐⌐⌐⌐

danger, *n.* - [**LA**·TĚDZ] ⌐⌐⌐

darken, *v.* - [ZĒNTH] ⌐⌐

darkness, *n.* - [**ZĒN**·DĚ] ⌐⌐⌐.

dart, *v.* - [ZASH] ⌐⌐

daughter, *n.* - [GO·**PA**·GA] ⌐⌐⌐.

dawn, *n.* - [HĚ·**ZOT**] ⌐⌐⌐

day, *n.* - [TAZL] ⌐⌐

daybreak, *n.* - [TU·**Z'L**] ⌐⌐⌐

daydream, *v.* - [KWĚCH] ⌐⌐⌐

dead, *adj.* - [A·LĒ·**TO**·TH'] ⌐⌐⌐

dear, *adj.* - [A·YĚDZ] ⌐⌐

death, *n.* - [Ē·**TOTH**·NA] ⌐⌐⌐.

debt, *n.* - [DVOBV] ⌐⌐

decisive, *adj.* - [A·H'·**MU**·NA] ⌐⌐⌐.

decisive (to be), *v.* - [**H'**·MUNTH] ⌐⌐⌐

decisiveness, *n.* - [H'·**MU**·NA] ⌐⌐⌐.

decorate, *v.* - [**TĚ**·'NTH] ⌐⌐

deep, *adj.* - [AR·**SOBV**·CHĚ] ⌐⌐⌐.

defeat, *v.* - [SHA·**THĚSH**] ⌐⌐⌐

defecate, *v.* - [**YĚ**·T'CH] ⌐⌐

defend, *v.*- [TH'·**BVĚSH**] ⌐⌐⌐

deflect, *v.* - [**LĒ**·TH'SH] ⌐⌐⌐

degree, *n.* - [O·**YĚ**·BVOT] ⌐⌐⌐

delicate, *adj.* - [A·TH'·LĒ·**GO**·M'] ⌐⌐⌐

delight, *v.* - [(H)**RAN**·DHONTH] ⌐⌐⌐

dematerialize, *v.* - [Ē·**WA**·YĚNTH] ⌐⌐⌐

depend, *v.* - [BVOCH] ⌐⌐

dependent, *n.* - [HA·Z'·**BVU**·CHA] ⌐⌐⌐.

deposit, *v.* - [BV'TH] ⌐⌐

descend, *v.* - [HOSH] ⌐⌐

descent, *n.* - [**HO**·SHA] ⌐⌐.

design, *v.* - [**PA**·DV'NTH] ⌐.℥'⌐

desire, *v.* - [CH'CH] ⅊

destruction, *n.* - [OM·**ZĔ**·THA] ℴ⌐℥:ℨ.

detail, *n.* - [**FVĔ**·NA] ⌐∴⌐.

develop, *v.* - [N'·YĔTH] ⌐'⌐∴ℨ

development, *n.* - ['N·**YĔ**·THA] '⌐⌐∴ℨ.

diamond (mineral), *n.* - [(H)RU·**W'**·DZA] ℴ⌐ℯℴℴ.

die, *v.* - [**Ĕ**·TOTH] :℥℥ℨ

die (singular of "dice"), *n.* - [**WUS**·YOT] ℧⌐℥ℴℴℐ

differ, *v.* - [SHĔNSH] ℥∴⌐ℑ

different, *adj.* - [A·**SHĔ**·N'] .℥∴⌐'

differential, *n.* - [SHĔ·N'·**LOK**·DĔ] ℥∴⌐'ℐℴℴℴℴ∴

dig, *v.* - [PWĔTH] ⌐ℐ∴ℨ

digestion, *n.* - [YA·**MĔ**·THA] ⌐.⌐∴ℨ.

dim, *v.* - [**ZA**·ZĔNTH] ℥.℥:⌐

direction, *n.* - [**FVĔ**·SHA] ⌐:℥.

dirty, *adj.* - [**ĔPS**·W'] :⌐ℐ'

disappear, *v.* - [Ĕ·**WU**·YĔTH] :℧⌐∴ℨ

discovery, *n.* - [PĔ·**WĔ**·(H)RA] ⌐:ℐ∴ℴ.

discussion, *n.* - [LO·J'·**LĔ**·NA] ℐℴℴℐ:⌐.

disease, *n.* - [**GĔM**·BVA] ℥℥:⌐℥.

disguise, *v.* - [NĔWSH] ⌐∴ℐ

disgust, *v.* - [**SKTHAR**·TOTH] ℥℥℥.⌐℥℥℥ℨ

disperse, *v.* - [Ĕ·LO·**MO**·MUTH] :℥ℴℴℴℴℴ⌐ℨ

disrobe, *v.* - [**MU**·GĔRSH] ℴ⌐℥:ℴ

disrupt, *v.* - [TSA·SHA·**BV'**·DZANTH] ℴ.℥.ℴ'ℴ.⌐

disruption, *n.* - [TSA·SHA·BV'·**DZA**·NA] ℴ.℥.ℴ'ℴ.⌐.

distance, *n.* - [HĔ·**DZ'**·TOM] ⌐∴ℴℐℴℴ

distribute, *v.* - [BVATH] ℥.ℨ

ditch, *n.* - [**YO**·'ST] ⌐ℴ'℥ℐ

divide, *v.* - [**THĔ**·NOTH] ℨ:⌐ℴℨ

divinity, *n.* - [BVOLM] ℥ℴℐℴ

division, *n.* - [**THĔN**·THOK] ℨ:⌐ℨℴℴ

do, *v.* - [(H)RĔSH] ℴ∴ℴ

dog, *n.* - [**LA**·MUDZ] ℐ.℥ℴℴ

dolphin, *n.* - [TS'·**HOS**·MA] ℴ'℥ℴ℥℥.

door, *n.* - [**HOG**·YO] ℥ℴℴℴ℥ℴ

doubt, *v.* - [**GĔ**·MURSH] ℥:⌐ℴℴ

down, *adj., adv. & prep.* - [SOBV] ℥ℴℴ

108

doze, *v.* - [ĔK·NOTCH]

dozing, *adj.* - [A·LĔK·NOT·**CHL'**·A]

dragon, *n.* - [**DV'N**·THA]

drain, *v.* - [**SO**·TSASH]

draw, *v.* - [**DZA**·YĔTH]

drawer, *n.* - [MU·**YAK**·LA]

dream, *n.* - [WO·**TUK**]

dream, *v.* - [WOTCH]

dress (garment), *n.* - [**SHAL**·KTHA]

drink, *v.* - [TSARSH]

drive, *v.* - [**THĔ**·SOTH]

drone (sound), *n.* - [SOK·(H)RO·**BVĔR**·TĔ]

drop (fluid), *n.* - [YU]

drum, *v.* - [THUMTH]

drunk, *adj.* - [ĔR·MOL]

dry, *adj.* - [A·FVĔTS]

duration, *n.* - [LĔDZ]

dusk, *n.* - [**TAZ**·LĔT]

dust, *n.* - [HĔM]

Dvarsh, dvarsh, *n.* - [DVARSH]

E

each, *adv., det. & pro.* - [FVAMT]

eager, *adj.* - [A·**DVĔBV**·CHĔ]

eagle, *n.* - [KHĔN·**YO**·NA]

ear, *n.* - [OK]

early, *adj.* - [A·**BVĔ**·P']

early, *adv.* - [BVĔPS]

earn, *v.* - [**(H)RA**·SĔTH]

earning, *n.* - [**(H)R'**·SA]

earth, *n.* - [HABV]

east, *n.* - [ZOM]

eat, *v.* - [**HA**·ZURSH]

ecstasy, *n.* - [THRDZ]

edge, *n.* - [TS(H)R'ST]

education, *n.* - [**J'T**·(H)RA]

effect, *n.* - [BVĔ·**SHO**·A]

effect pedal, *n.* - [M'K·(H)RĔ·'·DĔ]

egg, *n.* - [TUZL]

109

eight, *numb.* - [FVO] ～o

eighteen, *numb.* - [**FVO**·TU] ～o√ŧ

elapse, *v.* - [LOTH] ノ₆ξ

elastic, *adj.* - [A·TH'·**LOSH**·L'] ͺξ͵ノ₆ϣ͵

elbow, *n.* - [THO·**TOT**] ξ₆ノ₆ノノ

electricity, *n.* - [**TSUZ**·NA] Ϡͺϣ～.

eleven, *numb.* - [**MO**·TU] ～o√ŧ

embellish, *v.* - [**SOK**·LASH] ξ₆ϣϣͺϥ

ember, *n.* - [**DVABV**·NA] ϥͺϭ～.

embrace, *n.* - [**BVĚ**·TA] ϭ

embrace, *v.* - [**BVĚ**·TARSH] ϭͺͺ√₆

embroider, *v.* - [Ě·(H)R'N·**SĚ**·BVĚRSH] ͺ₆͵√ξͺϭͺϭͺ₆

embryo, *n.* - [ZABV] ϣͺϭ

eminence, *n.* - [**MO**·FV'] ～₆√͵

empathy, *n.* - [JĚ·NĚ·**BVĚ**·BVA] Ϡͺͺ√ͺϭͺϭͺ.

emptiness, *n.* - [**SHA**·KTHĚFV] ϥͺϣϣͺͺ～

encircle, *v.* - [O·**YĚS**·TATH] ₆ͺͺξͺξξ

enclose, *v.* - [O·**YĚS**·TANTH] ₆ͺͺξͺ√～

encounter, *v.* - [**O**·MOTH] ₆～₆ξ

end, *n.* - [**DZU**·THA] Ϡŧξ.

end, *v.* - [DZUTH] Ϡŧξ

energetic, *adj.* - [A·**HĚTS**·DĚ] ～ͺͺϣϣͺͺ

energize, *v.* - [**HĚ**·TSUNTH] ～ͺͺϠŧ～

energy, *n.* - [**HĚTS**·NA] ～ͺͺϠ～.

enforce, *v.* - [**SMA**·ĚTH] ξ～ͺͺξ

engine, *n.* - [SU·**THĚTS**·DVA] ξŧξͺͺϣϣ.

enjoy, *v.* - [**DZU**·TUTH] Ϡŧ√ξ

enough, *adj., adv. & pro.* - [MUCH·L'·O] Ϡŧξͺ√ͺ₆

enter, *v.* - [**Y'**·S'SH] ～͵ξͺϥ

entire, *adj.* - [A·DZU·**THOT**] ͺϠŧξ₆ͿͿ

entirety, *n.* - [**DZU**·THOT] Ϡŧξ₆Ϳ

entity, *n.* - [**NAN**·THA] ～ͺ～ξ.

entrance, *n.* - [**Y'**·**S'**·SHA] ～͵ξͺϥ.

envision, *v.* - [MOWSH] ～₆ϣ

equal, *v.* - [**M'**·HANTH] ϣ͵ϭͺ～

erase, *v.* - [Ě·**DZA**·YĚTH] ͺϠͺ～ͺξ

err, *v.* - [**SPO**·YUCH] ξ～₆√ͺϥ

error, *n.* - [SPO·**YU**·CHA] ξ～₆√ͺϥ.

essay, *n.* - [JĚTH·**LO**·TA] ϠͺͺξͿ₆√.

eternal, *adj.* - [A·LÊ·**DZUTH**·PA] ౿⌂⌂₃౿.

eternity, *n.* - [LÊ·**DZUTH**·PA] ౿⌂⌂₃౿.

even, *adv.* - [**Z'**·T'] ⌂⌂

event, *n.* - [**NA**·WA] ౿⌂.

ever, *adv.* - [**UBV**·MĚ] ⌂౿⌂.

every, *det.* - [**B**VAMT] ౿⌂⌂

everybody, *pro.* - [O·**MO**·FVĒ] ౿౿౿:

everyone, *pro.* - [O·**MO**·FVĒ] ౿౿౿:

evil, *adj.* - [A·GÊ·**THO**·KTHA] ⌂౿:₃౿⌂.

evil, *n.* - [GÊ·**THOK**] ⌂:₃౿⌂⌂⌂

evolution, *n.* - [**SON**·DĚ] ₃౿⌂⌂.

evolve, *v.* - [SONTH] ₃౿౿

example, *n.* - [NA·**W'**·MA] ౿⌂⌂.

exchange, *v.* - [**SHO**·KTHOSH] ⌂౿⌂⌂౿⌂

excrement, *n.* - [**YĚCH**·LA] ౿⌂⌂⌂.

exemplar, *n.* - [MA·'K·LAM·BV(H)RO·**SOT**] ౿⌂⌂⌂౿౿౿౿₃⌂⌂⌂

exist, *v.* - [NANTH] ౿.౿₃

existence, *n.* - [**NAN**·DĚ] ౿౿⌂.

expansion, *n.* - [TU·THA·**TĚ**·DĚ] ⌂₃⌂⌂.

expect, *v.* - [**WU**·Y'CH] ⌂౿⌂₃

experience, *v.* - [(**H)RU**·ONTH] ౿౿౿

experiment, *n.* - [CH'·**SĚ**·THA] ౿⌂₃.

experiment, *v.* - [**CH'**·SĚTH] ౿⌂⌂₃

expert, *n.* - [YU·**TĚ**·DĚ] ౿⌂⌂.

exploration, *n.* - [SAN·**TA**·NA] ₃౿⌂౿.

explore, *v.* - [**SAN**·TANTH] ₃౿⌂౿

extend, *v.* - [**LÊ**·DZUTH] ⌂⌂⌂₃

eye, *n.* - [**WO**·SHA] ⌂౿⌂.

eyesore, *n.* - [WÊK·(**H)RÊ**·NA] ⌂⌂⌂:౿.

F

fabric, *n.* - [FVO·'**SH**·A] ౿౿⌂.

face, *n.* - [YĚZL] ౿⌂⌂

fact, *n.* - [**WA**·NUK] ⌂౿⌂⌂

fail, *v.* - [LÊTH] ⌂:₃

fall (season), *n.* - [**MWA**·FVĚ] ⌂⌂⌂.

fall, *n.* - [**YU**·SHA] ౿⌂.

fall, *v.* - [YUSH] ౿⌂

falling, *adj.* - [A·YUSH·**L'**·A] ౿⌂⌂.

false, *adj.* - [Ē·JA·NO] ᪐
falsely, *adv.* - [Ē·JA·NĚ·']
family, *n.* - [HOS·MO·LOM]
far, *adj.* - [APS·Y']
far, *adv.* - [PA·Y']
farm, *n.* - [CHU·THAT]
fart, *v.* - [SO·LASH]
farther, *adj.* - [A·DZUTH·LOP·Y']
fashion, *v.* - [Y'·BVATH]
fat, *adj.* - [A·THOM·TUL]
fat (tissue), *n.* - [NA·MOL·TA]
father, *n.* - [TH'N·GU·'·GA]
fear, *v.* - [LAT·ZUCH]
feather, *n.* - [OTH·YAK]
feces, *n.* - [YĚCH·LA]
feeble, *adj.* - [A·TĒTS·L']
feed, *v.* - [HA·ZĒTH]
feel, *v.* - [JA·ZUCH]
feline, *adj.* - [A·GĒ·MO·T'·HA]
feline, *n.* - [GĒ·MOT]
female, *adj.* - [AG]
female, *n.* - [A·GA]
fertile, *adj.* - [A·TU·THAM·DZ']
fetus, *n.* - [ZABV]
few, *adj. & pro.* - [Ē·MO·MU·MU]
fiber, *n.* - [GĚS]
fickle, *adj.* - [Ē·LĒ·TU]
fickle (to be), *v.* - [Ē·LĒ·TUNTH]
fiction, *n.* - [BVĚCH·DĚ·NA]
field, *n.* - [HA·ZU·CHA]
fifteen, *numb.* - [DZA·TU]
fight, *v.* - [(H)RĒTCH]
find, *v.* - [JA·Z'TH]
finger, *n.* - [FVA·PUT]
finish, *v.* - [DZUTH]
fire, *n.* - [DV'N]
fire (as ceramics), *v.* - [YADTH]
first, *numb.* - [Ě·'·MO]
fish, *n.* - [NA·TSA]

fish, *v.* - [**NA**·TSACH] ⌐.⌐.⌐

five, *numb.* - [**DZA**·A] ⌐.

fixed, *adj.* - [A·LĔ·**HAN**·L'] .⌐.⌐.⌐.

flag, *n.* - [KTHASH·**T'**·SHA] ⌐.⌐.⌐.

flame, *n.* - [DV'·**W'**·GA] ⌐.⌐.⌐.

flat, *adj.* - [**A**·HOG] .⌐.⌐

flesh, *n.* - [**YAM**·DĔ] ⌐.⌐.⌐.

flicker, *v.* - [WA·**TH'**·MĔNTH] ⌐.⌐.⌐.⌐

flight, *n.* - [**KTHOSH**·NO] ⌐.⌐.⌐

flock, *n.* - [**KTHO**·BVOM] ⌐.⌐.⌐

flood, *n.* - [**TSO**·TSA] ⌐.⌐.

floor, *n.* - [**SOBV**·GA] ⌐.⌐.⌐.

flow, *n.* - [**TSON**·DĔ] ⌐.⌐.⌐.

flow, *v.* - [TSONTH] ⌐.⌐

flower, *n.* - [DZĔ·**W'**·GA] ⌐.⌐.⌐.

fluid, *adj.* - [A·**TSOL**·T'] .⌐.⌐.⌐

fluid, *n.* - [**TSOL**·TA] ⌐.⌐.

flush, *v.* - [HĔZ·**LO**·TUTH] ⌐.⌐.⌐.⌐

flute, *n.* - [PLU·**WĔL**·(H)RA] ⌐.⌐.⌐.

flutter, *v.* - [ZU·**L'**·MĔTH] ⌐.⌐.⌐.⌐

fly, *n.* - [**KTHO**·FVA] ⌐.⌐.

fly, *v.* - [**KTHO**·SHOSH] ⌐.⌐.⌐

fold, *v.* - [PĔSH] ⌐.⌐

foliage, *n.* - [**THA**·KTHO·MA] ⌐.⌐.⌐.

follow, *v.* - [SOSH] ⌐.⌐

folly, *n.* - [(H)RA·**BVO**·CHA] ⌐.⌐.⌐.

food, *n.* - [HAZL] ⌐.⌐

foolish, *adj.* - [AR·**BVO**·CHA] .⌐.⌐.⌐.

foolish (to be), *v.* - [**(H)RA**·BVOCH] ⌐.⌐.⌐

fool, *n.* - [(H)RA·BVO·**CHOT**] ⌐.⌐.⌐.⌐

foot, *n.* - [**FVA**·LOPS] ⌐.⌐.⌐

footing, *n.* - [HO·**GACH**·MA] ⌐.⌐.⌐.

for, *prep.* - [CH'] ⌐.

force, *v.* - [**U**·THANTH] .⌐.⌐

forest, *n.* - [**GA**·GOPS] ⌐.⌐.⌐

forever, *adv.* - [**BVA**·FVOM] ⌐.⌐.⌐

forge, *n.* - [Y'·**BVOT**] ⌐.⌐.⌐

forge, *v.* - [Y'·**BVATH**] ⌐.⌐.⌐

forget, *v.* - [Ĕ·**SHLO**·KTH'SH] .⌐.⌐.⌐.⌐

forgive, *v.* - [BVĚTH] ᠊᠊᠊

fork, *n.* - [**HAZ**·YA] ᠊᠊᠊

form, *v.* - [YONTH] ᠊᠊᠊

forward, *adj.* - [A·**LU**·Z'G] ᠊᠊᠊

forward, *adv.* - [U·**Z'G**·LA] ᠊᠊᠊

foul, *v.* - [**LO**·'TH] ᠊᠊᠊

found, *v.* - [**HO**·GACH] ᠊᠊᠊

foundation, *n.* - [HO·**GACH**·MA] ᠊᠊᠊

four, *numb.* - [CHO] ᠊᠊᠊

fourteen, *numb.* - [**CHO**·TU] ᠊᠊᠊

fourth, *n.* - [CHO·**W'**·THA] ᠊᠊᠊

fowl, *n.* - [BVA·**TAT**] ᠊᠊᠊

fox, *n.* - [GĚ·**LA**·MUDZ] ᠊᠊᠊

frail, *adj.* - [Ě·GOM] ᠊᠊᠊

frame, *n.* - [O·YĚS·**TA**·NA] ᠊᠊᠊

free, *adj.* - [A·**DZA**·N'] ᠊᠊᠊

free (to fr...), *v.* - [DZANTH] ᠊᠊᠊

free (to be fr...) , *v.* - [DZAN·**BVĚT**·ATH] ᠊᠊᠊

freedom, *n.* - [**DZA**·NADZ] ᠊᠊᠊

freely, *adv.* - [A·**DZA**·NOTZL] ᠊᠊᠊

freeze, *v.* - [TSĚTH] ᠊᠊᠊

frequent, *adj.* - [**ACH**·R'] ᠊᠊᠊

fresh, *adj.* - [**A**·TUZL] ᠊᠊᠊

freshen, *v.* - [**TU**·Z'TH] ᠊᠊᠊

freshing, *adj.* - [A·TU·**Z'TH**·L'] ᠊᠊᠊

friend, *n.* - [**HU**·THA] ᠊᠊᠊

from, *prep.* - [O·A] ᠊᠊᠊

front, *adj.* - [A·**Z'G**·LA] ᠊᠊᠊

front, *n.* - [Z'G·**LA**·A] ᠊᠊᠊

fruit, *n.* - [YUPS] ᠊᠊᠊

fuck, *v.* - [DZ'TH] ᠊᠊᠊

fuel, *n.* - [**HA**·ZĚM] ᠊᠊᠊

full, *adj.* - [**AM**·DZ'] ᠊᠊᠊

future, *n.* - [PUT] ᠊᠊᠊

G

galaxy, *n.* - [HĚ·Z'·**MOT**] ᠊᠊᠊

game (recreation), *n.* - [(H)RO·S'N·**YO**·LA] ᠊᠊᠊

garden, *n.* - [JA·**GU**·UM] ᠊᠊᠊

garment, *n.* - [FVO·'·**SHU**·LA] ꞁ

gas, *n.* - [**KTHO**·NA]

gate, *n.* - [Y'·S'·**SH'**·HA]

gather, *v.* - [O·**MO**·MUTH]

gathering, *n.* - [O·**MO**·MUTH·**LO**·A]

gear down, *v.* - [**P'**·BVĔCH]

gel, *n.* - [**TSU**·KTHA]

gem, *n.* - [**ZO**·BVA]

general, *adj.* - [AS·POT·**WA**·NA]

generate, *v.* - [TOM·DĔ·'·**BV'**·DZUNTH]

generosity, *n.* - [BVATH·**L'**·DĔ]

generous, *adj.* - [A·BVATH·**L'**·A]

genitalia, *n.* - [Y'·**BVU**·FVA]

gentleness, *n.* - [**YĔTH**·DZA]

get, *v.* - [**BVA**·ATH]

gibbon, *n.* - [MOS·**MĔ**·CHA]

gift, *n.* - [**DZA**·MO]

gild, *v.* - [**HĔ**·ZĔTH]

gin, *n.* - [SKTHA·**(H)RĔTS**·NA]

girl, *n.* - [**TA**·GA]

gist, *n.* - [DĔ·'·LĔ]

give, *v.* - [**BVĔT**·ATH]

glade, *n.* - [TAL·**TA**·GOPS]

glass, *n.* - [(H)RU·**WOK**]

glide, *n.* - [BV'·**ĔS**·KHA]

glide, *v.* - [BV'·**ĔS**·KHASH]

glisten, *v.* - [W'·**WO**·ZĔTH]

glitter, *v.* - [W'·**WO**·ZĔTH]

glove, *n.* - [FVA·**O**·LA]

glow *n.* - [ZA·**AN**·DĔ]

glow *v.* - [**ZA**·ANTH]

go, *v.* - [SHOSH]

goal, *n.* - [CHA]

goat, *n.* - [**SPAK**·LĔT]

god, *n.* - [BVOL·MU·'·**GA**]

godchild, *n.* - [BVRM]

goddess, *n.* - [BVOL·**MA**·GA]

gold (metal), *n.* - [**HĔZ**·NA]

good, *adj.* - [Y'ZL]

gorilla, *n.* - [HOM·SMA·**TĚ**·DZA] ⌒⌒⌒⌒. .⌒.

govern, *v.* - [**GĚ**·G'TH] ⌒.⌒⌒

grain, *n.* - [SPAPS] ⌒⌒

grass, n. - [**GA**·BV'ST] ⌒⌒⌒

gray, *adj.* - [**A**·HAG] .⌒⌒

gray, *n.* - [HAG] ⌒⌒

great, *adj.* - [**A**·TĚDZ] .⌒⌒

greater, *adj.* - [A·**TĚDZ**·CHĚ] .⌒⌒.

green, *adj.* - [A·**TO**·W'] .⌒⌒

green, *n.* - [**TO**·W'] ⌒⌒

grip, *v.* - [**FVAP**·BVOCH] ⌒⌒⌒⌒

group, *n.* - [LOM] ⌒⌒

grove, *n.* - [GAK·**MO**·'] ⌒.⌒⌒

grow, *v.* - [TUTH] ⌒⌒

growth (grown thing), *n.* - [**TU**·THOT] ⌒⌒⌒

guard, *n.* - [SHU·**BVĚ**·CHA] ⌒⌒⌒.

guard, *v.* - [**SHU**·BVĚCH] ⌒⌒⌒

guardian, *n.* - [SHU·BVĚ·**CHOT**] ⌒⌒⌒⌒

guess, *v.* - [CHANTH] ⌒⌒

guide, *v.* - [**TH'N**·GOTH] ⌒⌒⌒⌒

guild, *n.* - [**SĚTH**·LOM] ⌒⌒⌒

guitar, *n.* - [MAR·KLU·'·**SA**] ⌒⌒⌒⌒.

gull, *n.* - [TS'·HA·**T'K**·BVA] ⌒⌒.⌒⌒.

H

Habdvarsha, *n.* - [HAB·**DVAR**·SHA] ⌒⌒⌒⌒.

hair (collective), *n.* - [GĚ·JĚM] ⌒.⌒⌒

hair (individual), *n.* - [GĚ·JĚS] ⌒.⌒⌒

hallucinate, *v.* - [**FVA**·WOSH] ⌒⌒⌒

half, *n.* - [BVA·**W'**·THA] ⌒.⌒⌒.

hammer, *n.* - [THA·**YOT**] ⌒⌒⌒

hammer, *v.* - [**THA**·YOTH] ⌒⌒⌒

hand, *n.* - [FVAPS] ⌒⌒

hang, *v.* - [**SHO**·BVUCH] ⌒⌒⌒

hanging, *adj.* - [A·SHO·**BVA**·TA] .⌒⌒.⌒

happen, *v.* - [NAWSH] ⌒⌒

happiness, *n.* - [HO·**DZUK**] ⌒⌒⌒⌒

harbor, *n.* - [HA·**BV'TS**·NA] ⌒⌒⌒.

hard, *adj.* - [**LO**·BV'] ⌒⌒

116

harm, *v.* - [ZÊTH] ⠗⠺⠒⠃

harmony, *n.* - [SOK·**HU**·THAM] ⠎⠕⠍⠗⠼⠃⠁⠎

harp, *n.* - [DHON·LU·**U**·ZA] ⠚⠎⠕⠗⠝⠚⠞⠗⠗⠺⠄

harvest, *n.* - [OM·**WATH**·A] ⠕⠎⠣⠃⠄

harvest, *v.* - [**OM**·WATH] ⠕⠎⠣⠃

haste, *n.* - [TĔ·**OK**·SHA] ⠚⠒⠕⠍⠍⠟⠄

hat, *n.* - [**BVAG**·JĔK] ⠎⠄⠗⠍⠒⠍⠝⠗

hate, *v.* - [**LU**·DVÊRSH] ⠚⠞⠵⠒⠎

have, own, *v.* - [(H)RASH] ⠎

have/has, *aux. v.* - [APCH] ⠄⠗⠗

had - [**APCH**·LO] ⠄⠗⠗⠍⠲

having - [**APCH**·L'] ⠄⠗⠗⠵⠂

will have - [**APCH**·P'] ⠄⠗⠗⠎⠂

he, *pro.* - [MO] ⠗

head, *n.* - [GĔJ] ⠗⠲⠕

heal, *v.* - [SPATH] ⠎⠗⠄⠃

health, *n.* - [**SPATH**· DĔ] ⠎⠗⠄⠃⠕⠒

hear, *v.* - [SKTHURSH] ⠎⠗⠗⠞⠒⠎

heart, *n.* - [SHABV] ⠗⠄⠎

heat, *n.* - [YĔ·**DVOTH**·DĔ] ⠗⠒⠲⠒⠃⠒

heat, *v.* - [**YĔ**·DVOTH] ⠗⠒⠲⠒⠃

heavy, *adj.* - [**SPĔK**·TA] ⠎⠗⠒⠲⠗⠃⠄

hello, *exclam.* - [Y'Z·NA·**NĔTH**·NOFV] ⠗⠂⠣⠗⠄⠒⠎⠗⠎

help, *v.* - [(H)RO·'SH] ⠗⠕⠂⠗

hemorrhoid, *n.* - [DHUG·LĔ·NĔ·TA] ⠚⠗⠞⠗⠃⠒⠲⠒⠗⠗⠂⠄

hemp, *n.* - [GODZ] ⠗⠲⠕

herb, *n.* - [GOS·KTHA·(**H)ROK**] ⠗⠲⠒⠎⠃⠗⠄⠗⠲⠃⠃

herd, *n.* - [**TĔ**·LOM] ⠚⠒⠲⠲⠗

here, *adv.* - [HAFV] ⠗⠒⠝

hero *n.* - [Ĕ·'·MÊ] ⠒⠗⠂⠗⠒

hers, *adj. & pro.* - [**MĔ**·Ê] ⠗⠄⠄

hidden, *adj.* - [A·**NĔ**·W'] ⠂⠗⠒⠣⠂

hide, *v.* - [NÊWSH] ⠗⠒⠣

high, *adj.* - [**AR**·SĔK] ⠄⠗⠎⠄⠃

hill, *n.* - [CHĔG] ⠎⠒⠗⠺

hip, *n.* - [BVĔ·**TA**·AT] ⠗⠄⠞⠲⠞

his, *adj. & pro.* - [**MĔ**·Ê] ⠗⠄⠄

history, *n.* - [SHLO·**CHA**·TA] ⠲⠲⠲⠎⠗⠄

hit, *v.* - [**THU**·ZÊTH] ⠃⠞⠗⠒⠃

hobbit, *n.* - [SOK·**LU**·THA] ᗐₒᨆᨆ↑Ȝ.

hold, *v.* - [**(H)RĔ**·BVOSH] ᗐ∴ᨂₒᑫ

hole, *n.* - [**YO**·LO] ᔂₒᕽₒ

hollow, *adj.* - [A·**SHAK**·Y'] ᛫ᛂᨆᕽ'

hollow, *n.* - [SHA·**KTHĔ**·YA] ᛂᨆᛡᔂ.

home, *n.* - [HABV] ᔂ

honey, *n.* - [SWĔ·**DZA**·TSA] Ȝᨂᛙᛂᛂ.

hook, *v.* - [**HAG**·HONTH] ᗐᛙᔂ

hope, *n.* - [WA·A·**CHUK**] ᔌ᛫᛫ᛣᨆᨆ

hope, *v.* - [**WA**·ACH] ᔌ᛫ᛣ

horn, *n.* - [GĔ·TA] ᨆᛂᛂ.

horse, n. - [**SHO**·MOT] ᛣₒᛙᔌ

hospital, *n.* - [(H)RĔ·OS·**PĔ**·THA] ᗐᛂₒȜᛙ᛫᛫Ȝ.

hot, *adj.* - [HĔTS] ᗐᛂᛂᛡ

house, *n.* - [**HAB**·YĔTS] ᗐᛙ

house, *v.* - [HAB·YĔ·**BVĔT**·ATH] ᗐᛙᨂȜ

household, *n.* - [JAM·NO·**(H)RO**·TA] ᔌ᛫ᛙᗐₒᗐₒᛙ.

how, *adv.* - [SHĔTS] ᛂ᛫ᛡ

howl, *v.* - ['**Z**·LORSH] ᛬ᨆᕽᗐ

hug, *n.* - [**BVĔ**·TA] ᗐ

hug, *v.* - [**BVĔ**·TARSH] ᗐ᛫ᛢᗐ

human, *n.* - [HO·O·**MAN**·THA] ᗐₒₒᗐ᛫ᨆȜ.

humid, *adj.* - [A·**TSO**·OL] ᛫ᛢₒₒᔌ

humidity, *n.* - [**TSO**·OL] ᛢₒₒᔌ

humor, *n.* - [DZO·**ZAR**·NA] ᔌₒᛙᛂᗐ.

hundred, *numb.* - [TSA·**TSA**·TU] ᛂᛂᛂᛡ

hunger, *n.* - [TU·**NOCH**·NA] ᛡᗐₒᗐᛂ.

hunger, *v.* - [TUNCH] ᛡᗐᛣ

hurl, *v.* - [**CHA**·HOCH] ᛣᗐₒᛣ

hurry, *n.* - [TĔ·**OK**·SHA] ᛂ᛫ₒᨆᨆ᛫.

hurry, *v.* - [**TĔ**·OKSH] ᛂ᛫ₒᨆᨆᑫ

hurt, *v.* - [ZĔTH] ᔌᛂȜ

hypnarch, *n.* - [WOT·CHU·THA·**NOT**·CHA] ᔌₒᛡᛢȜ.ᗐₒᛡᛂ.

hypothesis, *n.* - [**GĔR**·SYOT] ᛡ᛫ₒᛣᗐₒᔌ

hypothesize, *v.* - [**GĔR**·SYOSH] ᛡ᛫ₒᛣᗐₒᑫ

I

I, *pro.* - [**MO**·FVĒ] ᛂᗐ

ice, *n.* - [TSĒT] ᔌ᛫ᔌ

118

ice, *v.* - [**TSĒ**·T'TH] ⟋⟍⟍

idea, *n.* - [S'·**GĔ**·JA] ⟋⟍⟍

ideal, *adj.* - [A·**S'**·KTH'] ⟋⟍

ideal, *n.* - [**S'**·KTH'] ⟋⟍

identity, *n.* - [**SMO**·OT] ⟋⟍

idiom, *n.* - [O·JA·**LĒ**·NO] ⟋⟍

idle, *adj.* - [A·**SHĒN**·DĔ] ⟋⟍

idle, *v.* - [SHĒNTH] ⟋⟍

idleness, *n.* - [**SHĒN**·DĔ] ⟋⟍

if, *conj.* - [**NU**·P'] ⟍⟍

ignite, *v.* - [DVATH] ⟍⟍

ignore, *v.* - [Ē·**LO**·WASH] ⟍⟍

ill, *adj.* - [A·**LĒS**·**PA**·TH'] ⟍⟍

image, *n.* - [WON·**THO**·TA] ⟍⟍

imaginary, *adj.* - [A·THU·WO·**N'**·HA] ⟍⟍

imagine, *v.* - [**THU**·WONTH] ⟍⟍

imp, *n.* - [NĔ·**SPAK**·ZA] ⟍⟍

important, *adj.* - [A·**WAT**·DZ'] ⟍⟍

improve, *v.* - [Y'CH] ⟍⟍

improvisation, *n.* - [**THO**·ADZ] ⟍⟍

impulse, *n.* - [DV'·**GĔ**·JA] ⟍⟍

in, *prep.* - ['·A] ⟍

increase, *v.* - [**OT**·YUTH] ⟍⟍

indecision, *n.* - [HO·O·**MA**·NA] ⟍⟍

indifference, *n.* - [ĒDZ] ⟍

individuality, *n.* - [SMO·O·**NOK**] ⟍⟍

individuate, *v.* - [**SMO**·ONTH] ⟍⟍

industry, *n.* - [THAS·**TH'**·OM] ⟍⟍

infinity, *n.* - [LĒ·**DZUT**·YA] ⟍⟍

infect, *v.* - [**DĔL**·TĒNTH] ⟍⟍

influence, *v.* - [TARCH] ⟍⟍

injury, *n.* - [**ZĒTH**·DĔ] ⟍⟍

ink, *n.* - [**ZĒL**·TSA] ⟍⟍

inn, *n.* - [**YA**·TA] ⟍⟍

inner, *adj.* - [**MA**·(H)R'] ⟍⟍

innocence, *n.* - [**ZUCH**·GO] ⟍⟍

insect, *n.* - [**SPA**·NA] ⟍⟍

inspiration, *n.* - [**CHATH**·DĔ] ⟍⟍

inspire, *v.* - [CHATH] ⟍⟍

instinct, *n.* - [DĔ·LA·**(H)RO**·SA] ⌒.⌒.⌒⌒⌒.

instrument, *n.* - [**PRĔS**·HA] ⌒⌒..⌒⌒.

insurance, *n.* - [H'·MUR·**LO**·THA] ⌒'⌒⌒⌒⌒⌐.

intelligence, *n.* - [MA·(H)R'·**CHAR**·LSA] ⌒.⌒'⌒.⌒⌒⌒.

interest, *v.* - [SH'BVCH] ⌒'⌒⌒

intervene, *v.* - [GA·**(H)R'K**·HĔNTH] ⌒.⌒'⌒⌒..⌒

into, *prep.* - [Y'] ⌒'

intoxicated, *adj.* - [ĔR·MOL] :⌒⌒⌒

intrinsic, *adj.* - [**S'**·G'] ⌒⌐⌒'

introduce, *v.* - [**USH**·ZARCH] ₊⌒⌐.⌒⌒

introduction, *n.* - [USH·ZAR·**CHOK**] ₊⌒⌐.⌒⌒⌒⌒⌒⌒

intuit, *n.* - [J'·KTH'·KTH'·**MOT**] ⌒⌐⌒⌒⌒⌒⌒⌐⌒⌐⌐

intuit, *v.* - [J'·KTH'·**KTH'TS**·(H)RASH] ⌒⌐⌒⌒⌒⌒⌒⌒⌐.⌒

intuition, *n.* - [J'·**KTH'**·KTH'] ⌒⌐⌒⌒⌒⌒'

invention, *n.* - [DV'·**JAL**·THA] ⌒⌐⌒⌐.

investigate, *v.* - [PACH] ⌒.⌒

iron (metal), *n.* - [**HAG**·HA] ⌒⌐⌒.

island, *n.* - [HĔ·**DZ'**·TSA] ⌒..⌒⌐.

isolate, *v.* - [**FVĔ**·N'TH] ⌒:⌒'⌐

isolation, *n.* - [FVĔ·**N'TH**·DĔ] ⌒:⌒'⌐⌒:.

it, *pro.* - [MO] ⌒

its, *adj. & pro.* - [**MĔ**·Ĕ] ⌒...

J

jay, *n.* - [KTHA·**BVO**·BVA] ⌒⌒.⌒⌒⌒.

jelly, *n.* - [**SWĔ**·TSUK] ⌒⌐..⌒₊⌒

jewel, *n.* - [**CHA**·ZA] ⌒.⌒.

join, *v.* - [**MO**·PONTH] ⌒⌐⌒⌒⌒

joke, *n.* - [**DZO**·G(H)ROT] ⌒⌐⌒⌒⌒⌐⌐

jouissance, *n.* - [(H)RADZ·NĔ·M'K·FVAR·**LAN**·DĔ] ⌒.⌒⌒:⌒'⌒⌒⌒.⌒.⌒⌒..

journey, *n.* - [SO·**SHO**·SHA] ⌒⌐⌒⌐⌒.

joy, *n.* - [DZA] ⌐

joyous, *adj.* - [ADZ] ₊⌐

judge, *v.* - [J'·HUNTH] ⌒⌐⌒⌒

jump, *v.* - [SĔSH] ⌒..⌐

K

keep, *v.* - [BVĔRSH] ⌒..⌐

kettle, *n.* - [**YOK**·DVOM] ⌒⌐⌒⌒⌒⌐

120

key, *n.* - [HAG·**LA**·(H)RA] ⌇⌇⌇⌇⌇

kick, *n.* - [CHĒ·'·CHA] ⌇⌇⌇

kick, *v.* - [**CHĒ**·'CH] ⌇⌇⌇

kicker, *n.* - [CHĒ·'·**CHOT**] ⌇⌇⌇⌇⌇

kill, *v.* - [ĒTH] ⌇⌇

kiln, *n.* - [**YAD**·THA] ⌇⌇⌇

kin, *n.* - [**HOG**·CHUM] ⌇⌇⌇⌇⌇

kind, *adj.* - [A·Y'·**ZUTH**·L'] ⌇⌇⌇⌇⌇

kind, *n.* - [**MA**·YOM] ⌇⌇⌇

kindness, *n.* - [Y'·**ZUTH**·DĚ] ⌇⌇⌇⌇

kiss, *v.* - [**YO**·DZ'CH] ⌇⌇⌇⌇

knee, *n.* - [**PO**·CHĒT] ⌇⌇⌇⌇

knife, *n.* - [HAZ·**W'**·OT] ⌇⌇⌇⌇⌇

knot, *n.* - [SHAFV·**KTHU**·(H)RA] ⌇⌇⌇⌇⌇

know, *v.* - [JA·(H)RASH] ⌇⌇

knowledge, *n.* - [**JA**·KA] ⌇

L

laboratory, *n.* - [HA·SĚ·**TH'**·CHA] ⌇⌇⌇⌇⌇

lake, *n.* - [**TS'**·NOT] ⌇⌇⌇⌇

lamp, *n.* - [ZAM] ⌇⌇

landmark, *n.* - [TH'N·**GO**·KTHĚK] ⌇⌇⌇⌇⌇⌇

language, *n.* - [O·JA·**LĒ**·NO] ⌇⌇⌇⌇⌇

large, *adj.* - [SPĚK] ⌇⌇⌇

last, *v.* - [LĒ·DZANTH] ⌇⌇⌇

late, *adj.* - [**ASH**·PL'] ⌇⌇⌇

late, *adv.* - [**SHOP**·L'] ⌇⌇⌇

later, *adj./adv.* - [**APS**·L'] ⌇⌇⌇

laugh, *v.* - [**DZO**·OTH] ⌇⌇⌇

laughter, *n.* - [DZO·**OTH**·DĚ] ⌇⌇⌇⌇

launch, *v.* - [**KHĚ**·BV'NTH] ⌇⌇⌇⌇⌇

law, *n.* - [CHA·**BVO**·TA] ⌇⌇⌇⌇

laze, *v.* - [SHĒNTH] ⌇⌇⌇

lazy, *adj.* - [A·**SHĒ**·NA] ⌇⌇⌇

lead (metal), *n.* - [HAG·**LO**·A] ⌇⌇⌇⌇

lead, *v.* - [GĚ·J'NTH] ⌇⌇⌇⌇

leader, *n.* - [GĚ·J'·**NU**·THA] ⌇⌇⌇⌇⌇

leaf, *n.* - [**THA**·KTHOT] ⌇⌇⌇⌇

learn, *v.* - [J'**TS**·(H)RASH] ⌇⌇⌇⌇

leather, *n.* - [WA·YO·FVA] ౨౸౯౧.
left (direction), *adj.* - [O·'G·NU] ౦౯౨౸ɾ
left (direction), *n.* - [GO·'·NU] ౸౦ɾ౸ɾ
leg, *n.* - [TA·AT] ౧౸౮
less, *adv. & pro.* - [Ĕ·CHĔ] ;౯౸
lesser, *adj.* - [A·LĔ·CHĔ·CHĔ] ౮;౯౸౯౸
letter (epistle) *n.* - [SHĔTH·L'·OT] ౨౸౩౸ɾ౮౮
level, *n.* - [HOG·SKTHA] ౸౦౨౯౮౨౨.
level, *v.* - [HOG·SKTHANTH] ౸౦౨౯౮౨౨.ɾ
library, *n.* - [JAZ·YĔTS] ౦.౨౸ɾ;౮
life, *n.* - [O·NA] ౦ɾ.
lift, *v.* - [SĔK·CHĔTH] ౯౸.౨౨౯౸.౩
light (weight), *adj.* - [ĔS·PĔK·T'] ;౯ɾ;.౨౨౩;
light, *n.* - [Z'ZL] ౨
light-colored, *adj.* - [GO·ZUL] ౸౦౨ɾ౮౮
like, *prep.* - [Ĕ·'] ;ɾ'
-like, *suff.* - ['·HA] ɾ౸.
like, *v.* - [DZU·TUTH] ౨ɾ౮ɾ౩
limit, *v.* - [TSAPS·Y'TH] ౮ɾɾɾɾ౩
line, *n.* - [W'ST] ౨ɾ౮౮
linen, *n.* - [SHĔN·FVO·SHA] ౨;ɾ౸౦౮౨.
lip, *n.* - [YOTS·(H)R'] ɾ౦౸౸'
liquid, *n.* - [TSO·NA] ౨౮ɾ.
liquor, *n.* - [TĔ·WON·CHA] ౮;౨౦ɾ౸.
list, *n.* - [G(H)RO·FVOM] ౸౨౦౦ɾ౦౸
list, *v.* - [G(H)RO·FVO·MOWSH] ౸౨౦ɾ౦ɾ౸౦౨
listen, *v.* - [SOCH] ౯౦ɾ౸
little, *adj.* - [SPAKZL] ;౯ɾ.౨౨౨
live, *v.* - [ONTH] ౦ɾ
lizard, *n.* - [HU·THAK·ZA] ɾɾ౩.౨౨౨.
location, *n.* - [HA·FVĔ·YA] ౸ɾ.ɾ;ɾ.
lock, *v.* - [THA·BVĔSH] ౩.౸ɾ;౩
long, *adj.* - [A·BV'] ;౸ɾ'
look, *v.* - [WO·HANTH] ౨౦౸.ɾ
loose, *adj.* - [A·NĔDZ] ;ɾ;;౨
lore, *n.* - [JA·KA] ౨
lose, *v.* - [ĔRSH] ;ɾ౸
lotus, *n.* - [TS'·GA] ౨ɾ౸.
loud, *adj.* - [A·SO·TĔDZ] ;౯౦౨;;౨

love, *n.* - [**DZWO**·SHA] ᴐᴊₑ₂.
love, *v.* - [DZWOSH] ᴐᴊₑ₂
lover, *n.* - [DZWO·**SHOT**] ᴐᴊₑ₂ₑᴊᴖ
low, *adj.* - [A·**SO**·'BV] ₊₃ₑᵗ₃
lucubrate, *v.* - [**GA**·JOTH] ₂ₜ.ᴐₑ₃
lunar cycle, *n.* - ['**Z**·LOT] ₊ᴣᴊₑᴖ
lust, *n.* - [NĚ·**DZACH**·DĚ] ₋₃.ᴐₜ₃ᴐ..
lust, *v.* - [**NĚ**·DZACH] ₋ᴣᴐ₃

M

machine, *n.* - [**SU**·THA] ₃ₜ₃.
mage, *n.* - [MO·**JABV**·THA] ₋ₑᴐₜᴣₜ₃.
magic, *n.* - [JOK] ᴐₑᴣᴖ
make, *v.* - [**A**·ATH] ₃
make up (cosmetics), *v.* - [TĚ·'NTH] ᴊₜ.ᵗ₋
male, *adj.* - [**U**·'G] ₊ᵗᴣᴐ
male, *n.* - [U·'**G**·A] ₊ᵗᴣᴐ.
man, *n.* - [SMO·TU·'·GA] ₃₃ₑᴣₜᵗᴣᴐ.
manage, *v.* - [**GĚ**·G'TH] ᴣᴐ..ᴣᴊᵗ₃
manager, *n.* - [GĚ·**GU**·THA] ᴣᴐ.ᴣᴊₜ₃.
manifest, *v.* - [**SMU**·JĚSH] ₃ᴣₜᴐ..ᴐ
many, *adj. & pro.* - [M'·MO·**MU**·MU] ᴣᵗᴣₑᴣₜᴣₜ
map, *v.* - [**HĚ**·DZĚTH] ᴣ..ᴐ..₃
mark, *v.* - [**JĚ**·WATH] ᴐ..ᴊ.₃
market, *n.* - [**SHOK**·HA] ᴣₑᴣᴣ₋.
market, *v.* - [**SHOK**·LĚSH] ᴣₑᴣᴣᴊ..ᴐ
marking, *n.* - [**WA**·A] ᴊ..
marriage, *n.* - [JAM·NO·(**H)RO**·TA] ᴐₜᴣᴣₑᴣₑᴊₜ
married, *adj.* - [A·JAM·**NO**·(H)R'] ₊ᴐₜᴣᴣₑᴣᴐᵗ
mask, *n.* - [**E**·WA] ₊ᴊ.
mask, *v.* - [ĒWSH] ₊ᴊ
mass *n.* - [WOM] ᴊₑᴣ
match (igniter), *n.* - [DVA·**L**·'PA] ₂.ᴊᵗ₋.
match, *v.* - [**M**'·HAWSH] ᴣᵗᴣ.ᴊ
mate, *n.* - [**MO**·DZA] ᴣᴐ
material, *n.* - [WA·**YĚN**·DĚ] ᴊ.ᴣ..ᴣᴐ..
materialize, *v.* - [**WA**·YĚNTH] ᴊ.ᴣ..ᴣ
mathematics, *n.* - [HOCH·GA·**BVO**·CHUM] ᴣₑ₃ᴐ..ᴣₑ₃ₜᴣ
matter, *n.* - [**WO**·NA] ᴊₑᴣ.

may, *v. aux.* - [PUTCH]

me, *pro.* - [**MO**·FVĔ]

meadow, *n.* - [**TAL**·TĔ]

meal, *n.* - [HA·**ZATH**·RA]

measure, *v.* - [**GA**·BVOCH]

meat, *n.* - [**HO**·YAM]

meddle, *v.* - [GARSH]

medical, *adj.* - [A·J'S·**PA**·THA]

meditate, *v.* - [Z'CH]

meet, *v.* - [OMTH]

melody, *n.* - [**KHAR**·LA]

melt, *v.* - [TSUNTH]

memory, *n.* - [**SHLOK**·FVA]

mend, *v.* - [Ĕ·ZĒTH]

mercy, *n.* - [**BVĔTH**·BVA]

mesa, *n.* - [**CHĔG**·NA]

meta-, *aff.* - [JO·**AN**·THĒ]

metal, *n.* - [**MĒ**·GA]

metamathemage, *n.* - [JOK·M'·HO·CHO·A·**NU**·THA]

metamathemagics, *n.* - [JOK·M'·HO·CHO·**AN**·THĒ]

microphone, *n.* - [PAL·KHU·U·LĔ]

middle, *adj.* - [AS·**MON**·TA]

military, *adj.* - [A·ZĒL·**BVO**·CHA]

milk, *n.* - [**HA**·TSA]

million, *numb.* - [ZO·**TSA**·TU]

mind, *n.* - [SHA·**BVO**·CH']

mine, *pro.* - [**MĔ**·FVĔ]

mineral, *n.* - [LĔ·**H'**·OT]

mint (herb), *n.* - [GOS·**KTHA**·(H)RA]

mirror, *n.* - [**ZĔTH**·SHOT]

miss, *v.* - [Ĕ·JOWSH]

mist, *n.* - [**OK**·TSOM]

mix, *v.* - [**YA**·LĔNTH]

modern, *adj.* - [ATH·LO·**BVA**·N']

modesty, *n.* - [DV'N·THA·**NĒ**·W']

mold (for shaping or casting), *n.* - [YA]

mold, *v.* - [YATH]

moment, *n.* - [LĔ·**(H)R'**·T']

money, *n.* - [MĔ·**GAR**·YA]

monkey, *n.* - [**SMĒ**·CHA] ⸚⸚:⸚.
month (lunar), *n.* - [**'Z**·LOT] ⸒⸜⸜₆⸌
moon, *n.* - [**'Z**·LO] ⸒⸜⸜₆
more, *adv. & pro.* - [CHĚ] ⸚:.
morning, *n.* - [ĒP·**MON**·TA] :⸜⸚⸚₆⸜⸌.
mosquito, *n.* - [TA·LOBV·**CHOT**] ⸌⸜₆⸚⸚₆⸜⸜
most, *adj. & pro.* - [**FV'**·CHĚ] ⸜⸌⸚:.
mother, *n.* - [TH'N·**GA**·GA] ⸝⸜⸚.⸚.
mother, *v.* - [TH'N·**GA**·GASH] ⸝⸜⸚.⸚.⸴
motion, *n.* - [YA·**MA**·(H)RA] ⸜.⸚.₆.
mound, *n.* - [CHĚMPS] ⸚:.⸚⸜
mountain, *n.* - [CHĚ·**GOK**] ⸚:.⸜₆⸜⸜
mourn, *v.* - [**DVO**·TSASH] ⸘₆⸜:.⸴
mouth, *n.* - [**YO**·LO] ⸜₆⸜₆
move, *v.* - [**YAM**·(H)RĚSH] ⸜.⸚₆:.⸴
much, *adv. & pro.* -[M'·MO·**MU**·MU] ⸚⸌⸚₆⸚⸝⸚⸝
muscle, *n.* - [TSO·**YAM**] ⸘₆⸜.⸚⸚
mushroom, *n.* - [**HON**·GO] ⸜₆⸜⸜₆
music, *n.* - [**SO**·KTHADZ] ⸚₆⸜⸜.⸜
must, *v. aux.* - [**'**·BVURSH] ⸒⸚⸝⸜
mute, *adj.* - [A·SĒK·**L'**] ,⸚:⸜⸜⸌
mute, *n.* - [SĒK·HA] ⸚:⸜⸜.
my, *pro.* - [MĚ·FVĚ] ⸚:.⸜:.
mystery, *n.* - [TA·**LO**·JĚM] ⸜⸜₆⸜:.⸚

N

nail (as on finger or toe), *n.* - [**FVA**·GĚ] ⸜.⸚:.
nail (carpentry), *n.* - [HA·**GĚ**·TA] ⸜.⸚:.⸌.
naked, *adj.* - [Ē·MU·**GĚ**·FV'] :⸜⸵⸚:.⸜⸌
name, *n.* - [G(H)ROM·FVĚ] ⸝⸵⸚⸚⸜:.
name, *v.* - [G(H)ROM·FVĚSH] ⸝⸵⸚⸚⸜:.⸴
nap, *v.* - [**Z'N**·TOCH] ⸜⸌⸜⸜₆⸚
narrow, *adj.* - [ASPS] ,⸚⸜
nation, *n.* - [PUPS] ⸜⸝⸜
natural, *adj.* - [A·**HO**·N'] ,⸚₆⸜⸌
nature, *n.* - [**HO**·NA] ⸚₆⸜.
near, *adj.* - [**USH**·L'] ,⸜⸜⸌
near, *adv. & prep.* - [**'SH**·LU] ,⸜⸜⸴
necessary, *adj.* - [A·**TAN**·CHL'] ,⸜⸜⸚⸜⸌

neck, *n.* - [TUG] 𝒥ᵢ∾

need, *v.* - [**TA**·N'CH] 𝒥ᵢ∼,ₛ

needle, *n.* - [U·THAN·**YO**·LO] ,ₐ.∼∾₀𝒥₀

negotiate, *v.* - [**SHOK**·P'SH] 𝒬₀∽∼,𝒬

nerve (bio.), *n.* - [ON·WĔ] ₀∼𝒥:

net, *n.* - [FVO·'**K**·THO] ∼₀,∞ₐ₀

network, *n.* - [MUM·**THOM**] ∾ᵢ∽ₐₒ∽

neuter, *adj.* - [Ĕ·GO] :∾₀

neuter, *v.* - [Ĕ·GOTH] :∽₀ₐ

neutral, *adj.* - [Ĕ·GĔ] :∾:

never, *adv.* - [Ĕ·BVAFV] :∾.∼

new, *adj.* - [UPS·FVĔ] ,∼∾:

new, *n.* - [**PU**·FVA] ∼ᵢ∾.

news, *n.* - [BVA·**NA**·TA] ∾.∼.𝒥.

night, *n.* - [**TA**·LO] 𝒥.𝒥₀

nine, *numb.* - [FVUM] ∼ᵢ∽

nineteen, *numb.* - [**FVUM**·TU] ∼ᵢ∽𝒥ᵢ

ninth, *numb.* - [Ĕ·'·FVUM] ∴∽ᵢ∽

nipple, *n.* - [**PA**·TSA] ∼.𝒥.

no, *adv. & det.* - [ZOT] ∾₀𝒥

nobody, *pro.* - [Ĕ·**MO**·O] :∽₀₀

Nod's Way, *n.* - [**SOS**·NODZ] ₐ₀ₐ∾₀𝒥

noise, *n.* - [**ZOL**·THA] ∾₀𝒥ₐ.

nomad, *n.* - [SMO·**SA**·TA] ₐ∽₀ₐ.𝒥.

nonsynthetic, *adj.* - [THAG] ₐ.∾

normal, *adj.* - [A·TA·Z'·**TA**·Z'] .𝒥.∾.𝒥.∾,

north, *n.* - [TSĔPS] 𝒥:∼

nose, *n.* - [AK·**THO**·LA] ,∞ₐ₀𝒥.

not, *adv.* - [ĔST] :ₐ𝒥

note, *n.* - [**JA**·GĔ] ₀.∾:

now, *adv. & conj.* - [BVANH] ∾.∽

number, *n.* - [**BVAT**·YOT] ∾.𝒥∾₀𝒥

nut, *n.* - [DVAPS] 𝒬.∼

O

obesity, *n.* - [THOM·**TU**·LA] ₐ₀∽𝒥ᵢ𝒥.

object, *n.* - [**MO**·(H)RA] ∾₀∾.

obligation, *n.* - [JAM·**NO**·(H)RA] ₀.∾∾₀∾.

oblivion, *n.* - [**SHLO**·KTHĔFV] 𝒬𝒥₀∞:∼

observed, *adj.* - [A·**WO**·NA] ⌒

obstruct, *v.* - [**BVO**·GANTH] ⌒

obtain, *v.* - [**BVA**·ATH] ⌒

occasion, *n.* - [BVAFV·**TA**·CHA] ⌒

ocean, *n.* - [TS'·**HA**·YĚ] ⌒

odor, *n.* - [SKTHART] ⌒

of, *prep.* - [O·A] ⌒

off, *adv. & prep.* - ['L·SHL'] ⌒

offer, *v.* - [WĚ·THACH] ⌒

office, *n.* - [SUP·**CHO**·NA] ⌒

ogre, *n.* - [Ě·WO·**NA**·THA] ⌒

oil, *n.* - [MOLT] ⌒

okay, *adv. & adj.* - [KTHĚ·'] ⌒

old, *adj.* - [CHĚZL] ⌒

on, *adv.* - ['·**Z'CH**·L'] ⌒

on, *prep.* - ['·A] ⌒

ondine, *n.* - [TS'·MOT] ⌒

one, *numb.* - [MO] ⌒

only, *adj.* - [AM·FVĚ] ⌒

ontotronic, *adj.* - [AP·(H)RĚ·SHA·NA·**NUK**] ⌒

open, *v.* - [ZUCH] ⌒

opening, *n.* - [YO] ⌒

operation, *n.* - [THA·**TA**·CHA] ⌒

opinion, *n.* - [**LO**·SHA] ⌒

opposite, *n.* - [M'·**SHĚ**·NA] ⌒

optimize, *v.* - [**P'**·BVĚCH] ⌒

or, *conj.* - [O·O] ⌒

orange (color), *n.* - [**HĚZ**·NAL] ⌒

orange (fruit), *n.* - [YU·**P'**·YOT] ⌒

orangutan, *n.* - [MO·S'·HO·**JĚN**·L'] ⌒

orca, *n.* - [MU·DZA·TS'·**HA**·TA] ⌒

order (arrangement), *n.* - [**HAL**·HA] ⌒

order (arrange), *v.* - [HA·**LĚ**·HATH] ⌒

order (command), *v.* - [LOCH] ⌒

organization (arrangement), *n.* - [**P'**·BVO·CHA] ⌒

organization (group), *n.* - [**P'**·BVOM] ⌒

organize, *v.* - [**P'**·BVOCH] ⌒

orgasm, *n.* - [DZAR·**TH'**·CHĚ] ⌒

orgasm, *v.* - [DZARTH] ⌒

ornament, *n.* -[DĔ·NA] ⌒
other, *n.* - [SHĒ·NOT] ⌒
our, ours, *pro.* - [MO·MĔ·FVĔ] ⌒
out, *adj.* - [A·Ē·Y'] ⌒
out, *adv. & prep.* - [Ē·Y'] ⌒
outlier, *n.* - [M'·FVĒ·NA] ⌒
outrage, *v.* - [U·THĔ·DVĔ·TSARSH] ⌒
oven, *n.* - [YAD·THO·KTHA] ⌒
over, *adv.* - [LO·SĔ] ⌒
over, *prep.* - [OSK] ⌒
overlook, *v.* - [Ē·JOWSH] ⌒
overweight, *adj.* - [A·THOM·TUL] ⌒
owe, *v.* - [BVORSH] ⌒
owl, *n.* - [TA·LĔM·SOK] ⌒
own, *v.* - [(H)RASH] ⌒
owner, *n.* - [(H)RA·OT] ⌒

P

pack, *v.* - [YOSH] ⌒
page, *n.* - [JA·KTHOT] ⌒
pain, *n.* - [K(H)RĒ·NA] ⌒
paint, *n.* - [TS'·YUK·NA] ⌒
pale, *adj.* - [A·GO·ZĔ] ⌒
pallor, *n.* - [GOZ·DĔ] ⌒
pants (garment), *n.* - [TAT·LĔM] ⌒
paper, *n.* - [JA·YĔ·GA] ⌒
parallel, *v.* - [BVĒMTH] ⌒
parasite, *n.* - [SHĔP·HUR·DĔ] ⌒
parcel, *n.* - [TA·MU·YA] ⌒
parent, *n.* - [TH'N·GUK] ⌒
parent, *v.* - [TH'N·GUSH] ⌒
part, *n.* - [YOT] ⌒
partner, *n.* - [MO·DZA] ⌒
pass, *v.* - [LO·'SH] ⌒
passage, *n.* - [LO·'SH·DĔ] ⌒
past, *n.* - [SHLO·A] ⌒
paste, *v.* - [NA·BVUTH] ⌒
'pataphysician, *n.* - [NA·JA·TH'·LO·PĔ·MU·THA] ⌒
'pataphysics, *n.* - [NA·JA·TH'·LO·PĔM] ⌒

path, *n.* - [SOS] ⟋

payment, *n.* - [MĚ·**GA**·(H)RA] ⟋⟍⟍

peace, *n.* - [**NĚCH**·TA] ⟍⟍⟋

peak, *n.* - [OK·**HA**·NUL] ₆⟍⟍⟋

peal, *v.* - [**DVO**·KTHASH] ⟍⟍⟍

pearl, *n.* - [HA·**BVĚTS**·DZA] ⟍⟍⟍

pen, *n.* - [JA·YA] ⟍⟍

pencil, *n.* - [JA·**'L**·WA] ⟍⟍⟍

penetrate, *v.* - [GOTH] ⟍⟍

penis, *n.* - [Y'·BVU·FVU·**'**·GA] ⟍⟍⟍⟍

perceive, *v.* - [JOWSH] ⟍⟍

percussion, *n.* - [KLA·**TĚ**·(H)ROM] ⟍⟍⟍⟍

performance, *n.* - [**WU**·DĚ] ⟍⟍

perseverance, *n.* - [DZU·THA·**BVĚ**·CHA] ⟍⟍⟍⟍

persevere, *v.* - [DZU·**THA**·BVĚCH] ⟍⟍⟍⟍

person, *n.* - [**MOS**·MA] ⟍⟍⟍

persona, *n.* - [**SMO**·OT] ⟋⟍⟍⟍

photograph, *n.* - [**BVĚZ**·NA] ⟍⟍⟍

photograph, *v.* - [**BVĚ**·Z'NTH] ⟍⟍⟍

physical, *adj.* - [A·**NU**·(H)R'] ⟍⟍⟍

physics, *n.* - [**NA**·JAM] ⟍⟍⟍

piano, *n.* - [KLA·(H)RA·LU·**WĚ**·ZA] ⟍⟍⟍⟍⟍

picture, *n.* - [**THUN**·WA] ⟍⟍⟍

piece, *n.* - [YOT] ⟍⟍

pierce, *v.* - [GOTH] ⟍⟍

pig, *n.* - [MO·**HĚPS**·WA] ⟍⟍⟍

pile, *v.* - [CHĚMTH] ⟍⟍⟍

pilot, *n.* - [MO·**KTHA**·HA] ⟍⟍⟍

pin, *n.* - [W'·**HA**·GA] ⟍⟍⟍

pink, *adj.* - [HĚ·**ZU**·UL] ⟍⟍⟍⟍

pink, *n.* - [HĚ·ZU·**UL**·DĚ] ⟍⟍⟍⟍

pipe, *n.* - [W'S·**TU**·(H)RA] ⟍⟍⟍⟍

pitch, *v.* - [CHACH] ⟍⟍

pitch (musical), *n.* - [P'BV·LĚ·**CHUK**] ⟍⟍⟍⟍⟍

place, *n.* - [**LĚ**·HA] ⟍⟍⟍

plan, *v.* - [**SU**·P'CH] ⟍⟍⟍

plane (geom.), *n.* - [**HO**·GA] ⟍⟍⟍

plank, *n.* - [HO·**GA**·KTHA] ⟍⟍⟍⟍

plant, *n.* - [**GA**·BVA] ⟍

plant, *v.* - [**GA**·BVATH] ∿.∽.ȝ

plant, domesticated, *n.* - [**GODZ**·MA] ∾₀∾.

plate, *n.* - [H'·**YA**·GA] ∽∽.∿.

play, *v.* - [DZOCH] ∾₀ᴧ

please, *adv.* - [BVA·**A**·L'] ∾..ᴧ,

please, *v.* - [DZA·**BVĚT**·ATH] ∾ᴧȝ

pleasure, *n.* - [DZA·**BVĚTH**·DĚ] ∾.∿.ȝ∾.

pleasure, *v.* - [DZA·**BVĚT**·ATH] ∾ᴧȝ

pledge, *n.* - [**BVĚ**·TA] ∿

pledge, *v.* - [BVĚPSH] ∿.∴∿ᴧ

plenipotentiary, *n.* - [WUS·**(H)RU**·THA] ᴧ.ᴧ₀ᴧȝ.

plow, *n.* - [HA·**W'**·THA] ∿.ᴧᴧȝ.

plug, *n.* - [**DHU**·GA] ∾∾ᴧ∿.

plus, *conj. & prep.* - [**O**·TA] ₀ᴧ,

pocket, *n.* - [YOL·**WĒ**·SHA] ∾₀ᴧᴧ.∿.

poetry, *n.* - [ZAR·**DZA**·(H)RA] ∾.₀∾.∿.

point, *n.* - [YĒT] ∿.ᴧ

poison, *n.* - [TĒ·**WON**·YA] ᴧ.ᴧ₀ᴧᴧ.

polish, *v.* - [**BVĚ**·ZONTH] ∿.∴∾₀ᴧ

political, *adj.* - [A·LUBV·**CHĚ**·NA] .ᴧ₀ᴧȝ.∴ᴧ.

polymer, *n.* - [HA·**BVOL**·TA] ∿.∿₀ᴧᴧ.

pond, *n.* - [**TS'N**·YA] ∾ᴧᴧ.

ponder, *v.* - [Z'CH] ∾ᴧᴧ

pool, *n.* - [**TS'N**·DĚ] ∾ᴧᴧ∾.

pool, *v.* - [TS'NTH] ∾ᴧᴧ

poor, *adj.* - [A·**LĒ**·LO] .ᴧ.ᴧ₀

porter, *n.* - [SĚK·**CHU**·THA] ȝ.∾ᴧȝ.

portion, *n.* - [BVĚT·**ATH**·RA] ∿.ᴧ.ȝ∿.

position, *n.* - [LĚ·**WO**·HA] ᴧ.ᴧ₀∾.

possession, *n.* - [(**H)RASH**·TU] ∿.ᴧᴧ

possible, *adj.* - [A·**NUT**·CH'] .ᴧᴧᴧ,

posterity, *n.* - [LĒ·**MOSH**·PA] ᴧ.∿₀∾ᴧ.

pot, *n.* - [**YA**·DVOM] ∿.ᴧ₀∾

potato, *n.* - [HA·**G'**·UPS] ∿.∾ᴧᴧ∿

potential, *n.* - [PUT] ∿ᴧᴧ

pour, *v.* - [**TSU**·'SH] ᴧᴧᴧᴧ

powder, *n.* - [**FVĒ**·YOM] ∿.ᴧ₀∾

power, *n.* - [**SĚTS**·DVA] ȝ.∾ᴧ.

precious, *adj.* - [**A**·YĚDZ] .ᴧ.∿

precipice, *n.* - [**YUSH**·L'] ⌐ₜ⧸ᴗ,

pregnancy, *n.* - [ZA·**BVAN**·DĚ] ᴗ₅⧹⌐ᴗₔ

pregnant (to be pr–), *v.* - [**ZA**·BVANTH] ᴗ₅⧹⌐

pregnant (to become pr–), *v.* - [**ZA**·BVĚTH] ᴗ₅ₔ₃

prelude, *n.* - [JA·TUPS] ᴗᴊ⌐

present, *v.* - [**ZAR**·BVĚCH] ᴗ₅⌐₅ₔₔ⌐

price, *v.* - [**G(H)ROM**·BVACH] ⌐ᴗ₅⌐₅ₔ⌐

print, *v.* - [THWOMTH] ₃ᴊₒ⌐₃

prison, *n.* - [**SHAFV**·(H)RĚTS] ᴗₒ⌐ₔᴊ

private, *adj.* - [A·LĚ·**HO**·TA] ⸴ᴊᵼ⌐ₒᴊ.

probable, *adj.* - [A·**SH'**·SA] ⸴ᴗᵼ₅.

probe, *v.* - [PACH] ⌐ᵼ⌐

process, *n.* - [M'·**MĚ**·(H)RA] ⌐ᴊ⌐ᵼᴗ.

process, *v.* - [**M'**·MĚRSH] ⌐ᴊ⌐ᵼᴗ

produce, *v.* - [YARTH] ⌐ᵼᴗ₃

profit, *n.* - [**(H)R'**·SA] ⌐ᴊ₅.

progress, *n.* - [TA·**(H)R'**·NA] ᴊᵼⱯ⌐.

progress, *v.* - [**TA**·(H)R'NTH] ᴊᵼⱯ⌐

progression, *n.* - [TA·**(H)R'N**·DĚ] ᴊᵼⱯ⌐ᴗₔ

progressive, *adj.* - [A·**TARN**·L'] ⸴ᴊᵼⱯᴗᴊ'

property, *n.* - [LĚ·**HAR**·YOT] ᴗₔᵼᴗᵼⱯᴗᴊ

prose, *n.* - [**MUM**·G(H)ROT] ⌐ᵼᴗᴗ⌐ᴗᴊ

prosper, *v.* - [DZARSH] ᴗᵼⱯ

prostitute, *n.* - [Ě·**NAR**·SHOT] ⸴⌐ᵼᴗᴊ⌐ᴊ

prostitute, *v.* - [**Ě**·NARSH] ⸴⌐ᵼⱯ

protect, *v.* - [LOS·**HO**·BV'CH] ᴊₒ⌐ᴗₒ₅ᴗ'⌐

protest, *v.* - [**SO**·BVĚCH] ⌐ₒ₅⸴⌐

protract, *v.* - [**LĚ**·DZUTH] ᴊⱯᴗᵼ₃

public, *adj.* - [A·**ZU**·TA] ⸴ᴗᵼᴊ.

publish, *v.* - [BVĚ·WOTH] ⌐Ɐᴗₒ₃

pull, *v.* - [SHOCH] ᴗₒ⌐

pump, *v.* - [TS'NCH] ᴗᵼⱯ⌐

punish, *v.* - [ZĚ·THURSH] ᴗⱯᴊ₃ₜⱯ

punishment, *n.* - [ZĚ·**THUR**·LA] ᴗⱯᴊ₃ᴗⱯᴊ.

purchase, *v.* - [FVĚ·GARSH] ⌐ⱯᴗⱯᴗ

purple, *adj.* - [A·HO·'·KTH'] ⸴⌐ₒ'ᴗᴗ'

purple, *n.* - [HO·'·KTH'] ⌐ₒ'ᴗᴗ'

purpose, *n.* - [**CHA**·SA] ᴗᵼⱯ.

push, *v.* - [SHATH] ᴗᵼ₃

put, *v.* - [LĔ·HATH]

Q

qualification, *n.* - [NĔ·DZA·**THUK**]
qualify, *v.* - [**NĔ**·DZATH]
quality, *n.* - [HOG·**YO**·TA]
quantum, *n.* - [(H)RO·**BVĔR**·TSA]
quartz, *n.* - [(H)RU·**WO**·MOZL]
queen, *n.* - [WOT·CHU·**THA**·GA]
quest, *n.* - [SHA·**THUK**]
question, *v.* - [JU·N'CH]
quick, *adj.* - [AP·**TĔ**·LĒ]
quiet, *adj.* - [A·**KTHOCH**·KTH']
quiet, *n.* - [KTHO·**CHOK**·TA]
quintessence, *n.* - [DĔ·'·LĒ]
quip, *n.* - [**DZO**·G(H)ROT]
quite, *adv.* - [UTS·**P'**·T']
quorum, *n.* - [NAN·SA·**LĔ**·YA]
quote, *v.* - [JA·ATH]
quotient, *n.* - [WON·**BVA**·TA]

R

radiation, *n.* - [ZO·THA·**GU**·KTHA]
rage, *n.* - [DVĒBV]
rage, *v.* - [DVĒBVCH]
rail, *n.* - [**LO**·BV'ST]
rain, *v.* - [KYUSH]
range, *v.* - [**(H)RĔ**·DZUTH]
raptor, *n.* - [KTHOBV·**CHOT**]
rat, *n.* - [**LUM**·HA]
rate, *v.* - [**BVO**·TOWSH]
raven, *n.* - [MOS·**MOK**·BVA]
ray (as of light), *n.* - [ZO·**THA**·GA]
reaction, *n.* - [ZUT·**(H)RO**·SHA]
read, *v.* - [Z'RSH]
ready, *adj.* - [A·**L'S**·TO]
real, *adj.* - [NOFV]
reason, *n.* - [GOR·**PĔ**·SHA]
reason, *v.* - [**GOR**·POSH]

receipt, *n.* - [BVAT·**YU**·LA] ⟿⟲⟲

receive, *v.* - [**SKTHO**·'RSH] ⟿⟲⟲

record, *v.* - [(H)R'TH] ⟿⟲

recover, *v.* - [SPATH] ⟿⟲

recovery, *n.* - [SPATH·**L'**·A] ⟿⟲⟲

recruit, *v.* - [THO·**M'**·MĔSH] ⟿⟲⟲

rectitude, *n.* - [**SOS**·NODZ] ⟿⟲⟲

red, *adj.* - [A·**HĔZ**·LO] ⟿⟲⟲

red, *n.* - [**HĔZ**·LO] ⟿⟲⟲

redden, *v.* - [HĔZ·**LO**·TUTH] ⟿⟲⟲

reek, *v.* - [**LO**·TSATH] ⟿⟲⟲

reflect, *v.* - [ZĔ·TH'SH] ⟿⟲⟲

refresh, *v.* - [**TU**·Z'TH] ⟿⟲⟲

regret, *v.* - [(**H)RO**·LASH] ⟿⟲⟲

regular, *adj.* - [A·BVA·**Z'**·T'] ⟿⟲⟲

reject, *v.* - [Ĕ·Z'RSH] ⟿⟲

related to (to be r–), *v.* - [**HOG**·MĔCH] ⟿⟲⟲

relation, *n.*- [**HOG**·CHUM] ⟿⟲⟲

religion, *n.* - [BVOM·FVO·**L'**·KTHA] ⟿⟲⟲

relish, *v.* - [**DVA**·(H)R'SH] ⟿⟲⟲

rely, *v.* - [BOCH] ⟿⟲

remember, *v.* - [**SHLOK**·FVASH] ⟿⟲⟲

remove, *v.* - [MORSH] ⟿⟲

renewal, *n.* - [TU·**Z'TH**·DĔ] ⟿⟲⟲

repair, *n.* - [GO·LO·**PU**·CHA] ⟿⟲⟲

repair, *v.* - [GO·**LO**·PUCH] ⟿⟲⟲

repeat, *v.* - [CHRĔSH] ⟿⟲

reply, *v.* - [**ZAG**·LARNTH] ⟿⟲⟲

repository, *n.* - [TS'·HA·**T'**·JAK] ⟿⟲⟲

representative, *n.* - [**WĔCH**·YOT] ⟿⟲⟲

request, *v.* - [BVACH] ⟿⟲

residue, *n.* - [**MO**·LO] ⟿⟲

respect, *v.* - [**TĔ**·DZORSH] ⟿⟲⟲

respond, *v.* - [**ZU**·TOTH] ⟿⟲⟲

responsible, *adj.* - [A·YĔ·**BVO**·(H)RA] ⟿⟲⟲

rest, *n.* - [**KTHOCH**·TA] ⟿⟲⟲

rest, *v.* - [KTHOCH] ⟿⟲

retain, *v.* - [(**H)RĔ**·BVOSH] ⟿⟲⟲

retreat, *n.* - [LO·**L'**·SHA] ⟿⟲⟲

retreat, *v.* - [**LO**·L'SH] ꒰꒱꒜꒰꒱

return, *n.* - [Ĕ·**BVO**·SHA] ꜀꜀ꜛ꜀꜀.

return, *v.* - [Ĕ·BVOSH] ꜀꜀ꜛ꜀꜀

reveal, *v.* - [BVĔCH] ꜀꜀꜡꜀

reward, *v.* - [**DZAM**·GURSH] ꜀꜀꜀꜀꜀꜀

rhythm, *n.* - [SHO·**SHO**·SH'M] ꜀꜀꜀꜀꜀꜀

rhythmic, *adj.* - [A·SHO·SHO·**SH'**·M'] ꜀꜀꜀꜀꜀꜀꜀

rice, *n.* - [**WOP**·TA] ꜀꜀꜀꜀

right (correct), *adj.* - [JOL] ꜀꜀꜀

right (direction), *adj.* - [**AG**·N'] ꜀꜀꜀

right (direction), *n.* - [**GĔ**·N'] ꜀꜀꜀

rigid, *adj.* - [**BVO**·'] ꜀꜀꜀

ring, *n.* - [HA·**GĔS**·TA] ꜀꜀꜀꜀꜀

ring out, *v.* - [**DVO**·KTHASH] ꜀꜀꜀꜀

rise, *v.* - [KTHĔSH] ꜀꜀꜀꜀

rising, *adj.* - [A·**KTHĔSH**·L'] ꜀꜀꜀꜀꜀

river, *n.* - [**SOTS**·TO] ꜀꜀꜀꜀

road, *n.* - [SA] ꜀꜀.

robust, *adj.* - [GOM] ꜀꜀꜀

rock (material), *n.* - [**HABV**·NA] ꜀꜀꜀꜀.

rock (object), *n.* - [H'·**OT**] ꜀꜀꜀꜀

rod, *n.* - [GA·**KTH'S**·TA] ꜀꜀꜀꜀꜀꜀

role, *n.* - [**BVRA**·MA] ꜀꜀꜀꜀.

roll, *n.* - [BVĔ·**ZA**·THA] ꜀꜀꜀꜀꜀.

roll, *v.* - [**BVĔ**·ZATH] ꜀꜀꜀꜀

roof, *n.* - [**HOG**·SĔK] ꜀꜀꜀꜀꜀꜀

room, *n.* - [HA·**CHO**·NA] ꜀꜀꜀꜀.

root, *n.* - [**HOG**·CHA] ꜀꜀꜀꜀.

root (bot.), *v.* - [HOGCH] ꜀꜀꜀꜀

rope, *n.* - [WAS·**GĔ**·SA] ꜀꜀꜀꜀꜀.

rough, *adj.* - [A·**H'**·YA] ꜀꜀꜀.

round, *adj.* - [A·SĔK·**YO**·T'] ꜀꜀꜀꜀꜀꜀

rub, *v.* - [**YU**·MĔSH] ꜀꜀꜀꜀

ruby (mineral), *n.* - [(H)RU·**WĔZ**·LO] ꜀꜀꜀꜀꜀꜀

rule, *n.* - [**CHA**·BV'] ꜀꜀꜀

rule, *v.* - [THRĔSH] ꜀꜀꜀꜀

rum, *n.* - [**TWOS**·WUK] ꜀꜀꜀꜀꜀꜀

run, *v.* - [FVASH] ꜀꜀꜀

rush, *v.* - [**TĔ**·OKSH] ꜀꜀꜀꜀꜀

S

saccharine, *adj.* - [A·WON·YAS·**WĚ**·DZA] ꒐꒐꒜꒜꒐꒜꒐꒐

sad, *adj.* - [A·**(H)RU**·LO] ꒐꒐꒜꒐

sadness, *n.* - [**(H)RUL**·DĚ] ꒜꒐꒜꒜

safe, *adj.* - [A·HA·**DZA**·N'] ꒜꒐꒜꒜

sage, *n.* - [H'·**YĚTH**·T'] ꒜꒜꒜꒜

sail, *n.* - [**OK**·SHGA] ꒜꒜꒜꒜

sail, *v.* - [OKSH] ꒜꒜꒜

salt, *n.* - [**SW'**·OT] ꒜꒜꒜꒜

same, *adj.* - [A·**M'**·HA] ꒜꒜꒜

same, *adv. & pro.* - [**M'**·HA] ꒜꒜꒜

sand, *n.* - [**W(H)RO**·MA] ꒜꒜꒜꒜

sasquatch, *n.* - [H'·**YĚTH**·T'] ꒜꒜꒜꒜

satellite, *n.* - [N'K·SKTHU·U·L'·**O**·SA] ꒜꒜꒜꒜꒜꒜꒜

satisfy, *v.* - [U·**THĚ**·DZANTH] ꒜꒜꒜꒜

save, *v.* - [**HA**·TH'SH] ꒜꒜꒜

say, *v.* - [ZARNTH] ꒜꒜꒜

scale, *n.* - [**BVO**·TOM] ꒜꒜꒜꒜

school, *n.* - [J'**T**·HA] ꒜꒜꒜

science, *n.* - [**JA**·KA] ꒜

scissors, *n.* - [BVA·**W'**·THOM] ꒜꒜꒜꒜

scream, *v.* - [**SOK**·W'TH] ꒜꒜꒜꒜

screw, *n.* - [SA·**BVĚ**·CHA] ꒜꒜꒜꒜

screw, *v.* - [**SA**·BVĚCH] ꒜꒜꒜

screwdriver, *n.* - [SA·BVĚ·**CHOT**] ꒜꒜꒜꒜꒜

scroll, *n.* - [BVĚ·**WĚTH**·NA] ꒜꒜꒜꒜

sea, *n.* - [TS'·**HA**·T'] ꒜꒜꒜

search, *n.* - [**CH'**·CHA] ꒜꒜

seat, *n.* - [**TSUL**·TOK] ꒜꒜꒜꒜

second, *numb.* - [Ě·'·**BVA**] ꒜꒜

secret, *adj.* - [A·**LĚ**·WOT] ꒜꒜꒜꒜

secret, *n.* - [**Ě**·WOT] ꒜꒜꒜

see, *v.* - [WOSH] ꒜

seed, *n.* - [GOPS] ꒜꒜꒜

seek, *v.* - [CH'CH] ꒜

seeking, *n.* - [**CH'CH**·L'] ꒜꒜

seem, *v.* - [WATH] ꒜꒜

seen, *adj.* - [A·**WO**·NA] ꒜꒜꒜

seen (to be s–), *v.* - [WONTH] ᴐₒↃ

selection, *n.* - [FVÊ·**THU**·LA] ↄᵋ₃ₜↄ.

self, *n.* - [SMO·O·**NOK**] ᵌↄₒₒᵧₒ₂₂₂

selfhood, *n.* - [SMO·**ON**·DĚ] ᵌↄₒₒↄ₂.

self-reliance, *n.* - [BVOCH·SMO·**ON**·DĚ] ₒₒᵌᵌↄₒₒↄ₂.

sell, *v.* - [MĚ·**G'**·ARSH] ↄↄᵌ'ₜᵌ

send, *v.* - [THUSH] ᵌₜↄ

sense, *v.* - [**KTHO**·JUCH] ₂₂ₒ₂ₜᵌ

separate, *v.* - [Ê·BVONTH] ₜↄₒↄ

serious, *adj.* - [A·**FVO**·NĚ] ₜↄↄₜ.

servant, *n.* - [SĚTH·**LU**·THA] ᵌₜᵌↄₜᵌ.

settle, *v.* - [MĚ·HANTH] ↄ₌ↄₜↄ

seven, *numb.* - [**FVA**·Ê] ↄₜ.

seventeen, *numb.* - [**FVAK**·TU] ↄₜ₂₂₂ₜ

sew, *v.* - [**FVO**·'NTH] ↄₒᵎↄ

sewing, *n.* - [FVO·'N·**L'**·A] ↄₒᵎↄↄ.

sex, *n.* - [**PU**·DZA] ↄₜↄ.

sex (to have), *v.* - [PLUSH] ↄↄₜↄ

shade, *n.* - [**LU**·LA] ↄₜↄ.

shadow, *n.* - [LO] ↄ

shake, *v.* - [**M'**·MĚSH] ↄᵎↄↄↄ

shame, *v.* - [**YU**·LÊTH] ↄₜↄ₌ᵌ

shape, *n.* - [YĚTS] ↄ

shape, *v.* - [YATH] ↄₜᵌ

share, *n.* - [BVĚT·**ATH**·RA] ₒₜↄₜᵌₒ.

share, *v.* - [BVĚT·**ATH**·RASH] ₒᵌₒ

sharp, *adj.* - [A·**THAN**·Y'] ₜᵌₜↄↄ'

she, *pro.* - [MO] ↄ

sheep, *n.* - [**GĚS**·LĚT] ↄₜᵌↄₜↄ

sheet, *n.* - [FVO·'·SHA·**TH'**·LA] ↄₒᵎↄₜᵌↄↄ.

shelf, *n.* - [**SKTHO**·GA] ᵌↄↄₒↄ.

shell, *n.* - [**HA**·BVĚTS] ↄₜↄₜↄᵌ

shield, *n.* - [LOSH·BV'·**CHO**·TA] ↄₒↄₒᵎᵌₒↄ.

ship, *n.* - [TSĚ·TA·**CHO**·MA] ↄₜↄₜᵌₒↄ.

shirt, *n.* - [**KTHUSH**·LA] ₂₂ₜ₂₂.

shock, *v.* - [**TSU**·ZANTH] ↄₜↄₜↄ

shoe, *n.* - [HA·**BVO**·LOM] ↄₜↄₒↄↄₒↄ

short, *adj.* - [A·GĚT] ↄₜↄ

shout, *v.* - [**SOS**·PĚKCH] ᵌₒᵌₒↄₜↄↄᵌ

show, *v.* - [BVĔCH] ᗡᖆᐟᔕ
shut, *v.* - [Ĕ·ZASH] ᗡ,ᗡ,ᖇ
sibling, *n.* - [HO·JĔM] ᐦᗡᗡᖆᔕ
sick, *adj.* - [A·GĔ·MA] ,ᖆᗡᖆᔕ.
sicken, *v.* - [GĔ·MĔSH] ᖆᗡᔕᗡᖇ
sickness, *n.* - [GĔ·MĔK] ᖆᗡᔕᗡᗡ
side, *n.* - [YĔS·TA] ᔕᖆᔕᖇ.
sign, *n.* - [WA·A] ᗡ,,
silence, *n.* - [ĔM·SO·KTHA] ᗡᔕᔕᗡᗡ.
silent, *adj.* - [A·LĔM·SO·KTHA] ,ᗡᔕᔕᗡᗡ.
silk, *n.* - [SPAN·GĔS] ᔕᔕ,ᔕᔕᔕᔕ
silver (color), *n.* - [GAZL] ᔕᗡᗡ
silver (metal), *n.* - [GAZ·HA] ᔕᗡᗡᔕ.
simple, *adj.* - [AN·DĔ] ,ᔕᗡᖆ
simpleton, *n.* - [J'·KTH'·KTH'·BVO·'] ᗡ,ᗡᗡ,ᗡᗡᖆᔕᖇᐟ
simplicity, *n.* - [NĔ·DZA] ᔕᗡ
simplification, *n.* - [P'·BVĔ·CHA] ᔕᖇᔕᖆᔕ.
simplify, *v.* - [P'·BVĔCH] ᔕᖇᔕᖆᔕ
sing, *v.* - [DZA·ACH] ᗡᖆᔕ
singer, *n.* - [DZA·CHOT] ᗡᖆᔕᗡᖇᖇ
single, *adj.* - [AM·FVĔ] ,ᔕᔕ:
singularity, *n.* - [FVĔ·N'·THA] ᔕᖆᔕᖇᖆᖇ.
sister, *n.* - [HO·JA·GA] ᐦᗡᗡᖆᔕ.
sit, *v.* - [TSUK·TOCH] ᗡᖇᗡᗡᖆᔕ
six, *numb.* - [FVĔ·'] ᔕᖇᐟ
sixteen, *numb.* - [FVĔK·TU] ᔕᖆᗡᗡᖇ
size, *n.* - [TĔ·HA] ᗡᖆᔕ.
sketch, *v.* - [JA·'WSH] ᗡᖇᗡ
skin, *n.* - [WA·YA] ᗡᔕ.
skirt, *n.* - [BVUG·SA] ᔕᖇᔕᖇᔕ.
sky, *n.* - [KTHO] ᗡᗡ
sleep, *n.* - [NOT·CHA] ᔕᔕᔕᖇ.
sleep, *v.* - [NOTCH] ᔕᔕᔕᖇ
sleeper, *n.* - [NOT·CHU·THA] ᔕᔕᖆᖇᔕᖇ.
sleeping, *adj.* - [A·NOT·CHL'] ,ᔕᔕᖇᖇᖇᐟ
slice, *v.* - [TĔNTH] ᗡᖆᔕ
slip, *v.* - [G(H)RĔSH] ᔕᔕᖇᖇ
slip (undergarment), *n.* - [SPAN·GĔ·LA] ᔕᔕ,ᔕᔕᖆᔕᖇ.
slope, *v.* - [S'·YUSH] ᔕᔕᖇᖇ

slow, *v.* - [SHLASH] ᒐᒎᒐ

small, *adj.* - [ASPS] ᵎᔑᖸ

smash, *v.* - [PLANTH] ᖸᒎᖸ

smell, *v.* - [SKTHARTH] ᔑᒎᵔᔑᔜ

smile, *n.* - [**YOL**·DZA] ᖸᵔᒎᒎᵎ

smile, *v.* - [**YOL**·DZAWSH] ᖸᵔᒎᒎᒎᒎ

smith, *n.* - [Y'·BVO·**TU**·THA] ᖸᵔᖹᒋᔜᵎ

smithy, *n.* - [Y'·BVO·**TUK**] ᖸᵔᖹᒋᒎᒎᒎ

smoke, *n.* - [OK·**NĒ**·ZA] ᖺᒎᖸᵔᒎᵎ

smoke, *v.* - [**OK**·NĒNTH] ᖺᒎᖸᵔᖸ

smooth, *adj.* - [AS·**PAN**·G'] ᵎᔑᖸᒎ

snack, *n.* - [GA] ᒎᵎ

snake, *n.* - [W'S·**TAK**·ZA] ᒎᖸᔑᒎᒎᒎᵎ

sneeze, *n.* - [**KTHOSH**·TA] ᒎᒎᖺᒎᒎᵎ

sneeze, *v.* - [KTHOSH] ᒎᒎᖺᒐ

snow, *v.* - [DVĒNTH] ᒐᖸᖸ

so, *adv.* - [CHUL] ᔑᖸᒎ

so, *conj.* - ᒎ['T] ᒎ

soap, *n.* - [POLT] ᖸᖺᒎᒎ

soar, *v.* - [**KHĚN**·YUNTH] ᒎᒎᖺᖸᖸᖸ

sober, *adj.* - [**A**·(H)RO] ᵎᖺᖸ

sobriety, *n.* - [(H)R'·**NUK**] ᖸᖸᖸᒎᒎᒎ

society, *n.* - [**SMOM**·TA] ᔑᔑᖺᒎᒎᒋ

sock, *n.* - [FVAL·**PU**·TA] ᖸᒎᖸᒋᒋ

soft, *adj.* - [**TSU**·(H)R'] ᒎᖸᖸᖸ

solid, *adj.* - [A·HABV] ᵎᖺᖸ

solid, *n.* - [HABV] ᖺᖸᖸ

solidify, *v.* - [**HA**·BVĒTH] ᖺᖸᖸᔜ

some, *adj.* - [**A**·LĚM] ᒎᖺᖸ

some, *pro.* - [LĚM] ᒎᖺᖸ

somebody, *n.* - [**LĚ**·MO] ᒎᖺᖸᖺ

someone, *n.* - [**LĚ**·MO] ᒎᖺᖸᖺ

somewhere, *n.* - [LĚ·**LA**·HABV] ᒎᖺᒎᖸᖸ

son, *n.* - [GO·PU·'·GA] ᒎᖺᖸᖸᵎ

song, *n.* - [**DZA**·DĚ] ᒎᒎᖸ

songbird, *n.* - [KTHO·**BVA**·TA] ᒎᒎᖺᖸᒋ

sorrow, *n.* - [(H)**RASH**·LO·'] ᖺᒎᒎᖺᖸ

sort, *v.* - [**HĚ**·GĒCH] ᖺᖸᔑᔜ

sound, *n.* - [SOK] ᔑᖺᒎ

soup, *n.* - [TS'·**NA**·ZA] ⟡⟡⟡

sour, *adj.* - [A·(**H**)**R'**·NA] ⟡⟡⟡

sour, *v.* - [(H)R'NTH] ⟡⟡

sourness, *n.* - [(**H**)**R'**·NA] ⟡⟡⟡

south, *n.* - [BVOK] ⟡⟡⟡

sow, *v.* - [**GA**·BVATH] ⟡⟡⟡

space, *n.* - [U·**CHO**·NA] ⟡⟡⟡

space ("outer"), *n.* - [**U**·CHOK] ⟡⟡⟡

spade, *n.* - [**PWĔTH**·YA] ⟡⟡⟡⟡

special, *adj.* - [Ē·**BVĒ**·Z'] ⟡⟡⟡

sphincter, *n.* - [LĔ·**NĔ**·TA] ⟡⟡⟡⟡

spin, *v.* - [SPOCH] ⟡⟡⟡

spinner, *n.* - [SPO·**CHOT**] ⟡⟡⟡⟡

spirit, *n.* - [**Ē**·NO] ⟡⟡

spirituality, *n.* - [Ē·**NOK**] ⟡⟡⟡⟡

spoil, *v.* - [**LO**·ASH] ⟡⟡⟡

sponge, *n.* - [NOM·**TSA**·(H)RA] ⟡⟡⟡⟡⟡

spoon, *n.* - [**YO**·YA] ⟡⟡⟡

spoor, *n.* - [**MO**·LO] ⟡⟡⟡

spread, *v.* - [SMUSH] ⟡⟡⟡

spring (season), *n.* - [**TUT**·FVĔ] ⟡⟡⟡⟡

sprout, *n.* - [TUT] ⟡

square, *n.* - [**YĔM**·CHO] ⟡⟡⟡

stage (developmental), *n.* - [SO·**SHO**·YOT] ⟡⟡⟡⟡⟡

stage (theatrical), *n.* - [DZO·**CHO**·GA] ⟡⟡⟡⟡

stamp, *v.* - [YĒLTH] ⟡⟡⟡

stand apart, *v.* - [**M'**·FVĒNTH] ⟡⟡⟡

stand still, *v.* - [Ē·(**H**)**RĔ**·OSH] ⟡⟡⟡

standard, *adj.* - [A·BVATH·**RAL**·DZA] ⟡⟡⟡⟡⟡

standard, *n.* - [BVATH·**RAL**·DĔ] ⟡⟡⟡⟡

star, *n.* - [YĔZL] ⟡⟡

start, *v.* - 1. [POTH] ⟡⟡⟡

    2. [THĔTH] ⟡⟡⟡

statement, *n.* - [**BVĔCH**·GA] ⟡⟡⟡⟡

station, *n.* - [SOSH·**YA**·TA] ⟡⟡⟡⟡

steal, *v.* - [(**H**)**RA**·OTH] ⟡⟡⟡

steam, *n.* - [**KTHON**·TSA] ⟡⟡⟡⟡

steel (metal), *n.* - [**HAG**·ZA] ⟡⟡⟡⟡

steep, *adj.* - [A·**YUSH**·DĔ] ⟡⟡⟡⟡

stem, *n.* - [**T'**·GĔT] ꙩꙩꙩ

step, *v.* - [**FVAL**·POSH] ꙩꙩꙩ

stewpot, *n.* - [YA·**DVO**·MAZL] ꙩꙩꙩ

stick, *n.* - [**GAK**·LA] ꙩꙩꙩ.

stiff, *adj.* - [ĔN·DZ'] :ꙩꙩ'

still, *adj.* - .ꙩꙩꙩ' [A·KTHO·**CHO**·'] .ꙩꙩꙩ'

still, *adv.* - [PSĔ] ꙩꙩ

stillness, *n.* - [KTHO·**CHO**·YA] ꙩꙩꙩ.

sting, *v.* - [**DV(H)RU**·THANTH] ꙩꙩꙩ

stink, *v.* - [**SKTHA**·(H)R'CH] ꙩꙩꙩ

stitch, *n.* - [FVO·'·NA] ꙩꙩꙩ.

stocking, *n.* - [FVAL·**PU**·CHĔ] ꙩꙩꙩ:

stomach, *n.* - [**HA**·SHOK] ꙩꙩꙩ

stone (material), *n.* - [**HABV**·NA] ꙩꙩꙩ.

stone (object), *n.* - [H'·**OT**] ꙩꙩꙩ

stop, *v.* - [ĔSH] :ꙩ

store, *v.* - [**HA**·DZĔRSH] ꙩꙩꙩ

store (retail), *n.* - [**FVĔG**·HA] ꙩꙩꙩ.

story, *n.* - [BVĔ·**CHA**·TA] ꙩꙩꙩ.

straight, *adj.* - [A·**W'**·S'] .ꙩꙩ'

strand (fiber), *n.* - [W'·GĔ·SA] ꙩꙩꙩ.

strange, *adj.* - [Ĕ·JĒZ·L'] :ꙩꙩ'

stream, *n.* - [TS'·**FVA**·SHA] ꙩꙩꙩ.

stream, *v.* - [**TS'**·FVASH] ꙩꙩꙩ

street, *n.* - [H'·**A**·SA] ꙩꙩ.

strength, *n.* - [**TSA**·DVA] ꙩꙩ.

stretch, *v.* - [**TH'**·LOSH] ꙩꙩꙩ

strew, *v.* - [BVATH] ꙩꙩ

string, *n.* - [SPO·**CHUK**] ꙩꙩꙩꙩꙩ

strong, *adj.* - [A·TSA·**DVA**·TA] .ꙩꙩꙩ.

structure, *n.* - [SU·P'·**CHO**·THA] ꙩꙩꙩꙩ.

student, *n.* - [MO·**J'T**·(H)RA] ꙩꙩꙩ.

study, *v.* - [JO·SOSH] ꙩꙩꙩ

subjectivity, *n.* - [**KTH'**·KTH'] ꙩꙩ'

substance *n.* - [NOM] ꙩꙩ

such, *adj. & pro.* - [**FV'**·U] ꙩꙩ

suck, *v.* - [DVUSH] ꙩꙩ

sudden, *adj.* - [**ZA**·M'] ꙩꙩ'

sugar, *n.* - [SWUK] ꙩꙩꙩ

suggest, *v.* - [**Z'**·GAWSH] ∂,ᘛ,ᴗ

suggestion, *n.* - [Z'·**GA**·WA] ∂,ᘛ,ᴗ.

sum, *n.* - [BVA·**TA**·CHA] ᘛ.ᴣ.ᘔ.

summer, *n.* - [**YĔD**·FVĔ] ᴖ.ᴦᘔᴖ.:

sun, *n.* - [HĔZL] ᴖ.ᴦᴗ

support, *v.* - [**SĔK**·(H)ROSH] ᘔ.ᴣᴗᴖᴝᴣ

surface, *n.* - [WA·**YĔ**·NA] ᴗᴖᴦᴖᴦ.

surprise, *n.* - [**FVĔ**·ZA] ᴖ.ᴦᴗ.

swear, *v.* - [**BVĔ**·(H)R'SH] ᘛᴦᴖ'ᴣ

sweat, *v.* - [**LĔ**·TSOSH] ᴗᴦᴦᴣ

sweet, *adj.* - [**AS**·WĔDZ] .ᘔᴗᴦᴦ

sweetheart, *n.* - [TA·**(H)R'N**·YOT] ᴗᴦᴝ'ᴖᴖᴝᴞ

swim, *n.* - [SA·**TSU**·SHA] ᘔ.ᴣᴦᴣ.

swim, *v.* - [SA·TSUSH] ᘔ.ᴣᴦᴣ

swimmer, *n.* - [SA·TSU·**SHOT**] ᘔ.ᴣᴦᴦᴞᴞ

swimming place, *n.* - [SA·TSUSH·**T'**·TA] ᘔ.ᴣᴦᴣᴝᴞ.

synthesis *n.* - [TO·MAS·**FVAN**·GA] ᴞᘔᴦᘔᴖᴦᴖᴝ.

synthesize, *v.* - [TO·MAS·**FVAN**·G'TH] ᴞᘔᴦᘔᴖᴦᴖᴝ'ᴣ

synthesizer, *n.* - [TO·MAS·FVAN·**GU**·THA] ᴞᘔᴦᘔᴖᴦᴖᴝᴦᴣ.

system, *n.* - [SHU·**PUK**] ᴣᴦᴦᴦ∂∂∂

T

table, *n.* - [**THO**·GA] ᴣᴝᴦᴦ.

tail, *n.* - [**W'S**·TOT] ᴗᴦᴣᴞᴝ

tailor, *v.* - [SHNA·**'**·DĔRSH] ᴣᴦ.ᴦᴦᴣᴖ

take, *v.* - [ARSH] .ᴦᴣ

talk, *v.* - [**OJ**·LÊNTH] ᴦᴦᴞᴦᴖ

tall, *adj.* - [**A**·THĔT] .ᘔᴦᴞ

tally, *n.* - [BVA·**TA**·CHA] ᘛ.ᴣ.ᘔ.

tamper, *v.* - [GARSH] ᴦᴦ.ᴦᴣ

tapeworm, *n.* - [MA·**(H)R'**·SHĔP·**HUR**·DĔ] ᴦᴦᴦ'ᴣᴦᴦᴖᴦᴖᴦᴦᴦ:

taste, *v.* - [SWĔTH] ᴣᴗᴦᴣ

tax, *v.* - [**MĔ**·GORSH] ᴦᴦᴦᴝᴖᴖ

tea, *n.* - [**TO**·TSA] ᴞᴦᴣ.

teach, *v.* - [JA·BVATH] ᴦᴦᴣᴦᴣ

teacher, *n.* - [MO·**JABV**·THA] ᴦᴦᴦᴦᴣᴣ.

technology, *n.* - [SĔTH·YO·**SHUK**·YA] ᘔ.ᴣᴦᴦᴦᴦ∂∂ᴖ.

tell, *v.* - [BVĔCH] ᘛᴦᴣ.

template, *n.* - [MO·**N'K**·HA] ᴦᴦᴝ'∂∂ᴖ.

temple, *n.* - [ĒR·BVYĚTS] ︓⟋⟋⌒ᵔᵔꜛ⟋

ten, *numb.* - [TSA·TU] ⟋ᵔ⟋ꜛ

ten days, *n.* - [TAZL·TSA·TU] ⟋ᵔ⟋⟋⟋ᵔ⟋ꜛ

tendency, *n.* - [SO·TA·(H)RA] ⟋ᵔ⟋ᵔ⟋ᵔᵔ⟋ᵔᵒᵔ

test, *v.* - [W'·P'NTH] ⟋ᵔ⟋ᵔ⟋⌒⟋⌒

than, *conj. & prep.* - [KRUT] ⟋⟋⟋ᵔᵔ⟋

thank you, *exclam.* - [KH'·DZAR·LO] ⟋⟋⟋⟋ᵔ⟋ᵔᵔ⟋ᵒ⟋ᵒᵒ

that, *adj.* - [YĚBV] ⌒ᵔᵔᵔᵒ

the, *def. art.* - [FVĒ] ⌒

them, *pro.* - [MO·O·MO] ⟋ᵒᵒ⟋ᵒ

then, *adv.* - [BVA·FVU] ᵒᵔᵒᵔꜛ

theorist, *n.* - [GĚ·RU·THA] ⟋ᵔᵔᵒᵔꜛ3ᵔ

theorize, *v.* - [GĚRTH] ⟋ᵔᵔᵔᵒᵔ3

theory, *n.* - [GĚR·THA] ⟋ᵔᵔᵔᵒᵔ3ᵔ

therapize, *v.* - [GĚS·PATH] ⟋ᵔᵔᵔ⟋ᵒ⟋ᵔᵔ3

therapy, *n.* - [GĚS·PA·THA] ⟋ᵔᵔᵔ⟋ᵒ⟋ᵔᵔ3ᵔ

there, *adv.* - [KTHĚFV] ⟋⟋ᵔᵔᵔ⌒

these, *adj., adv. & pro.* - [BVU·M'M] ᵒᵔᵔ⟋ᵒ⟋ᵒ

they, *pro.* - [MO·O·MO] ⟋ᵒᵒ⟋ᵒ

thick, *adj.* - [SPOCH·TĚ] 3ᵔᵒᵔ⟋ᵔᵔ

thief, *n.* - [(H)RA·THOT] ᵔᵔ3ᵒ⟋⟋

thigh, *n.* - ['·TUT] ⟋ᵔᵔ⟋

thin, *adj.* - [TH'L] 3ᵔ⟋

thing, *n.* - [N'·OT] ⌒ᵔᵒ⟋

think, *v.* - [GORSH] ⟋ᵒᵒᵒᵔ

third, *numb.* - [Ě·'·TA] ᵔᵔ⟋ᵔ

third (portion), *n.* - [TA·W'·THA] ⟋ᵔ⟋ᵔ⟋3ᵔ

thirst, *n.* - [TSOCH·DĚ] ⟋ᵒᵔ⟋ᵒᵔ⟋ᵔᵔ

thirst, *v.* - [TSOCH] ⟋ᵒᵔ⟋ᵒ

thirteen, *numb.* - [TA·TU] ⟋ᵔ⟋ꜛ

this, *adj., adv. & pro.* - [BVUM] ᵒᵔᵔ⟋ᵒ

those, *adj.* - [YĚ·BV'M] ⌒ᵔᵔᵒ⟋ᵒ

thought, *n.* - [GO·(H)RA] ⟋ᵒᵒᵔᵔᵒ

thousand, *numb.* - [GĚ·TSA·TU] ⟋ᵔᵔᵔ⟋ᵔ⟋ꜛ

thread, *n.* - [SPO·CH'K] 3ᵔᵒᵒᵔ⟋ᵔᵒᵒ

three, *numb.* - [TA] ⟋ᵔ

thrm, *n.* - [THRM] 3ᵒᵒ

throat, *n.* - [HA·ZĚS·TA] ᵔᵔ⟋ᵔᵔᵔ3ᵔ

through, *prep.* - [(H)RU] ᵒᵔ

throw, *v*. - [CHACH] ⟨symbols⟩

thumb, *n*. - [**SMU**·PUT] ⟨symbols⟩

thunder, *n*. - [ZOT·**KTHOL**·THA] ⟨symbols⟩

ticket, *n*. - [MĚ·**G'**·SA] ⟨symbols⟩

tie (as a knot), *v*. - [**SHA**·FVURSH] ⟨symbols⟩

tight, *adj*. - [(H)RUS·P'] ⟨symbols⟩

time, *n*. - [BVAFV] ⟨symbols⟩

time, *v*. - [**BVAFV**·TACH] ⟨symbols⟩

tin (metal), *n*. - [Z'·HO] ⟨symbols⟩

tire, *v*. - [HÊT·NĚRSH] ⟨symbols⟩

tired, *adj*. - [A·HÊT·**NĚR**·L'] ⟨symbols⟩

to, *prep*. - [U·SHĚ] ⟨symbols⟩

today, *n*. - [**TA**·ZUM] ⟨symbols⟩

toe, *n*. - [FVA·**LOT**] ⟨symbols⟩

together, *adv*. - [USH·**MO**·MĚ] ⟨symbols⟩

tomorrow, *adv*. - [**TA**·SHOPS] ⟨symbols⟩

tomorrow, *n*. - [TA·**SHO**·PA] ⟨symbols⟩

tongue, *n*. - [**YOL**·MĚT] ⟨symbols⟩

tool, *n*. - [**SĚTH**·YA] ⟨symbols⟩

tooth, *n*. - [**NA**·YO] ⟨symbols⟩

top, *n*. - [**WA**·SĚK] ⟨symbols⟩

torc, *n*. - [HA·GĚS·**TA**·THA] ⟨symbols⟩

total, *n*. - [BVA·**TA**·CHA] ⟨symbols⟩

touch, *n*. - [MU·**SHĚ**·SHA] ⟨symbols⟩

touch, *v*. - [**MU**·SHĚSH] ⟨symbols⟩

toward, *prep*. - [**SHU**·SHĚ] ⟨symbols⟩

town, *n*. - [M'TH·L'·**MA**·TA] ⟨symbols⟩

trace, *n*. - [**MO**·LO] ⟨symbols⟩

track, *n*. - [**MO**·LO] ⟨symbols⟩

trade, *v*. - [**SHO**·KTHOSH] ⟨symbols⟩

train, *n*. - [**MO**·SHOM] ⟨symbols⟩

train, *v*. - [J'T·SĚTH] ⟨symbols⟩

transcendence, *n*. - [NAN·FVĒ] ⟨symbols⟩

transcendent being, *n*. - [NAN·FVĒ] ⟨symbols⟩

transit, *n*. - [KĚ·**FVOSH**·L'] ⟨symbols⟩

transit, *v*. - [**KĚ**·FVOSH] ⟨symbols⟩

transparent, *adj*. - [A·(H)RU·WO] ⟨symbols⟩

transport, *v*. - [YO·**Y'**·MĚSH] ⟨symbols⟩

travel, *v*. - [**SO**·SHOSH] ⟨symbols⟩

tray, *n.* - [THO·GĔ·CHA] 〰️

treasure, *n.* - [**DZA**·MO] 〰️

treat, *v.* - [(H)RĔ·**OS**·PATH] 〰️

tree, *n.* - [**GA**·KTHO] 〰️

triangle, *n.* - [**YĔM**·TA] 〰️

trick, *v.* - [**DZO**·CHĔNTH] 〰️

troll, *n.* - [DZA·**ZA**·NA] 〰️

trouble, *n.* - [LODZ] 〰️

trousers, *n.* - [**TAT**·LĔM] 〰️

truck, *n.* - [TĔD·**SHOT**] 〰️

true, *adj.* - [A·**JA**·N'] 〰️

trumpet, *n.* - [TOM·WĔ·LĔ·(H)RA] 〰️

trust, *n.* - [Y'Z·**WO**·SHA] 〰️

trust, *v.* - [**Y'Z**·WOSH] 〰️

truth, *n.* - [**JA**·NO] 〰️

tryst, *n.* - [BVĔ·**SHOSH**·L'] 〰️

tryst, *v.* - [BVĔ·**SHOSH**] 〰️

tube, *n.* - [W'·**YĔS**·TA] 〰️

tune, *v.* - [**P'BV**·LĔCH] 〰️

tunnel, *v.* - [**NĔL**·SONTH] 〰️

turn, *v.* - [**SA**·OCH] 〰️

turn on, *v.* - [DVATH] 〰️

twelve, *numb.* - [**BVA**·TU] 〰️

twenty, *numb.* - [BV'·**TSA**·TU] 〰️

twenty-one, *numb.* - [BV'·TSA·**TO**·MO] 〰️

twice, *adv.* - [**BVAM**·BVAPS] 〰️

twilight, *n.* - [ZA·**ZĔ**·NA] 〰️

twist, *v.* - [U·**THAK**·YĔNTH] 〰️

two, *numb.* - [BVA] 〰️

U

ugly, *adj.* - [A·**WĔK**·(H)RĔ] 〰️

ukulele, *n.* - [GLĔN·LU·'·SA] 〰️

umbrella, *n.* - [LU·LAK·**YU**·LA] 〰️

under, *adj.* - [A·**LĔ**·CH'] 〰️

under, *adv. & prep.* - [**LĔCH**·L'] 〰️

understand, *v.* - [**CHO**·OTH] 〰️

understanding, *n.* - [CHO·**OTH**·DĔ] 〰️

undine, *n.* - [**TS'**·MOT] 〰️

undo, *v.* - [Ē·(H)RĒSH] ⟨glyphs⟩
undress, *v.* - [**MU**·GĒRSH] ⟨glyphs⟩
union, *n.* - [SĒTS·**DVA**·LOM] ⟨glyphs⟩
unique, *adj.* - [AM·**BV(H)RO**·S'] ⟨glyphs⟩
unit, *n.* - [BVOT] ⟨glyphs⟩
unite, *v.* - [MĒTH] ⟨glyphs⟩
unity, *n.* - [**MĒTH**·DĚ] ⟨glyphs⟩
unless, *conj.* - [WĒPS] ⟨glyphs⟩
unnoticed, *adj.* - [A·Ē·**WO**·NA] ⟨glyphs⟩
unseen, *adj.* - [A·Ē·**WO**·NA] ⟨glyphs⟩
unseen (to be uns–) , *v.* - [Ē·WONTH] ⟨glyphs⟩
until, *conj. & prep.* - [PU·**U**·TABV] ⟨glyphs⟩
up, *adj., adv. & prep.* - [SĚK] ⟨glyphs⟩
upland, *n.* - [CHĚG] ⟨glyphs⟩
urinate, *v.* - [**YĚ**·TSATH] ⟨glyphs⟩
us, *pro.* - [MO·**MO**·FVĒ] ⟨glyphs⟩
use, *v.* - [THA·SĚTH] ⟨glyphs⟩
utensil, *n.* - [LA·HA·**GUK**] ⟨glyphs⟩

V

vacate, *v.* - [**O**·MORSH] ⟨glyphs⟩
vaccinate, *v.* - [BVAK·Z'·**NĚ**·'TH] ⟨glyphs⟩
vagina, *n.* - [Y'·BVU·**FVĚ**·GA] ⟨glyphs⟩
value, *n.* - [ĒR·**BVĚTH**·YA] ⟨glyphs⟩
vast, *adj.* - [A·SA·**KTHUSH**·TA] ⟨glyphs⟩
vastness, *n.* - [SA·KTHUSH·**T'**·TA] ⟨glyphs⟩
vehicle, *n.* - [THĚ·**SHOT**] ⟨glyphs⟩
vein, *n.* - [TSĒJ·**S'**·A] ⟨glyphs⟩
venerable, *adj.* - [A·TĚ·DZOR·CHĒM·**THL'**·A] ⟨glyphs⟩
verse, *n.* - [SPAK·**DZA**·(H)RA] ⟨glyphs⟩
very, *adv.* - [(H)RO] ⟨glyphs⟩
vessel, *n.* - [**YA**·DVOM] ⟨glyphs⟩
view, *v.* - [JU·WORSH] ⟨glyphs⟩
village, *n.* - [**M'TH**·LOM] ⟨glyphs⟩
villager, *n.* - [M'TH·LO·**MO**·TA] ⟨glyphs⟩
viola, *n.* - [SPA·**CHĚ**·DZA] ⟨glyphs⟩
violence, *n.* - [MO·**ZĒTH**·LA] ⟨glyphs⟩
violent, *adj.* - [A·MO·**ZĚ**·TH'L] ⟨glyphs⟩
violet (color), *adj.* - [A·KTHA·**BVĒZ**·LO] ⟨glyphs⟩

145

violet (color), *n.* - [**KTHA**·BVĒZL] ⠿⠿
violin, *n.* - [**SPAZ**·CHO] ⠿⠿
vision, *n.* - [**MO**·WA] ⠿⠿
vocation, *n.* - [**WA**·SOBV] ⠿⠿
voice, *n.* - [SOK·**YO**·LA] ⠿⠿
vulture, *n.* - [PA·**WOT**·BVA] ⠿⠿

W

waist, *n.* - [PRUST] ⠿⠿
wait, *v.* - [Ė·**LO**·'SH] ⠿⠿
waiting, *n.* - [Ė·LO·'**SH**·DĖ] ⠿⠿
walk, *v.* - [**FVA**·LOSH] ⠿⠿
wall, *n.* - [**BVO**·GA] ⠿⠿
wander, *v.* - [**SA**·KTHUSH] ⠿⠿
wanderer, *n.* - [SA·KTHU·**SHOT**] ⠿⠿
want, *v.* - [CH'CH] ⠿
war, *n.* - [ZĖL] ⠿⠿
warm, *adj.* - [Ė·CHĖTS] ⠿⠿
warmth, *n.* - [CHĖ·**TSUK**] ⠿⠿
wash, *v.* - [ZUTH] ⠿⠿
waste, *n.* - [Ė·**DZUTH**·PA] ⠿⠿
watch, *v.* - [**LO**·WASH] ⠿⠿
water, *n.* - [**TS'**·NA] ⠿
waterlily, *n.* - [TS'·**GO**·GA] ⠿⠿
wave *v.* - [**ZU**·LĖTH] ⠿⠿
waver, *v.* - [HO·**O**·MANTH] ⠿⠿
wax, *n.* - [**BVA**·MOLT] ⠿⠿
way, *n.* - [SOS] ⠿
we, *pro.* - [MO·**MO**·FVĖ] ⠿⠿
weak, *adj.* - [Ė·GOM] ⠿⠿
weather, *n.* - [**OK**·THOM] ⠿⠿
weave (of fabric), *n.* - [**FVO**·'·SHA] ⠿⠿
weave, *v.* - [**FVO**·'SH] ⠿⠿
weaver, *n.* - [FVO·'·**SHOT**] ⠿⠿
weaving, *n.* - [FVO·'·**SHU**·KTHA] ⠿⠿
weigh, *v.* - [**NAS**·PĖRSH] ⠿⠿
weight, *n.* - [**NAS**·PĖ] ⠿⠿
welcome, *exclam.* - [DZĖ·BV'DZ] ⠿⠿
welcome, *v.* - [DZĖ·BV'DZCH] ⠿⠿

weld, *v.* - [**BVO**·BVOTH]

well, *adj.* - [A·**Y'M**·DĔ]

well, *adv.* - [**Y'M**·DZ']

well (shaft), *n.* - [YO·**LOTS**·NA]

west, *n.* - [ZĒ·LA]

wet, *adj.* - [A·**TSĔ**·FV']

whale, *n.* - [TS'·**HA**·HOT]

what, *adv. & pro.* - [Ĕ·BVU]

wheel, *n.* - [SĒ·**THO**·YA]

when, *adv. & conj.* - [**U**·BVAFV]

where, *adv. & conj.* - [**A**·SHAFV]

which, *det. & pro.* - [**DVA**·BVU]

while, *adv. & conj.* - [**(H)RU**·BVĚ]

whip, *v.* - [**MĒ**·GĒTH]

whiskey, *n.* - [TĒ·WO·**ZĒ**·NA]

whisper, *v.* - [SOK·**YO**·LĒWSH]

whistle, *v.* - [**SOK**·(H)RUSH]

white, *adj.* - [A·**WO**·MUZL]

white, *n.* - [**WO**·MOZL]

who, whom, *pro.* - [**MO**·BVU]

whole, *adj.* - [A·**MO**·FV']

why, *adv.* - [SHOK]

wide, *adj.* - [**SPOCH**·TĔ]

wild, *adj.* - [A·SHA·BV'·**DZA**·NA]

wild, *n.* - [SHA·BV'·**DZA**·NA]

wilderness, *n.* - [SHA·BV'·**DZANTH**·DĔ]

wildness, *n.* - [SHA·BV'·**DZA**·NA]

will, *v.* - [GĔRSH]

win, *v.* - [**THRA**·ATH]

wind, *n.* - [**KTHASH**·TA]

window, *n.* - [**KTHASH**·TYO]

wine, *n.* - [YU·**PĔM**·LOT]

wing, *n.* - [**KTHO**·FVOT]

winter, *n.* - [**TSĒT**·FVĔ]

wire, *n.* - [MĔ·**GĔ**·SA]

wisdom, *n.* - [JĒ·NO]

wise, *adj.* - [A·**JĒN**·L']

wish, *n.* - [WON·**CHUK**]

wish, *v.* - [WONCH]

with, *prep.* - [O·'] ౦౸

wolf, *n.* - [MUDZ] ౸౸౦

woman, *n.* - [SMO·**TA**·GA] ౸౦౦౸౦.

wood (material), *n.* - [GA·**KTHO**·MA] ౸.౦౦౦౸.

wool, *n.* - [GĔZL] ౸:.౸

word, *n.* - [G(H)ROT] ౸౸౦౦

work, *n.* - [**SĔ**·THA] ౸:.౸.

work, *v.* - [SĔTH] ౸:.౸

worker, *n.* - [SĔ·**LU**·THA] ౸:.౸౸.

workshop, *n.* - [HA·**SĔ**·THA] ౸.౸:.౸.

world, *n.* - [**CHAR**·LSA] ౸.౦౸౸.

worm, *n.* - [HA·**W'S**·TA] ౸.౸౸౸.

wound, *n.* - [**TSĔ**·YO] ౦:.౸౦

wren, *n.* - [KTHO·BVA·**CHA**·SA] ౦౦౸.౸.౸.

wrist, *n.* - [**(H)RAP**·SA] ౸.౸౸.

write, *v.* - [**JA**·YĔTH] ౦.౸:.౸

writing, *n.* - [**JA**·**YĔTH**·L'] ౦.౸:.౸౸'

wrong, *adj.* - [ĔJL] :౦౸

X

X-ray (image), *n.* - [BVĔZ·NAH·**YOT**] ౸:.౸౸.౸౸౦౸౸

X-ray (radiation), *n.* - [ZO·THA·GAH·**YOT**] ౸౦౸.౸.౸౸౦౸౸

xylophone, *n.* - [JĔ·GAK·MA·**SOK**·YOT] ౦:.౸.౦౦౸.౸౦౦౸౦౸

Y

yarn (fiber), *n.* - [SPO·**CHA**·TĔDZ] ౸౦౦౸.౸:.౦

year, *n.* - [**LOTH**·GO] ౸౦౸౸౦

yearly, *adj.* - [A·**LOTH**·GO] .౸౦౸౸౦

yearn, *v.* - [**T'**·TUNCH] ౸౸౸౸౸

yellow, *adj.* - [**A**·HODV] .౸౦౦౸

yellow, *n.* - [HODV] ౸౦౦౸

yellow, *v.* - [**HO**·DVUTH] ౸౦౦౸౸

yes, *adv.& det.* - [**KTHĔ**·'] ౦౸:.'

yesterday, *n.* - [**TA**·ZĔPS] ౸.౸:.౸

yet, *adv.* - [PĔ] ౸:.

yet, *conj.* - ['·PĔ] ,౸:.

yeti, *n.* - [H'·**YĔTH**·T'] ౸.౸:.౸౸

yodel, *v.* - [**DZA**·ZANTH] ౦.౸.౸

yodeler, *n.* - [DZA·ZA·**NOT**] ౦.౸.౸౦౸౸

you (sing.), *pro.* - [MĒ·FVA] ⌒:⌒.
you (plur.), *pro.* - [MĒM·**FVA**·'M] ⌒:⌒⌒.'⌒
young, *adj.* - [APS·T'] .⌒⌒
your, yours (sing.), *pro.* - [MĒ·Ē·FVĚ] ⌒::⌒∴
your, yours (plur.), *pro.* - [M'·**MĒ**·FVĚ] ⌒'⌒:⌒∴

Z

zero, *numb.* - [Ē·MO] ：⌒ᵒ
zinc (metal), *n.* - [ZA·HOL] ⌒,⌒ᵒ⌒

Aath'm. Word art attributed to Emo Azek, a figure at once trickster and mage in Dvarsh folklore.

Non-capitalization, punctuation and other symbols

As mentioned previously, the *dvarsh* have no convention like capitalization. Vertical text generally signals more emphasis than horizontal text, and is often used for headings and titles. Scholarly practice adheres to principal text formatted in vertical blocks, with adjacent glosses oriented horizontally.

Dvarsh punctuation is minimal and used sparingly. The set of formal marks were a relatively recent introduction, and there is still considerable variation in their use. Marks correspond to commas, periods, question marks, exclamation marks, and parentheses / quotation marks. There is also a general purpose "long stroke," found in the earliest writing and still the only punctuation used by some scribes. A mix of long strokes and formal marks is not uncommon.

As in English, parentheses / quotation marks are placed in mirror pairs enclosing the part of a sentence to which they apply. Unlike in English, exclamation marks and question marks are also placed in mirror pairs, and also enclose only the part of a sentence to which they apply. This is very clear with questions, which are typically formed by making a statement with a question word (e.g. how, what, when, where, who, why) added at the end. Only the question word is enclosed by the marks.

comma / pause	'
period / stop	"
exclamation	⸸ ⸷
question	⸑ ⸒
parentheses / quotes	⸌ ⸍
long strokes	∼ ⌣
ota (ampersand)	℘
ordinal mark	⸱
equal	⸚
not equal	⸝
multiply	⸭
divide	∫

Numbers

The *dvarsh* use a base 10 number system, which they claim to have originated. Dvarsh numerals derive from the writing tradition of Hazl-speaking clans, an altogether different system than the characters of the *jayĕlu*. One authority (Wobvul, Fvemor, "Haz'm, the Contrarians of the Glades," *Annals of the Dvarsh Repository, Vol. 16332 no. 7* [English redaction]) argues that the ancient Hazl writing system—and therefore the numerals in use today—was inspired by blades of grass at forest margins. Subsequent scholarship admires the poetry of this invention. A preponderance of evidence taps flint pen nibs during the pre-metallurgical period of *hazl* paleoliteracy as a more likely factor shaping the numerals.

In practice, the *dvarsh* rarely write out the names of numbers, using numerals in almost every situation. A dictionary is one of the few places where names of numbers are spelled out.

Ordinal numbers are specified by an ordinal superscript [ʸ] placed in front of any cardinal number. The superscript consists of three dots arranged two over one.

Dvarsh attachment to numericism could be a fascinating study in and of itself. Their cultivation of number driven and number derived sciences—e.g. conjuration, mathematics, metamathemagics, 'pataphysics, physics, probabilization and statistics—has produced a body of achievement that includes the entire version of reality they inhabit. Provocatively, clues to a complex system of numericist divination are embedded in the wisdom book, *sosnodz*, or *Nod's Way*. It is as though within the oracle anyone can access is another requiring a withheld key. To the disappointment of the curious, the entire *dvarsh* population seems to have taken an oath of secrecy on the topic, and no explanation is forthcoming.

The *dvarsh* zero [ₒ], called *ĕmo*, is distinct from other numerals in having an unrelated source. Originally drawn by a mage of the *zĕkth'm*, it is both a numeral and an object of contemplation much like the Daoist "Yin Yang," which it somewhat resembles. Reliable details about the individual who actually drew the figure have been lost, but folktales abound of a Nod-like trickster/mage, Emo Azek. The cognomen means "*zĕk*-person Zero." Her daughters, 'M and Bva, feature as allies or butts in many of the stories.

Numerals

၀	:ᘐ၀	*ēmo*	zero	0
၊	ᘐ	*mo*	one	1
၇	ᗏ.	*bva*	two	2
၇	ᒎ.	*ta*	three	3
၇	ᐟ၀	*cho*	four	4
၇	ᒐ..	*dzaa*	five	5
၄	ᘐ:'	*fvē'*	six	6
၄	ᘐ.:	*fvaē*	seven	7
၄	ᘐ၀	*fvo*	eight	8
၇	ᘐᑉᘐ	*fvum*	nine	9
၊၀	ᒎ.ᒎᵣ	*tsatu*	ten	10
၊၊	ᘐ၀ᒎᵣ	*motu*	eleven	11
၊၇	ᗏ.ᒎᵣ	*bvatu*	twelve	12
၊၇	ᒎ.ᒎᵣ	*tatu*	thirteen	13
၊၇	ᐟ၀ᒎᵣ	*chotu*	fourteen	14
၊၇	ᒐ.ᒎᵣ	*dzatu*	fifteen	15
၊၄	ᘐ:ᒐᒐᒎᵣ	*fvēktu*	sixteen	16
၊၄	ᘐ.ᒐᒐᒎᵣ	*fvaktu*	seventeen	17
၊၄	ᘐ၀ᒎᵣ	*fvotu*	eighteen	18
၊၇	ᘐᑉᘐᒎᵣ	*fvumtu*	nineteen	19
၇၀	ᗏ'ᒎ.ᒎᵣ	*bv'tsatu*	twenty	20
၇၊	ᗏ'ᒎ.ᒎᵣ၀ᘐ၀	*bv'tsatomo*	twenty-one	21
၊၀၀	ᒎ.ᒎ.ᒎᵣ	*tsatsatu*	one hundred	100
၊၀၀၀	ᘐ:.ᒎ.ᒎᵣ	*gĕtsatu*	one thousand	1000
၊'၀၀၀'၀၀၀	ᒐ၀ᒎ.ᒎᵣ	*zotsatu*	one million	1,000,000

Ordinal Numbers

ᵛ	.ᒎ.	*ata*	[ordinal mark]	
ᵛ၊	.:'ᘐ၀	*ě'mo*	first	1st
ᵛ၇	.:'ᗏ.	*ě'bva*	second	2nd
ᵛ၇	.:'ᒎ.	*ě'ta*	third	3rd
ᵛ၇	.:'ᘐᑉᘐ	*ě'fvum*	ninth	9th

Time

The day divides into ten *(h)rot'm* [⟡] of just under two and a half hours each. The singular is *(h)rot* [⟡].

A *(h)rot* divides into 100 *(h)r't'm* [⟡], singular *(h)r't'* [⟡].

A *(h)r't'* divides into 100 *(h)r't't'm* [⟡], singular *(h)r't't'* [⟡].

Every measured period, no matter how large or small, has a rising half followed by a falling half, thus doubling the divisions at every level. A century, for instance, rises for fifty years and falls for fifty. Similarly, a *(h)r't'* rises for half its period and falls for half.

In practical terms, demarcation of rising and falling *(h)rot'm* on a clockface represents a day with twenty divisions. To illustrate, *mo akthĕshl'* [⟡], Rising One, is distinct from and precedes *mo ayushl'a* [⟡], Falling One. Together they are halves of the first period of a day, *(h)rot mo* [⟡].

The rising half of a period is sometimes described as inhaling, and the falling as exhaling. The rising is also called the *yĕts* [⟡], or shape, of the period and the falling is called the *lo* [⟡], or shadow.

To compare to human periods, one *(h)rot* equals 2.4 hours, making each rising or falling half 1.2 hours. One *(h)r't'* works out to 1.44 minutes, and each *(h)r't't'* is a hair longer than .86 second.

The daily count of *(h)rot'm* begins at midnight. Noon is the boundary between the fifth and sixth *(h)rot'm*.

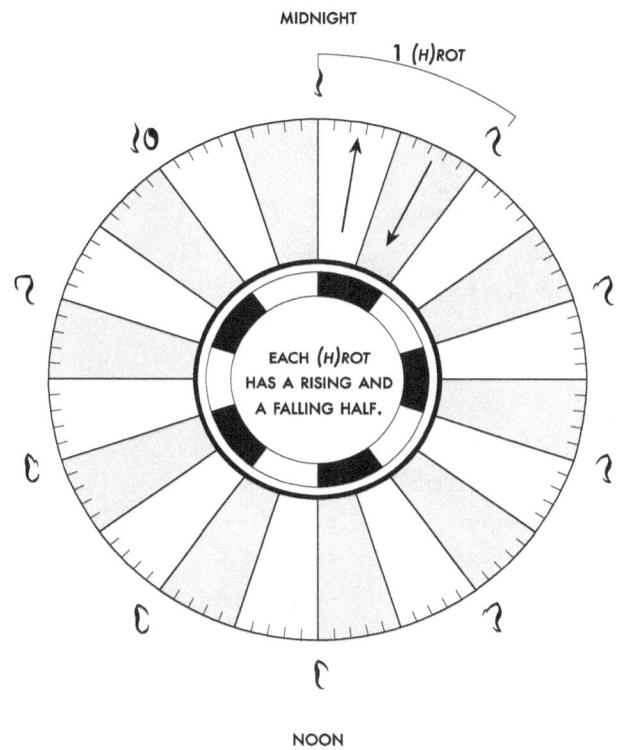

Key words relating to time

ꙧꙅꙷꙧꙬ	*lothgo*	(n) year
Ꙉ.ꙧꙬ	*talo*	(n) night
Ꙉ.ꙩ	*tazl*	(n) day
Ꙉ.ꙩꙈ.Ꙉꙉ	*tazltsatu*	(n) period of ten days
ꙧꙬꙈ	*(h)rot*	(n) a tenth of a day
ꙧꙈꙧ	*(h)r't'*	(n) 1/100th of a (h)rot
ꙧꙈꙧꙧ	*(h)r't't'*	(n) 1/100th of a (h)r't'
.ꙩꙩ꙳.ꙩꙧ	*akthĕshl'*	(adj) rising
.ꙬꙈꙩꙧ.	*ayushl'a*	(adj) falling

The Nod Calendar

	tazl mo	DECEMBER 22	Day One
	dzuthaha ota gabvatha psutafvē	DEC 23 - JAN 1	Completion & New Beginning
	kthofvē	JAN 2 - JAN 11	The Sky
	habvfvē	JAN 12 - JAN 21	The Earth
	kthochta	JAN 22 - JAN 31	Rest
	dzubvchafvē	FEB 1 - FEB 10	The Collective
	lal'sha	FEB 11 - FEB 20	Retreat
	jagumfvē	FEB 21 - MAR 2	The Garden
	dzuthabvĕcha	MAR 3 - MAR 12	Perseverance
	zuchgo	MAR 13 - MAR 22	Innocence
	tazl abvĕshl'	MARCH 23	Trysting Day
	yadvomazlfvē	MAR 24 - APR 2	The Stewpot
	tsashabv'dzana	APR 3 - APR 12	Disruption
	ē(h)rĕosh	APR 13 - APR 22	Stand Still
	shubvĕchótfvē	APR 23 - MAY 2	The Guardian
	golopucha	MAY 3 - MAY 12	Repair
	mĕthdĕ	MAY 13 - MAY 22	Unity
	tazl atuz'thl'	MAY 23	Freshing Day
	talojĕmfvē	MAY 24 - JUN 2	The Mystery
	yĕthdza	JUN 3 - JUN 12	Gentleness
	zuchdĕ	JUN 13 - JUN 22	Courage
	tazl ashēna	JUNE 23	Lazy Day
	dza	JUN 24 - JUL 3	Joy
	(h)rashlo'	JUL 4 - JUL 13	Sorrow
	ĕbvosha	JUL 14 - JUL 23	Return
	tsadva	JUL 24 - AUG 2	Strength
	(h)rabvocha	AUG 3 - AUG 12	Folly
	nĕthdzafvē	AUG 13 - AUG 22	The Simple
	aathl'	AUG 23 - SEP 1	Building

156

৭.ం,౨.౧.ౖ:	*shabv'dzanafvē*	SEP 2 - SEP 11	The Wild
౦౦৭ৎ৭	*hogchum'm*	SEP 12 - SEP 21	Relations
౨.౨ .౧..౨	*tazl ayaat*	SEPTEMBER 22	Berry Day
౧,౨౨,	*y'zwa*	SEP 23 - OCT 2	Trust
৭౨౧	*modzafvē*	OCT 3 - OCT 12	The Beloved
౧.ৢ౦৭. ,ౖ,౨৭౧.	*(h)rĕosha ah'muna*	OCT 13 - OCT 22	Decisive Action
౨,౧ৢ.౧:౨,	*dv'nthanēw'*	OCT 23 - NOV 1	Modesty
৭౨,	*ch'chl'*	NOV 2 - NOV 11	Seeking
౧.ৢ౨,౨.	*bvathl'dĕ*	NOV 12 - NOV 21	Generosity
౧.ৢৢ౨.	*bvĕthbva*	NOV 22 - DEC 1	Mercy
৭౦৭ৎৎ౦౦৭౨.	*bvochsmoondĕ*	DEC 2- DEC 11	Self-Reliance
:౨,౨౨.	*ēlo'shdĕ*	DEC 12 - DEC 21	Waiting
৭:,৭౦౧:	*chē'chotfvē*	LEAP DAY	The Kicker

The *dvarsh* may count moons, but their calendar includes neither weeks nor months. Instead, they divide the year into thirty-six ten-day periods, called *tazltsatu'm* [౨.౨౨.౧,౧], (sing. *tazltsatu*), and five holidays, with a sixth holiday every fourth year.

Day One, *tazl mo*, the first day of the *dvarsh* year, corresponds to December 22 in the Gregorian calendar used by many humans. Curiously—or not, to hear them tell it—their leap year coincides with ours as much as the slight misalignment of calendars allows. Every fourth year, a leap day, *chē'chotfvē* [౭:,৭౦౧:], The Kicker, is added to keep the calendar in sync with the seasons. The fact that the *dvarsh* add their leap day at the end also means the table provided here is off throughout most of each leap year. Most of the time, in most years, the relationship is stable.

Tazl mo 16,786 in the Nod calendar corresponds to December 22, 1999 CE in the human West. As old as it is, the Nod calendar was not the first. Adopted as a unifying standard, it replaced the earlier, competing counts of the individual clans. Called "the Nod calendar," *bvatachatazlnodzfvē* [౧.౨.౭.౨,౨౦౦౧:], because the periods of the year are given names of auspices from *sosnodz*, or *Nod's Way*, the calendar preserves a sequence that does not follow the order of the book.

Index